AN AFFAIR OF STATE

AN AFFAIR OF STATE

PART ONE

THE CRISIS

I

ON a winter's evening, not long ago, a man was walking along Bond Street in London, in a downpour of rain. Beneath his rather shabby over-coat was a suit of evening clothes, although a pair of thick boots and a bowler hat did not suggest its presence. It was a dirty night. At frequent intervals the wind, in sudden, fitful gusts, came shrieking round the corners of the by-streets that run into the famous thoroughfare. Every yard of his progress had to be fought for, but there was some-thing about the compact and powerful figure which seemed to welcome this contention with the elements.

The face of the man, undefended by an umbrella, was full of power. The large aggressive nose and the fighting jaw literally clove their way through wind and water. There was a look of subtle satis-faction about him, as of a full-blooded animal occupied worthily. In the square-fronted march through the teeth of the gale, in the drive of the athletic limbs, there was the stern delight that warriors feel. Wind and water furiously contested every yard that he made; but this Titan, chin in the air, a grim smile upon his face, abated not a point in his course.

At the Grafton Street crossing an unseen power, subtle and mysterious, which is called Chance in the present age of science, leaped suddenly to the aid of the agents of the air. The wayfarers stepped off the pavement boldly, perhaps a little unwarily, for the shops were closed and the street lamps gave none too much light, just as a taximeter cab dashed noiselessly round the corner of the street. Only a man of uncommon quickness and presence of mind could have saved himself.

He sprang back to the pavement, but quick as he was the lamp of the vehicle missed him by a hairbreadth, while its wheels flung a liberal supply of mud over his garments. Further agility was necessary to avoid a collision with a policeman who had just tried the door of a jeweller's shop.

"Constable, did you notice that fellow?"

The tone was challenging, imperious, and yet by some miracle it was perfectly polite.

Constable X94 paid the involuntary homage of a demeanour that was both alert and respectful.

"Yes, sir, I did. I wish I could have seen his number."

"LC 00942. Take it down. I shall try my best to have an example made of him. The law ought to have the power to hang such scoundrels."

Constable X94 stepped into the jeweller's doorway and produced his notebook.

"You are quite right, sir," he said with an air of conviction equal to that of the man who had so narrowly escaped being run over. "It's cruel the way they come round these corners at night. Only last week a gentleman was killed not a hundred yards from here. What might be your name and address, sir?"

"James Draper, 200 Queen Anne's Gate."

The policeman entered the information in his book.

"Not *the* Mr. Draper, sir?"

"If you will have it so." The laugh accompanying the words was deep and musical.

"A nice thing for the country if he had run over you, sir!" There was fervour in the tone of Constable X94.

"He would have made a few friends for himself, I dare say."

The Mr. Draper was pleasantly sardonic, but Constable X94 remained stolid and quite serious.

"Not among those who know, sir, I give you my word. He'd have done a bad evening's work for his country."

"Thank you, constable." A sudden accession of feeling vibrated in the deep voice of the man in the bowler hat. "Although, mind I don't say you are right," and then he added with a cordiality that was somehow magnetic, "Good-night!"

"Good-night, sir!" said Constable X94.

The pedestrian turned to make another attempt to cross the street. This time he was successful. Doggedly he fought his way until he came to Bruton Street. Turning down that thoroughfare he came at last to a famous house at the extreme end of the street. It was a large cheerless mansion of Georgian aspect, with an ugly courtyard to keep it sacred from the passers-by.

Mr. Draper crossed the courtyard and rang the bell of the imposing entrance.

The doors swung back at once with a sweeping swiftness that was half majestic, half magical. There was a gorgeous vision of powdered wigs and silk stockings; of a grave, patriarchal presence in the background; there was a fairylike glimpse of a gorgeous interior; there was a sensuous rush of warmth and light.

One overdressed functionary at once relieved Mr. Draper of his hat, a second helped him to remove his soaked chesterfield overcoat, a third and a fourth closed the doors; and while the pedestrian turned down the ends of his trousers, an office he was fain to perform for himself, a senior servant in the background made his way gravely forward through the press of his satellites to greet his visitor.

"Good evening, Harpole." The air of the visitor had the composure of one who so far from being impressed by such a reception was a little bored by it. "A nasty night! The Duke is at Lobourne, I suppose?"

"Yes, sir, his Grace went down to Lobourne on Friday. He is expected back in the course of to-morrow."

The servant led the way up a staircase of white marble, through a suite of reception rooms which had a number of famous pictures set in their satin-wood panels, until, coming to the threshold of an inner room, he announced his visitor.

This apartment, much smaller than the others, had a slightly obtrusive note of luxury which suggested the feminine. Its cushions were profuse, oriental, languorous; there were evidences of taste and perception in the charming trifles with which it was carelessly strewn; the rug on the floor was a delight to the foot; and the seductive warmth of the place was not rendered less fragrant by the fumes of a scented tobacco.

Howbeit, merely to catalogue these details is to render only half their signficance. The room had another, an austerer aspect. There was a case full of books and a table full of magazines; there was a small plaster cast of a well-known statesman on the chimneypiece; Plato in bronze was on the top of the bookcase; the *Constitutional Review* was lying face down on a sofa. On this sofa was seated the only person the room contained: a woman in a plain black gown smoking a cigarette.

She was an impressive, formidable, handsome person, large and rather masculine of feature. At the temples the thick black hair was turning gray, and this lent a touch of picturesque austerity to the face which was that of a woman of forty. It was a sensitive face, full of fineness and perception. About the mouth there was perhaps a faint trace of cynicism, the curves of the nose and chin held the love of power, but, beyond everything, in the gray eyes was the high light of a humorous candour.

"Eh bien, mon cher!" The occupant of the sofa aimed a cigarette, three parts consumed, at the fireplace and missed it easily. "Mayn't I tempt you?" She held out her gold case.

The visitor in his soaked and bespattered thick boots, in his old dinner jacket and rather muddy trousers, looked curiously out of harmony with his surroundings. But somehow he had the subtle air of one who did not move in the plane of the merely objective.

"Thanks, no." Mr. Draper picked the lighted end of the cigarette off the hearthrug and dropped it in the fire. "I have only once smoked a cigarette. And then I thought it a waste of time and money.   I was a shop assistant then," he added re-flectively.

"Autres temps, autres mœurs?"

"I don't agree with you, madam.   Once a shop assistant, a shop assistant always.   It is something in the blood.   One couldn't change it if one would, and one wouldn't if one could."

The Duchess of Rockingham laughed.   Her very large and singularly attractive mouth displayed two dazzlingly symmetrical rows of white teeth.

"I don't believe you," she said.   "You know it's only a pose.   You know in your heart you simply hate 'em."

"You've no right to say that, Evelyn," said Mr. Draper.   "Shop assistants are just as essential as duchesses.   More I think.   I won't have you say it."

Mr. Draper took the *Constitutional Review* off its face, closed it and laid in on the table.

"A book also, to my mind, has its corporate dignity and its fixed habit of life.   It is subversive of both to be left open, face down, on a sofa."

Evelyn Rockingham chose a cigarette.

"Now you have lost my place," she said plain-tively.   "Still, I forgive you."   Her eyes brimmed with humour.   "You are in your best form to-night."

"Page 996 — but life is too short for such twad-dle."

Mr. Draper handed the cigar-lighter and assisted her Grace with a quiet efficiency eminently honourable in a confirmed non-smoker.

"Yes, it is twaddle."

"Of course it is twaddle."

"Well, sit here you Berserk." Her Grace took in a reef, and indicated a vacant space on the sofa. "There is just room for our *tête-à-tête*."

Mr. Draper sat on the sofa.

"Do you know what I want to say to you?"

"Not in the least." Mr. Draper's words were light, but there was something in his manner which belied them.

"Guess!"

"I don't believe in guessing when there is exact information to be had for the asking."

"Don't be too sure of that." There was a shade of pique in the tone. If such a self-security did not actually call for rebuke, it jarred a little on the feminine mechanism. "And suppose, my dear James, it is not to be had for the asking, how, pray, are you going to get it?"

"By grasping the throat of Metternich, milady."

The answer came clear, pat, immediate.

Milady laughed.

"One doesn't seem to recognize the tone of 'the nobleman with the bald head,'" said she.

Mr. Draper laughed also.

"Ah, you are all alike in that," he said. "You, none of you quite realize that if you scratch the shop assistant you come up against the genus Englishman, the G— d— Britisher. Perhaps you'll find it out."

"I'm afraid we have found it out already."

Evelyn's laugh was rich, clear, spontaneous. She lit another cigarette.

II

I DON'T know about that," said Mr. Draper with the air of a man thinking. "I have a theory that you never find out anything."

"Whom do you mean by ' you '? "

"You patricians."

"Are there any these days?"

Mr. Draper reflected a little.

"Yes," he said, "I think there are a few. But," he added with his engaging frankness, "as far as I am concerned the discovery is comparatively recent. I used to think that caste was only a veneer, but since I've married Aline I find that it isn't."

Evelyn was amused.

"A graceful compliment, neatly turned," she said. "I am sure you didn't learn *that* from Aline. In fact, my dear James, one can't imagine you learning anything from that poor child. I am quite sure the Carlows have nothing to teach you."

"Oh, yes, they have," said Mr. Draper with his eyes glowing. " Everybody has something to teach me. I am always learning things. Nicholson, my butler, has taught me a lot. He is another of your patricians."

"I hope you don't talk like this to Aline."

"No, of course one can't, poor child. And there's the rub for both of us. I'm sometimes afraid of the future."

"My dear James, you need not fear that," said his mentor. "Still, you ought never to have married her, you know; although, of course, she is rather a darling."

"Yes, it is all a glorious mistake — if one can only keep from making her too unhappy."

Mr. Draper's extremely agreeable voice vibrated with feeling. A look of pain came into his eyes.

"Yes, it was very rash and wicked," said his friend. "It very nearly ruined you."

"I am not sure it hasn't."

"You need have no fear now. At this moment you are stronger in the country than you have ever been before."

"Oh, I know!"

Somehow her words seemed to touch a hidden spring. With a sudden gesture the Minister covered his face with his hands. A strange wave of emotion seemed almost to overmaster him.

"Evelyn," he said in a tone which thrilled her, "I am a lost soul in Hades."

"Poor fellow!" said his friend in a voice in which sympathy and kindness were mingled. "I thought you had finally put all that behind you."

"No, upon my soul, I can't."

Evelyn placed his hand gently in hers, as if she must soothe his pain.

"Yes," she said, "I suppose it is only natural that a true-blue democrat should bleed when he begins to have his doubts of democracy."

"Yes, it's something to abjure the faith in which you have been bred," said the Minister. "A man doesn't like to kick away the stepping-stones by which he has risen. But there seems to be no alternative now." Suddenly he turned to confront the fellow occupant of the sofa, tapping the palm of his right hand with a finger of his left. "The fact is, Evelyn, this Bill will give them ultimately every card in the game."

"Do you really think so?"

"Yes, I do. Looking ahead, that is the real meaning of Clause Nine. Of course it is very artfully dissembled. But that is my deliberate opinion, and I have made it quite clear to Grundy.

"And what says that prince of opportunists, the Prime Minister?"

"He either won't see it or he can't — one hesitates to say which."

"Mr. Facing-both-ways, as usual."

"No, Evelyn, we must be fair. His task is stupendously difficult."

"I have no patience with cowards."

"No, you must be fair. Grundy has done better than any other man could have done in his place. But il a les défauts de ses qualités, that is all."

"Well, what are you going to do?"

A slow perspiration gathered upon the face of the Minister.

"There is something right here," he said, clasping his forehead, "that seems to tell me that the time has come when we who love England must start to back the engine."

"I am sure you are right."

"I believe in the people, I love the people, I have bled for the people, I have gone to gaol for them, but a still small voice persists in telling me that we mustn't let this Bill go through."

"Yes," said Evelyn Rockingham in a lowered tone, "no one can deny that you have fully earned your title of the people's friend. And you have now the opportunity of earning the still more comprehensive title of your country's friend."

"They are all so blind," said the Minister. "They can't see far enough."

"One can't expect a pack of placemen to look into the future," said Evelyn Rockingham contemptuously.

"Oh, we have good men. We have honest men. They have done work for which the country ought to be grateful. All honour to Grundy and sensible

old George Bryant for keeping things going during
this last terrible year.   You see, Evelyn, we are on
the verge of the chasm all the time."

"Yes, I know."

"I was with Grundy till two o'clock this morning.
And his parting words to me were, 'For God's sake,
Draper, don't undo us.   If anything happens to this
Bill there is not a man of us who dare contemplate
the consequences.'"

"He means there will be an end of his precious
Coalition?"

"Unfortunately, he means much more than that."

"Yes, I suppose he does."

"Both sides have played it up so high, you see,
that if the Coalition goes we have absolutely nothing
to put in its place."

"There is Evan Mauleverer!"

"The North wouldn't stand him for an hour.   We
should have the Northumbrian miners sacking the
metropolis."

"It hasn't forgiven his fatuous Conscription Bill?"

"No; and it never will.   The most colossal blunder
of modern times.   It lies at the root of half our
troubles."

In one of his sudden accesses Mr. Draper covered
his face with his hands.

"One realizes, of course," said Evelyn Rockingham
while she watched the man's vivid emotion, "that

the North is the *clou* of the whole thing. And that reminds me that last evening out at dinner Evan Mauleverer himself made a rather impressive remark. He said that any man who had the North behind him could drive a wedge through the three estates."

The words of the famous leader of the Right, whose precision of phrase was admired as much as his reactionary spirit was deplored by moderate people, caused the president of the Board of Conciliation to remove his hands from his rather drawn and haggard face.

"My God, that's true!" he said.

"James Draper, those are words for you to remember."

"Don't tempt me," said the Minister.

"Let me remind you," said Evelyn, whose face was now mobile and luminous with its own emotion, "that it is the North that has put you where you are."

"I know."

"If Evan Mauleverer is right, and I think he is, you are the strongest man in the country to-day."

The Minister clenched his hands.

"Yes, perhaps," he said softly. "At least if it were put to the test the only man I should fear would be Galloway."

"Galloway?"

"Yes — the infamous rapscallion."

"We won't talk of *him*. Let us try to realize where you stand, my dear James, and what lies ahead of you."

"No, no," said the Minister. "As I say, we are on the verge. If the Coalition goes, everything is darkness and eclipse."

Evelyn Rockingham seized him by the arm. "No, my dear James," she said, speaking with decision and intensity. "England looks to you for more than that. You are the strongest man in the country and you are the straightest man in politics in spite of all that the Right has to say of you. If this Conciliation Bill is not an honest measure, and is going to give the Left every card in the game, it seems to me that there is only one thing for such a man as you to do."

"Which at the moment is to ring for a whisky and soda," said the Minister, in a rather dry voice.

III

WHEN this refreshment had been brought Mr. Draper became very thoughtful, while his companion kept her eyes fixed upon his face.

"It all turns upon my position in the country," he said at last. "Have I the weight, my dear Evelyn, the strength, the authority?"

"To form your own administration and carry on the Government if you wreck the Coalition?"

"Yes, it amounts to that. If I am not, or if the country loses its head and allows Evan Mauleverer to ride me off — and he will try all he knows to do that — it will mean the end of England as we know it."

"He either fears his fate too much ——" Evelyn quoted.

"Yes, I know — but they would be taking the tumbrils down Piccadilly. You see, Evan Mauleverer has endangered the monarchy with his tomfool tricks. There is always that lion in the gate. It's an awful responsibility. Upon my soul, I don't think any man ought to take the risk."

"You would have taken it three years ago — before you married Aline."

"I shouldn't have wanted to take it then."

"No, you were then the friend of the people. We expect you to be the friend of England now."

"What sort of a friend shall I be if I overthrow the monarchy?"

"You must be the first president of our republic." There was something in the manner in which the words were spoken which brought him abruptly to his feet.

Again the perspiration gathered on his forehead. His face grew deadly white.

He began to pace the room. He was like a lion in a cage. The brooding eyes, the mane of hair, the massive jaw, the pervasive sense of power suggested not inadequately the king of beasts.

Suddenly he stopped, took the occupant of the sofa by the wrist, and peered with grim intensity into the unflinching eyes.

"Look here, you sibyl," he said, "you shall prophesy! What if we send these cravens packing?"

The woman on the sofa closed her eyes and laid back her head among the cushions.

"Well?"

"A Cromwell will arise and put the key of the House of Commons in his pocket."

"Phrases, madam!"

"Have I ever misled you?"

"Never. Without reservation I say that. But I ask for more light."

Evelyn Rockingham sat up and flicked the ash from her cigarette.

"If you only had imagination! But you have, of course, else you would not have got so far in so short a time. Use your imagination, my friend!"

"I have not enough imagination to see myself a Cromwell, if that is what you mean."

"Then I must supply you with some of mine." The syllables were soft, delicate, deliberate. The sound of them was also sibilant, almost like the drawing of a sword.

The Minister breathed heavily.

"If one could only see a little further," he said.

"Yes, the little more! But at least you are aware that the three parties fear James Draper like the plague?"

"No, I was not aware of it," said the Minister. "At least not quite so specifically. That is," he went on rounding, clarifying, developing his thought, "they may have to fear him if they decline to play the game."

"Have they played it? — are they playing it?"

"Perhaps not the game, the whole game, and nothing but the game — but then who does play that?"'

"James Draper."

Again Mr. Draper stayed his course. He looked his companion full in the eyes. The accomplished woman of the world sustained the whole force of his gaze without a tremor. The cool and smiling candour seemed to pierce him.

He swooped down upon her and bore her hand to his lips.

"Thank you," he said, "thank you!"

She remained sphinxlike, immovable. Her eyes were veiled with an almost imperceptible laughter.

"You have only to walk into the Opposition lobby on Tuesday night to bring down the whole house of cards."

"Better a house of cards than no house at all."

"Why not regard it as a preliminary clearance of the ground for a little house-building of your own?"

"Castle-building, more likely."

"Is it that even now you don't realize your strength in the country?"

Again the Minister began to pace up and down the room. Evelyn Rockingham watched his every movement with an intentness that was a little cruel.

"And if I do!" he said, again facing her abruptly. "Don't you see that we are on the verge? Assuming that I fire them out on Tuesday night, don't you see that one slight miscalculation might send those tumbrils down Piccadilly?"

"Oh, yes, but for the grace of God working through James Draper."

The Minister had the look of a man tormented by a thousands imps.

"Oh, I know you are right!" he cried. "These muddlers — timid sophists — one-step-at-a-time — look-before-you-leap — bah! —— " Short, rough, crackling, half-coherent sentences were flung out of this volcano at intervals. "They can't see far enough. They can't grasp the meaning of it all."

He took her by the wrist.

"Evelyn," he said imperiously, "tell me what has put the idea of Cromwell into that wise and clever head?"

"Events, circumstances. Circumstances, events."

"You have every means, of course, of knowing the play of forces."

"You must continue to trust me, James."

"Oh, I trust you. I shall always trust you. Whatever happens I shall trust you always."

There was a directness and a simplicity about the words that brought the colour slowly to her face.

"Then if I hail you as a Cromwell, I ask you to believe me — a Cromwell who shall deliver my unhappy country lest a worse fate befall."

The voice of the sibyl was musical, deep, and dominant. With a gesture, almost of anguish, which he made no attempt to conceal, the man sank slowly to his knees before her and buried his face in her lap. It was the colour of death.

"Pray for me!" he said in a broken tone.

"I pray for you continually. The man and the the hour — the hour and the man, my prince."

She kissed the bowed head gravely. Issuing slowly from her cushions she rose to her feet. Tall and splendid she looked in her black gown, a daughter of a noble race. There was a fine strength about her that was strangely impressive.

"On Tuesday you must fire them out. I shall be there behind the grille — in my best hat!"

The man had the look of one who is being driven beyond his limit.

"You are absolutely right," he said, and the words seemed to tear him. "I see it all now. I see where my duty lies. But who am I that I should apply the match which may blow up the country."

"There will be no explosion, my friend, if you keep your nerve. On the contrary, you are the only man who can save the country now."

The Minister stood rigid, with head upflung, like a stag of ten.

"Yes, my God — you have spoken the truth!"

He wiped the sweat from his face.

IV.

The Duchess of Rockingham to the Honourable Mrs. George Glen-Maitland, Secretary of the Woman's League

DEAR LAURA: I scribble this at 2 A.M. in a very excited state. Sleep is out of the question, so, as usual, my dear, I sit down to bore you in the hope of calming weak feminine nerves in the process. Why were we born women, you and I? —I more particularly. I am wretchedly overwrought, the result of a three hours' *tête-à-tête* with that amazing man.

He is now keyed up to the pitch of throwing out this infamous Coalition on Tuesday night. God grant that he is right! God grant that his vision be just and true! He has had the perception to realize that if Clause Nine of the Bill goes through it is the last straw as far as we are concerned, and that it is the end, politically, of the classes who have a tradition to conserve.

What an irony it is that this man of all people, the red republican, the intellectual rawhead and bloodybones of a few short years ago, should now be

ready to risk everything to save us from extinction.
It may mean political suicide for him; for the country
it may mean civil war—the air is heavy with rumours
— but if he keeps his nerve I think he will be able
to point a course for this crazy ship of state.

When one comes to think of it, it is a wonderful
career. It seems only yesterday that he made his
first failure in the House of Commons. I shall
never forget his coming to me that evening. He was
an utterly broken man. And I remember I comforted him with the words of Dizzy, "The time will
come when they will hear you." And he burst into
tears and wept like a child.

Well, the time has come now with a vengeance.
He is the strongest man in the country. Of course,
he has many perils to face. There is an odious cabal
against him, and one is afraid he is too simple to
suspect it. At least he has an air of supreme uncon-
sciousness.

Last night, at a party, an amusing thing happened.
A. cut me deliberately, in the most open way. I
felt like boxing the ears of the little spitfire; it was
such a fine exhibition of the Carlow insolence. The
little fool is frantically jealous, and the tragedy is,
my dear, that Mr. D. is still very much in love
with her.

It is a quaint, mad world. To think of such a man
marrying A.; to think of such a woman as myself

having married Robert. How I hate and despise that parcel of vanities, yet I continue to eat his salt and to sustain him in his degree.

This odious cabal, a survival of Victorian England at its worst, suits his Grace's book pretty well. You know how mischievous he can be; and like the narrow, sterile, over-civilized bigot, which at heart he is, he simply loathes "the Haberdasher," as the Bloods call him. The cynical wretch goes about telling everybody that he and I lead a cat and dog life because it amuses us; and to keep the ball rolling, my wicked husband flirts with A. in the most shameless manner, and stuffs her head with all sorts of nonsense about Mr. D. and myself.

Of course I worship the man. But we are no more than friends. He has all the uneasy, ill-timed scrupulousness of the bourgeoisie. And yet one cannot help admiring it, even if it is a little inhuman at times. But it only makes this cabal more devilish. Robert, of course, is bent on his ruin. He makes no secret of that. He keeps prodding up the Pecksniffs in the most masterly manner. I saw him coming out of Brooks's yesterday, hanging on the arm of St. John Becher, the "pi" editor. I could tell by the look on his face that he despises the breed as much as he despises all things under the sun, but that it seemed good to the king to amuse himself.

I wish Robert no harm, but one of these days he

deserves to be severely punished for his levity. Rome is burning, and Robert and his faction saunter out of the Turf, and White's and the Travellers, like a parcel of overdressed bookmakers, backbiting and criticising and weaving their miserable plots. What have they ever done for the country, one would like to know, that they should give themselves such airs at the expense of their betters?

To be in politics, nowadays, they say you must belong to the Right, because the Right are sportsmen first and politicans afterward. That is the kind of cant which has brought the whole country to the verge of ruin. Evan Mauleverer has packed his front bench with amateurs like himself; the horny-handed "pros" on the Left score every point that they want to score; and the Centre, the real brains and backbone of the nation, finds it impossible to carry on the business of the state.

We live in parlous times, my dear. If the Coalition goes, as it certainly will on Tuesday evening, there is absolutely nothing to put in its place, unless Draper is strong enough to force the hands of his enemies and form a government. I think he is; otherwise I would not have urged him to put his fortune to the proof. But to quote his own phrase, "The slightest miscalculation might send the tumbrils down Piccadilly."

Yes, my dear, the hour and the man are here. The

time has come to "back the engine"— another of his phrases — unless we are tamely to consent to being uprooted by an insolent and overweening proletariat. Clause Nine will make it impregnable; and our noble Roman, who entered public life on the extreme Left, less than fifteen years ago, has had the wit to see it, and he is going to have the courage and the honesty to act on his knowledge.

Robert and his faction hate him upon instinct. His early indiscretions, the fruit of an imperfect education, are still remembered; and of course his shockingly imprudent marriage, his one real blunder, will never be forgiven. But this is a bid for their friendship. If they have the sense to rise to an appreciation of the man's real value, so much the better for them; if they continue to let their prejudices override their judgment, so much the worse for the country. Some one will have to carry on the King's Government. Of course the Bloods will try to run Evan Mauleverer, but even they must realize that the game is up. There is the monarchy to consider after that last terrible fiasco.

No, my dear, as far as one can see at present, it is Draper or none. It is possible that one overrates him, but he is a splendid creature. He has developed at an amazing rate and now he hardly bears any traces of his origin. He is a Whig, modernized and brought up to date, with all the latest improvements, and a noble genius added. Moreover, he is implicitly to be trusted. He says what he means and he means what he says. I suppose that is the secret of his power. Evan Mauleverer, with his usual affectation of depth, says the man is too transparent to be other than negligible. Certainly he is honest to a fault, but then, as I told him, the country may be in a mood to welcome a new kind of *malaise.*

Tuesday evening looms before me as I write in a kind of red haze. The deed is so momentous. Will it mean chaos? Perhaps — who knows? Or shall we live to see his statue erected at the bottom of St. James's Street? At any rate the die is cast. I pray God that He may arm our champion!

I shall be there to hear him "put the Government to sleep." I find myself continually using his phrases, as I dare say you have noticed. It will be an emotional treat at any rate. He is the greatest orator since Bright, and cast in a mould still ampler than that man of genius. With the Chamber in its present state of decomposition he is bound to overthrow it. The groundlings — 75 per cent. of the godless Coalition — will be carried off their feet.

My prediction is that a week from to-night the King's Government will be carried on by — no, I dare not prophesy!

Good-night, my dear. Forgive all this. I am
miserably overwrought.

Right Honourable James Draper, 200 Queen
Anne's Gate, to Mrs. Elizabeth Draper,
5 Beaconfield Villas, Newcastle-on-Tyne.

My dear Mother: I am writing to you my weekly
letter on the eve of a great crisis, certainly in my own
life, and, as I believe, in the life of the nation. I have
decided to take a very hazardous step, and by the
time this reaches you, you will be able read what has
happened and be in a position to draw inferences of
your own.

The step I contemplate is bound to have very
grave and far-reaching consequences. Indeed it is
only after the profoundest searchings of heart that I
have decided to embark upon it. There is no need
for me to rehearse the state of affairs in the country.
Substantially the situation is as it was a week ago,
except that there is a further perceptible weakening
in the Centre.

It may be that I am committing political suicide.
Should that be the case, although public life is very
dear to me, I am prepared to abide the issue, because
I am convinced that such an action, whatever may
be the immediate consequences springing out of it,
must result in the ultimate benefit of the country.

As I wrote last week, the present state affairs is hopeless. Grundy, with all his virtues, is not a strong enough man to hold the Left, which is able to bring enormous pressure to bear upon him. It is my firm conviction that if this Bill goes through in its present form we shall cease to be a free nation. Don't shake your head at me, but there is no tyranny like the tyranny of a half-educated democracy. It has all the power now, and is putting it to unfair uses. Grundy in his anxiety to carry on the Government is unable to see that, but we who love England must not be the slaves of expedience, nor must we ignore the truth. I am a man of the people, my dear mother. We have broken the back of more than one tyranny; but now in the flush of our triumph we must see that the pendulum does not swing too far. Let no man blind himself to injustice.

Unless a trustworthy Pilot can be found, a plain man good at need, as sure as fate we shall have the ship on the rocks — even if she is not on them already. Plainly, I don't like the Bill. It won't bear examination. Dress it up as they please, it is not a just measure. Sincere its authors may be; and on the surface the thing has the appearance of an honourable compromise which by judicious stage management may pose as a perfectly innocent matter. But it means much more than that for those who have eyes to see.

No, it is an unprincipled measure, which can and will be put presently to other uses than those for which it is designed. Grundy cannot or will not see it, but old George Byrant understands it well enough. They say it means revolution if we tear it up. Perhaps, but we of the faith must do battle though the heavens fall. And after all, as I tell them, the Bill itself is a mere attempt to postpone the day of reckoning.

It will be a spring in the dark. Perhaps I am undoing the work of years. Perhaps I am plunging the country into indescribable chaos. But I must take the risk. It will be vain to struggle when the fetters are riveted. It may be that my position in the country is not what I think it to be. But the North is with me — I feel that in my veins. I am one of themselves; there is my Northumbrian burr to prove it — and as there is a God in heaven they will rally when they hear it calling them. God bless them!

There is no hope of help from the Right. They are blind with self-love. They "have no use for the Haberdasher," these superfine, lily-white gentlemen. Well, we shall see. Time brings some queer revenges. Meanwhile Evan Mauleverer has misread all the signals, as usual. He is bound to make a bid for office. Elegant, insolent trifler! Vain fool posing as the saviour of his country!

I am going for "the knock-out." The master-secret in fighting is to strike once, but in the right place. This evening I must use every ounce I possess. Somehow I seem very confident now the time is so near. My duty is clear and God has given me wonderful strength. If I get home I shall put the Government to sleep; if I don't, all parties will conspire to rule me out of the ring forever.

I have been the best hated man in the country these twelve months past. They say I am too ambitious. They say my growing power is contrary to the public interest. Well, we shall see. They only let me into their precious Government out of sheer cowardice; and they are not able to keep me in it now they have got me there. Considered as individuals there are good men and true among them, but in their corporate capacity they are arrant cowards. Perhaps this trumpet-call will rally the true men of all creeds to the standard.

If it be the will of God that the strength is vouchsafed to James Draper to point a course for the old ship, so be it. . . . God works in a mysterious way His wonders to perform. Say a little prayer for me, my dear mother!

P.S. —I have not the time, nor am I in the mood, for domesticities. Aline is spending the week-end in the country with her aristocratic friends. I haven't much use for them — and they, you may be sure, are not overfond of "the Haberdasher." Well, I suppose it is only natural that they should distrust me. All the same, I am convinced they do A. no good. Still, she is one of themselves, and it is hardly fair to expect a charming she-leopard to change her spots all at once. Perhaps my marriage *was* a mistake, but it was a delicious folly of which I don't intend to repent. These barbarians have something that makes them fascinating, irresistible. You know you are charmed with A. yourself, although you shake your wise head over her.

V

MR. DRAPER'S interview with the Duchess of Rockingham had taken place late on the evening of Saturday. On the morning of the Wednesday following he was seated about twelve o'clock in the small and cosy study of his official residence. The appearance he presented was the reverse of elegant. There was rather more than twenty-four hours' growth of beard upon his chin. A white silk handkerchief did duty for a collar; a somewhat dilapidated dressing-gown fulfilled the functions of a coat, and in lieu of the stout and comfortable-looking boots, which were already rather famous, he wore a pair of carpet slippers.

On a small table, near the fire, a tray was set. It contained a teapot, a liberal supply of toast, and three boiled eggs. The *Planet* newspaper was propped against the teapot. With an adroitness that must have been the fruit of long practice, Mr. Draper ministered impartially to the needs of the mind and the needs of the body.

Line by line he read his speech of the previous night. The report of it in the famous journal was a miracle of accuracy and completeness. Every sentence was there in its integrity, as the speaker had delivered it. Almost every comma was in place. The orator could almost catch the subtle inflections of his own voice as he used the magical words. Paragraph by paragraph as he read, he nodded his head in a kind of rapturous unison.

Yes, it was a wonderful piece of reporting. It was a wonderful speech. The clear, simple, spontaneous Saxon English, as lucid as a crystal; the flashes of luminous imagery that had fused the minds of his hearers; the air of high sincerity; the masculine force of reasoning and the deep note of conviction which had given it such an irresistible momentum, all were here.

There came a point halfway down the second column where the Minister forgot all about his breakfast. His mind began to race ahead. He was reading now in a kind of entrancement with his brain on fire. Now he was the æsthete listening with a sense of emotional luxury to a symphony of exquisite music; now he was the acute and clear-sighted thinker, almost painfully conscious of the special conditions that had called it forth.

Suddenly he rose from the table. His sombre eyes were blazing out of a deeply lined face. Something seemed to have turned his veins to molten fire.

"Oh, my God!" he cried to his peers all around

him, the crowded shelves of his study, "Oh, my God, what a power you have given me!"

Demosthenes, Cicero, Burke, Bright, and Gladstone were with him in the room.   He trembled violently. He was almost overpowered by a desire to pray.

The words of the sibyl flamed across his brain: "You are the only man now who can save the country."

The remainder of his breakfast was forgotten.   He turned to another page of the *Planet* to read the leading article upon his speech.   He hardly expected it to interest him.   The art of the party journalist always left him cold.   He knew the source to be tainted; his instinct told him that here would be criticism of the man, not an appreciation of his motives.

Yes, the great newspaper was marshalling its barbs.   A look of pity came into his face.   But, steeled as he was, somehow this morning this obtuse partisanship was like a knife between his ribs.   At such a moment in the life of the nation it was very ill done.

Curiosity, however, enabled him to read on.   Very soon there began to emerge from the welter of partisan spleen a genuine note of alarm:

"By this foul stroke, the President of the Board of Conciliation, who of all men should have held his

hand in this acute national crisis, has undone with a
single blow the work to which the three great parties
in the realm have so painfully and so precariously
addressed themselves during the last twelve months.
It is the work of an incendiary; the work of one who
sets an ignoble personal ambition before the claims
of his Sovereign and the love of his country.   At such
a moment as this, every sane and responsible Englishman, acquainted with the true facts of the situation,
will view with nothing short of horror the downfall of
the Coalition Government whose doom was pronounced last night in the House of Commons by the
man of all others who, by the nature of his office, was
pledged to uphold it.   It is never the part of good
citizenship to yield to panic, but we are forced to
affirm that by his wicked and immoral action the
President of the Board of Conciliation has plunged
his country into the gravest internal crisis since that
which overwhelmed it on the fourth of January,
1642."

The source was polluted; but for once the cry of
"Wolf!" was sincere.   The *Planet* had cried "Wolf"
so often and so loudly that impartial minds, for all
the prestige to which it was justly entitled, no longer
heeded its voice.   But the note of fear was unmis-
takably genuine this morning.

VI

THERE came a peremptory knock on the door. A tall woman enveloped in a sealskin coat entered the study. It was Evelyn Rockingham.

"Don't blame Nicholson," she said. "He did his best, but he couldn't keep me out."

With a powerful effort of the will the Minister came back into the world of affairs. He set a chair for his visitor.

"You'll be losing a good servant his place," he said.

The duchess laughed. Her humorous eyes had already traversed the unrazored chin, the scarf, the dressing-gown and the carpet slippers.

"I think he deserves to lose it," she said.

"Poor fellow — if you knew his sufferings!"

"Why does he stay?"

"Personal magnetism, I suppose. He believes in me. He was there last night."

Evelyn nodded, suddenly grave.

"Is the door closed?" She looked round. "There is no possibility of our being overheard?"

"None."

"James Draper," she said, "no matter what happens now, you must keep your head. If you don't, God help us all."

The face of the Minister was haggard.

"There is quite a pleasant little family party at the Palace this morning," said the duchess.

"Yes, I expect so."

"Mr. Grundy was there by nine o'clock. Evan Mauleverer was sent for at ten. Daventry was sent for at a quarter-past, and even our poor, dear Robert had to dress in a desperate hurry before eleven."

"Poor Robert!" said the Minister. "Called into the councils of the nation at such an ungodly hour."

"Yes, it's an unjust world. All those nincompoops as blameless as the babe unborn; and here is the author of the mischief lingering in dressing-gown and slippers over his breakfast at twenty minutes past twelve by the clock. By which token I presume you have not yet been summoned to the councils of the nation."

"Oh, no, it's much too early. Things will have to be pretty hopeless before that happens."

"Yes, I suppose. Yet that time is very near. By the way, I see you have the *Planet* there."

"Yes."

"A pitiful exhibition!"

"Yes, rather pitiful." The face of the Minister grew suddenly sad. "If only it would learn to play fair politically, what a power it might be!"

"One can never understand why it doesn't."

"Bred in a bad old tradition. Yet it tries so hard to be honest in everything else."

Evelyn Rockingham shrugged her shoulders a little contemptuously.

"I don't think women have much cause to revere it. Give me a cigarette to purify the atmosphere."

The bell was rung and cigarettes were sent for.

"When are you going to try one?"

"I shall have to try something to stop the pressure," said Mr. Draper in a hollow tone. "I haven't closed my eyes for four nights."

"Poor fellow! You must really begin. Try this."

She chose a cigarette from the box that had been brought, placed it between his lips and gravely lit it for him.

"Take it gently at first. It ought to do you good." Suddenly she knitted her brows. "I wonder," she said, "if the collective wisdom of that precious crew will rise to the only possible solution?"

"What is the only possible solution?"

"Do you honestly mean you don't know?"

"Oh, I think I know; it is merely that I crave confirmation of my own prescience."

"Evan Mauleverer is the man who frightens me."

"Surely he must realize that all the signals are set dead against him."

"He realizes nothing beyond the fact that one Evan Mauleverer has a morbid craving for office. We were boy and girl together; I know the nature of the animal; he had always to be the cock of every walk."

"The Right in its furious valour will spur him on, of course, but unless the man is a fool he must know what there is against him."

"He is so arrogant; and he has always surrounded himself with inferior people. I hope there is one among that precious conclave who can read the writing on the wall."

"Well, we ought to know very soon now."

Mr. Draper looked at his watch.

"Perhaps we can find out now," said Evelyn Rockingham. "Ask Mr. Renshaw to telephone to Number 10."

"It will be more dignified to wait," said the Minister, rebuking this feminine impatience with a gentle show of indifference.

"You have such a force of will," she said. "You have a force of will so much greater than any one I have ever met. Oh, I hope these fools will realize it!" Her voice broke a little queerly.

"We none of us know what we have," said Mr. Draper, "until we are brought to the test. Evelyn"

— he lifted his sombre eyes half-deprecatingly, and she coloured a little at the curious note of intimacy — "Evelyn, I am going to make you a little confession. I almost wish now — at this moment — that I was a little nearer to my God."

"Yes, I understand. But I've always thought it was only we weak women who felt that sort of need."

"There is the woman in all of us," said Mr. Draper. "And she is never quite strong enough, poor soul. Cromwell was always very close to his God. It must have given him a great pull, I think."

As he spoke he pointed to a small cast in plaster of the Lord Protector which adorned the chimney-piece.

"Forgive my asking the question, but are you on terms with your own God?"

"I have not lost the habit of addressing Him on occasion."

"Then if you don't mind " — the Minister spoke quite humbly and a little shyly — "I want you, in your capacity of a friend to whom I owe a very great deal, always to say a special little prayer for James Draper."

As he spoke he collected the scattered sheets of the *Planet*, placed them together and folded the paper neatly. He had hardly done this when his wife came into the room.

Lady Aline Draper was a slight, petite, charm-

ingly dainty woman, ten years younger than her
husband. She had at that moment returned from
a week-end in the country.

On the threshold of the room she suffered an
instant of embarrassment.

"How are you, Aline?" said Evelyn Rockingham,
going forward to meet her.

Lady Aline's self-possession was equal to the moment, but the rather childish face turned the colour
of snow.

"How are you, Aline?" said Evelyn with marked
kindness.

They shook hands.

The Minister kissed his wife affectionately.

"Forgive my rags, darling," he said simply
enough. "Somehow I had got it into my head that
you would come back by the afternoon train."

Lady Aline had now flushed rather vividly. She
bit her lip. Evelyn Rockingham was not proof
against a little stealthy, slightly malicious amusement.

"It's not his fault," she laughed. "Poor Nicholson couldn't keep me out. I said, 'It's no use,
Nicholson, I know where to find him'; and I marched
right in here. And there was the wrecker of ministries in what he is pleased to call his dressing-gown
— you must really buy him a new one, my dear, and
insist on his wearing it — struggling with the *Planet*
and recalcitrant egg-shells."

This speech, carelessly genial and with perhaps an undercurrent of malice, did nothing to lessen the flush in the cheeks of Lady Aline. She made no immediate response beyond the rather lame and conventional rejoinder that she was sorry to disturb them.

"I hope you have read the speech," said Evelyn Rockingham.

"Yes, some of it."

"Some of it?"

"It was so long."

"So long?"

The two women looked at one another steadily. Their eyes had narrowed till they shone like rapiers.

"Yes, so long," said Lady Aline upon a note of defiance.

"I was there," said Evelyn, "in the House. I heard every word. I have read every word since. I can repeat passages by heart."

"Really!" The tone was cold and biting.

Evelyn flushed now. Her fine face was alive with emotion.

"It was a very wonderful speech," she said in a falling voice.

"I thought it read like a rather dangerous speech," said Lady Aline, with her eyes upon the other's face. "I hope it won't turn out the Government."

"It has turned out the Government."

The face of the Minster's wife was frankly incredulous. The Minister himself stood at his ease, his hands in his pockets and his back to the fire.

"Jim!" said his wife, the picture of consternation.

Mr. Draper smiled at her with a genuine tenderness in his eyes.

"Poor darling!" he said. "Go and get some lunch."

The slight figure stood the picture of dismay.

"Jim, what have you done?" she said. "That is the meaning of that dreadful article in the *Planet*. They say you have destroyed everything."

"One man cannot destroy everything, my dear child," said the Minister.

"But the Coalition! As long as that held there was a hope of keeping things together, wasn't there? Oh, Jim! what have you done?" Suddenly the daughter of the feudal aristocracy, to whom the security of the existing order meant so much, began to expound the dire truth as it was flashed across her mind. "Oh, it's madness, madness. If you have turned out the Coalition you have ruined your party, you have ruined your country, you have ruined yourself."

"O ye of little faith!" said Evelyn softly.

The other woman, for all her childish air, gathered herself with a gesture of fierce disdain. She almost bit her lip through in the vain attempt to repress the tempest that was raging within. The struggle left her white and trembling, but silent.

"Aline," said the Minister in a singularly gentle voice, which yet was full of pain, "I don't think you quite understand what lies behind all this. Pay no attention to the newspapers. Things are not always what they seem."

But Lady Aline was not listening to the words of her husband. She was looking at the rather mocking face of her rival.

"You wicked woman!" The words were chosen deliberately. "It was you who set him on to this. I see everything. You think if he overturns the monarchy it may help your miserable Woman's League. But it won't. Where will any of us be if we have a revolution? You wicked woman, to try to ruin the country. Evelyn, if there is a God in heaven I hope He will punish you."

In the manner of a small whirlwind Lady Aline withdrew from the room.

VII

MR. DRAPER and Evelyn Rockingham were left gazing at one another rather blankly.

"Poor child!" said Lady Aline's husband. There was something odd in his voice.

"She can't understand, poor child," said Evelyn Rockingham. "They are all alike, the Carlows. They have such limitations. Up to a point they are splendid. Beyond that point they are pathetic, tragic, hopeless."

"Yes, she is past her limit." Not only the voice but the face of the Minister was full of pain. "She can't understand. She doesn't know where we are, my dear Evelyn, you and I; she doesn't know in what relation we stand toward the civic liberties of our country."

With a gesture of homage the Minister bore her hand to his lips.

"That is how I think of you," he said. "I think of you as the first woman of your time."

The perfect simplicity of the action rendered Evelyn silent. There was something childlike in his trust of her and it made her wince.

"I hope you will never be undeceived," she said, half involuntarily.

"How can I be?"

His sombre eyes sank into hers.

"I only ask you not to raise the pedestal too high," she said. "Mortal men, you know, mortal men, as Falstaff said — and more than mortal women."

The door opened. "May I come in?"

A handsome, acute-looking, lawyer-like man about thirty entered carrying his hat and wearing an overcoat.

"Oh, it's you, Renshaw, is it? What are the tidings from Number 10?"

"A hopeless muddle, I'm afraid, sir," said the private secretary. "They all seem to have lost their heads. Nobody is willing to assume responsibility for anything. Mr. Grundy resigned at a quarter-past nine, and Mr. Mauleverer cannot be persuaded to accept office."

"What is the source of your information, Mr. Renshaw?" said Evelyn Rockingham. "It is not like Evan Mauleverer to be so modest."

"Sir John Hooper has just come from the Palace. He says the Centre has put in such a strong requisition that Mr. Mauleverer has asked the King to allow him to postpone his decision until to-morrow."

"Let us hope to-morrow will continue to bring

wisdom, Mr. Renshaw, even to Evan Mauleverer,"
said Evelyn Rockingham, "although personally I
take leave to doubt it."

"Things are in a hopeless muddle at Number 10
in the meantime," said the private secretary. "The
Chief Constable of Manchester has telephoned for
six battalions of the line and three companies of
artillery to guard the permanent way, but Sir George
has declined to undertake the responsibility, and
no one seems to know what to do in the circumstances."

"Asses!" said the ex-president of the Board of
Conciliation. "Why don't they go to the King.
The old sentimental humbug, I suppose, of safe-
guarding the popularity of the Throne, which has
done as much as anything to put us where we are.
What's a King for, if in the last resort he can't take
upon himself to defend the lives and uphold the
liberties of his subjects." The Minister strode up
and down the room. "Tell me, Renshaw, what are
they going to do?"

"I'm afraid nothing will be done, sir, until after
the meeting of the Privy Council, which is called
for to-morrow morning at ten o'clock."

"Monstrous! By that time the whole service of
the country may be dislocated."

Mr. Draper continued to stride up and down the
room.

"Do you really mean to say they are going to do nothing?"

"I am afraid that is their intention, sir. I understand that Mr. Grundy has consulted Professor Pery on the point of constitutional law involved, and on his advice action will be deferred until the Privy Council has met to-morrow."

"Oh, my God, it's like a comic opera," groaned the Minister.   "Isn't *anybody* going to take the thing in hand.   There isn't a moment to lose."

"Now that the Government is out, sir, they don't seem to know quite where they are, or what they should do.   They all seem to be waiting for somebody else to move."

"It's so like them," said Evelyn Rockingham.

"I think I had better go and see the King myself," said Mr. Draper.

"Yes, do," said Evelyn.

"I will.   And I hope he'll excuse my chin."

VIII

"I HAVE invited myself to lunch."

Lady Aline, seated alone at the table in the large and gloomy dining-room, rose to greet an impressive-looking personage who had been announced. He was a fine-looking man, verging upon fifty. In his black satin cravat was a very brilliant diamond, and he wore a decidedly fanciful frock-coat.

"I am so glad to see you," she said. There was a cordiality in her manner which showed they were great friends. "It was very disappointing you were not at Cloudesley."

"Yes, my dear Aline, very disappointing. But we are rather making history, you know, just at present."

Robert Conway, seventh duke of Rockingham, was a man to whom his country should have been able to turn with confidence in its hour of need. He came of a race of statesmen, he was a highly educated man of the world, he was familiar with the art of government in its most specialized and intricate phases. At more than one European court he was a popular and familiar figure; he had an extraordinary personal charm when he cared to exert it; and had it pleased Providence to call him to a humbler sphere, where an honourable ambition might have seemed not unbecoming, he had many of the gifts which would have enabled him to go far. Had he chosen to cultivate his garden he might have rendered signal service to the country. Unfortunately, life had always been made easy for him. He was content to toy with statesmanship. The only things he treated seriously were women and fly-fishing.

"Did you hear the speech last night?" asked Lady Aline as they seated themselves at the table.

"Unfortunately, no," said the Duke with an odd grimace.

"I want you to answer me one question, Robert," said Lady Aline. "Has it ruined him?"

His Grace took a little time for his answer.

"Yes, of course it has," he said. "And it's quite on the cards that it's ruined the country. Things are in a hopeless state this morning."

"One would have thought Evan Mauleverer ——"

"They'll never stand poor dear Evan for a quarter of an hour. Of course we might try him, but it's taking a frightful risk. The working classes have got conscription on the brain — and I don't blame 'em. Antrobus says we should have the Northumbrian miners pulling down the Houses of Parliament in twenty-four hours."

"Well, there's nobody else — is there?"

"Nobody, absolutely — that is, at the moment. There is an extraordinary conflict of opinion."

"Why don't they ask you, Robert?"

The Duke shrugged his shoulders placidly.

"This is a job for a professional," he said. "I am only an amateur, my dear Aline, and by the courtesy of Providence I'm content to remain one. It's not a gentleman's work to fight those dirty dogs on the Left. I hold my nose every time I go into the place and carry carbolic in my handkerchief. The fact is, my dear Aline, that filthy scum has been presented with every card in the game."

"Yes," said Lady Aline with intense bitterness.

"Of course those unwashed beasts will demand a referendum if we don't come to some agreement mighty soon, and then it will be a case of Citizen Galloway or a certain gentleman who shall be nameless."

"Do you think he had that in his mind?"

Rockingham laughed, not very pleasantly.

"Undoubtedly. At least a certain person had it in hers."

Lady Aline's face hardened.

"I knew she had set him on," she said. "I knew she was serving her own miserable ends."

"There is one thing she has forgotten though."

"What is that?"

"The Seventh Commandment," said his Grace, looking his companion imperturbably in the eyes.

The face of Lady Aline was the colour of flame. The glass of water she was about to drink slopped over on to the tablecloth.

"England is a very moral country," said the Duke, "and her Grace has forgotten it. There is the prettiest little cabal going on since Bulstrode, poor devil, was hounded out of politics. St. John Becher is the most important man in London just now. The purity brigade have got their ears back properly, I can tell you."

The face of Lady Aline was now the colour of ashes.

"It seems a pity that a fine career should end in that way," said the Duke imperturbably. "I'm rather sorry," he added with a somewhat sinister air of magnanimity. "He has such possibilities. When he's up he's the most interesting man in the House. By the way, I met him striding along the Mall just now as though his life depended on it. That is why I looked in. And as I came to the door, lo and behold! her Grace was driving away from it."

"She simply haunts the place now."

"I know," said the husband of her Grace with calm indifference. "Well, she has the satisfaction of having ruined a man of genius. I suppose it is a satisfaction of a kind."

"I can't think it is ruin."

"You would have thought so had you heard what passed this morning at the Palace. The studiously well-bred manner in which one and all avoided the mention of his name in my hearing was the choicest bit of comedy I've seen for years. Molière never surpassed it. And as though one cared a continental damn." His Grace was suddenly overwhelmed by laughter which sounded absolutely unforced and spontaneous. "It's a quaint, mad world, my masters. I must say the atmosphere was rather overpowering. By Jove, Aline," the Duke laid down his knife and fork, "if I didn't dislike the man so intensely, I'd rather like to see him play a coup. Somehow Mr. Pecksniff always gets one on the raw."

Lady Aline was silent. She and Rockingham were very old friends, and she was well accustomed to his frankness. But this morning it had a note of confidence that was almost brutal. He had always chosen to ignore the fact that she had married "the Haberdasher," but even he had never quite permitted himself his present degree of license.

"I wonder if the man is capable of playing a coup. But no" — the tone regained its assurance — "the fellow is not big enough and deep enough for that."

"What do you mean by a coup, Robert?"

"They seem to think in the Centre, those omniscient Moderates" — Rockingham's tone was bitingly satirical — "that Mr. D. having crabbed all parties, having cut the ground from under the feet of everybody, might make a trial of his own strength. They seem to think he has an enormous and growing power in the country."

The Duke's laugh was not agreeable. It may have been an emanation of the offended patriot; on the other hand, it had a note which did not exactly proclaim an unalloyed altruism.

"I suppose Evelyn might help him there?" said Lady Aline.

"She is mischievous enough for anything. And of course that infernal League, now that women have become so important, has, in a way, to be reckoned with. They say he has a strange power over women. But of course he must have, else you wouldn't have married him."

"I married him for love," said Lady Aline quite simply.

Rockingham nodded his head in a kind of pity.

"Poor girl," he said very gently. "I wish I understood more about women. They are so amazing. That Aline Carlow, of all people, should have married the Haberdasher!"

"He has genius."

"That is to say, he suffers from a rather obscure mental disease."

"He has given me my moments though. My life

would have been nothing without him. It has been a great experience. I am proud to have been his wife."

The slow tears gathered in her eyes. Rockingham was silent.

"It is all over now," she said. "I cannot hold him now, and I have ceased to try. He has gone beyond me. I suppose my marriage was a tragic mistake, as everybody said it would be. But I don't regret it."

Lady Aline rose abruptly from the table and left the room. Rockingham rose and followed her upstairs to her boudoir. In that seclusion she burst into a sudden, uncontrollable paroxysm of tears.

He regarded coolly the exhibition of her weakness.

"Aline," he said at length very softly, taking her hand very tenderly, "you must avenge yourself."

The slender shoulders were shaken with uncontrollable sobs.

He kissed her.

"Poor little soul!" he said.

She trembled from head to foot. He made to take her in his arms, but like a small child who is frightened she put him off. He gathered the charming fair head firmly against his shoulder.

"There," he said, stroking her hair, "have a good cry."

He kissed her again. She shivered in his arms, but she was a little comforted.

"If our child had lived, it would never have happened."

Again the slender frame was shaken.

"One can never tell," said Rockingham. "The idol, as a rule, has feet of clay. You remember the old saying about the silk purse —— ?"

"Don't, Robert!" said Lady Aline piteously. "I can't bear it. He is the noblest man I have ever known."

"A good man perverted by a miserable, mischief-making woman. She perverts everybody. It seems to be her *métier*."

By a supreme effort Lady Aline managed to regain self-control.

"Why did you marry her, Robert?"

"I married her for her intellect," said the Duke. "And any man who marries a woman for her intellect deserves to pay for it."

Lady Aline smiled sadly.

"I think I understand now, Robert, why they call you a reactionary. No wonder the masses hate you!"

"Oh, but they don't, now I've won the Derby twice. And perhaps you think the classes consider me an insolent trifler, eh? You mustn't believe it, my dear Aline. I merely expound the faith as it walks abroad in me. I try to have the courage of my convictions, that is all."

"One wonders if they are worth the courage that they call for, Robert."

"Oh, yes, to the individual, although perhaps they have no *national* significance. Hullo, what have we here!"

Nicholson, the butler, a responsible-looking patriarch, had entered the room, bearing on a salver a small white envelope with a black seal.

"A special messenger, my lady, so I thought I had better give it to you personally, as Mr. Draper is not in."

"Thank you," said Lady Aline. "Put it on the table, please."

Nicholson was a little surprised by the detachment of the tone. All the same he withdrew with the air of a maker of history.

"In his own hand too, by Jove," said Rockingham, taking a quizzical glance at the envelope as it lay on the table. "It is entirely on his own initiative, whatever it is. Evan Mauleverer and I found occasion this morning, when the others had left, to warn him strongly against taking Mr. D. into his counsels. But he had got that fatuous Archbishop coming to lunch. What a pity it is he is so impressionable!"

"Oughtn't a Sovereign to be impressionable?"

"Of course he oughtn't to be. At his birth he should have just a few definite and settled convictions given to him, and he should hang on to them like grim death. If every little side current of opinion can turn him this way and that, what is he going to do when the floodgates are opened?"

The Duke, for all his mantle of cynicism, was plainly discomposed by the modest-looking little packet on the table.

"Evan and I were both at particular pains to warn him. Mark my words, Aline, if that husband of yours once comes out on top the monarchy will not be worth *that!*" And Rockingham snapped his fingers.

"What *can* have moved him to write it, I wonder?"

He shook a finger in the direction of the envelope. Clearly, he was possessed by an itch of curiosity.

"Are you sure the writing is his?" asked Lady Aline, with her eyes fixed upon the letter.

"Quite. One would know that hand anywhere. It is the most characteristic thing about him. A special messenger besides."

Lady Aline kept her gaze pinned upon the letter.

"What can it mean?" said Rockingham, twisting his moustache in his perplexity. "But whatever it may mean it ought not to be."

"You are quite clear upon that point, Robert?" said Lady Aline, with a strange look in her eyes.

"Oh, quite. He oughtn't to be writing to any-body, least of all to Mr. Draper, at this hour of the day. It's most unconstitutional. I expect it's that confounded parson."

Rockingham was a picture of discomposure. And then suddenly, without a word, Lady Aline took the letter from the table and quietly placed it in the fire.

"Good God, Aline, are you mad!"

Rockingham gave a cry of dismay. Instantly he plunged his hand right into the fire and plucked out the scorched envelope. He burnt himself rather severely.

"Aline," he said with a wry mouth as he wrapped his handkerchief round his hand, "you ought not to have done that."

Her eyes had a curious light; her lips were set in a straight line.

"It's not quite the game, Aline." The pain of his fingers was beginning to make him swear a little.

"I am so sorry you are hurt, Robert," she said penitently.

"Oh, that's nothing," he said, valiantly stifling a groan. "But it was a near thing, by Jove!"

"And if it had been destroyed?" said the defiant, thin-lipped mouth.

"Oh, no, my dear girl." He reproved her gently as if she were a small but naughty child. "It isn't cricket, you know."

As she stood looking at him she made an odd picture, half acute remorse, half impenitence.

"You must please let me put something on your fingers," she said, conquered finally by the courage with which he bore his affliction.

He smiled at her rather wryly through the sharp pain that twisted his face.

"Oh, that's nothing at all, my dear girl." He held out his rather mutilated fingers. "But if you are really sorry you had better kiss them to make them better."

IX

WHEN Mr. Draper returned at four o'clock to Queen Anne's Gate, almost the first thing that caught his eye was the charred envelope lying on his study table. He picked it up, and as he was already acquainted with its contents, he examined its exterior closely without breaking the seal.

"It's abominably careless!" he said, and he rang the bell rather tempestuously.

The butler appeared in person.

"Nicholson," said his master sharply, "what is the meaning of this? A most important document partly destroyed."

"I can only say I very much regret it, sir," said the butler with lowered gaze.

"How did it happen?"

"I can't explain, sir, how it came to happen," said the butler, "but I accept full responsibility for the occurrence."

"It won't do, Nicholson," said his master sharply. "There's a mystery here. Where is Mr. Renshaw?"

"He is out, sir. He was not in when the letter arrived, and he knows nothing about it."

"To whom did you give the letter on its arrival?"
Nicholson answered without hesitation.

"I gave it to no one, sir. I brought it straight in
here, and it got partly destroyed by mistake."

"Where was Lady Aline when it arrived?"

"At luncheon, sir."

"Why didn't you give it to her?"

"Yes, sir — I ought to have done. I realize that.
I am very sorry indeed, sir."

Mr. Draper looked perplexed. Obviously he was
a good deal disturbed.

"I am not satisfied with your explanation, Nicholson," he said. "I know you to be an invaluable
servant. You have been in the service of three
prime ministers. I know you to be a discreet and
responsible man. This letter was delivered to you,
I believe, by special messenger. Such gross negli-
gence in a matter of such grave importance is quite
unlike you."

The butler bowed.

"I thank you, sir," he said. "I hope I understand the great responsibility of my position."

The Minister tapped the charred envelope with
his finger.

"This was not an accident, Nicholson," he
said. "That is the kind of accident that doesn't
happen. Did any one lunch with Lady Aline?"

For the fraction of an instant the butler hesitated.

"No one, sir."

"She lunched alone?"

"Yes, sir — alone."

"Very well. That will do for the present. But I am by no means satisfied. I intend to probe this matter to the bottom."

The butler withdrew. When he had closed the door of his master's study he hesitated for a moment like a man in doubt. Then he made his way upstairs to the boudoir of his mistress. She was indulging in a lonely cup of tea and a cigarette.

"May I speak to you, my lady?"

"Certainly, Nicholson," said his mistress amiably.

"It's about that letter, my lady. Mr. Draper has questioned me about it."

"Well?" said his mistress with amiable indifference.

"I thought I would like you to know, my lady, that I have taken full responsibility for it. I have informed Mr. Draper that it was not delivered to you, and I have also informed him that you lunched alone."

"That was rather indiscreet, wasn't it, Nicholson? — from your point of view, I mean." The tone of Lady Aline was one of rather bored indifference.

"I hope your ladyship approves of what I have done."

"On the contrary, I disapprove of it very strongly."

"I am exceedingly sorry, my lady."

The butler's face was rather blank.

"Was it necessary to lie about it, Nicholson?" said his mistress. "Is it necessary to lie about anything?"

"I can only say, my lady, that I have been in the service of three prime ministers, I am an old man, and experience has taught me that when two evils are presented to one it is generally wise to choose the lesser."

Lady Aline was rather amused by this statesman-like omniscience.

"In other words," said she, "you think it is better that you should lie and that I should lie rather than state the simple fact that a piece of paper was thrown in the fire. I am sorry, Nicholson, but I am afraid that kind of ethics is a little too advanced for me. I have always been brought up to believe, you know, that it is well for a servant to keep his place."

The butler bowed humbly and gravely.

"I am sorry, my lady," he said, "that you take this view. Having regard to the special circumstances I thought, after careful consideration, that that was the right course to take. I still venture to think so, my lady, having regard to the special circumstances. We are making history just at present, my lady, if you will excuse my freedom in mentioning it."

"So I believe," said his mistress, "but it seems rather unwise, Nicholson, that you should be mixed up in the process."

"It is not the first time, my lady," said Nicholson with the pride that apes humility, "that I have tried to do my best for the country in a national crisis. But since your ladyship disapproves of my action, I beg to be allowed to give notice."

"Very well, Nicholson," said his mistress, lighting a fresh cigarette; "I am inclined to think, in the circumstances, that is the best thing you can do. Your notice had better take effect a month from to-day. And as you have been quite a good servant, with whom I'm sure Mr. Draper will be sorry to part, I shall be pleased to give you a good character."

"Thank you very much, my lady," said the butler, who appeared to be deeply moved.

He made to withdraw. Before he could leave the room, however, Mr. Draper himself had entered. In his hand was the charred envelope.

"Aline," said the Minister, speaking in a manner more than usually direct, "this is a mystery I am anxious to clear up."

He showed his wife the letter.

"I am not aware," said Lady Aline, "that it is a mystery at all."

"Nicholson appears to treat it as one."

"Oh, yes. But that is an error of judgment on his

part. At least that is the view I take of it, although he still seems rather unconvinced. The whole thing is really quite simple. Nicholson delivered the letter to me. I chose to throw it in the fire, and Rockingham at the cost of his fingers chose to pull it out."

"Rockingham?"

"Yes, he lunched here."

"And you threw it in the fire?"

"Yes," said his wife coldly.

"And Rockingham pulled it out?"

"Yes, at the cost of his fingers. One rather respects him for it, I think."

For the moment the Minister stood in silence, looking a little unnerved. Still holding the charred envelope in his hand he seemed like a man in a dream.

The silence was broken by the quiet and low voice of the butler. It vibrated with feeling.

"I acted as I thought right, sir. I am sorry if I have not done so. But I now beg to be allowed to give notice, sir."

The Minister's drawn face had turned very white. At last, putting forth a powerful effort of the will, he was able to regain command of himself. He placed his hand on the butler's shoulder.

"You were right, Nicholson," he said. "You were quite right."

They went out of the room together.

X

MR. DRAPER and his wife were engaged for dinner that evening and they had to go on to a party afterward. On the plea of public business the Minister asked to be excused. Lady Aline went without him, and he dined alone.

The butler noticed that he ate and drank very little and that he seemed even more preoccupied than usual. It was clear that the business of the letter was weighing upon his mind. But there were other things that were weighing upon it too.

A little before nine o'clock Nicholson was summoned to his master's study.

"Suppose you consider yourself off duty for an hour, Nicholson," said the Minister. "Come and smoke a pipe and let us discuss the present discontents."

Had Nicholson been a dull man he would have been not unlikely to resent this unconventional behaviour of his master. A butler of high caste has his own private code of the ethics of his calling no less than a Minister of the Crown. Only a very bold man would have ventured to ignore the fact.

Each one of Nicholson's prime ministers would as lief have flown to the moon as invite him to his study to smoke a pipe after dinner and discuss the political situation. Happily, Nicholson was in nowise a small-minded man. Humbly and readily he sank the dignity of his calling in the exigencies of the crisis.

"Mix yourself a whisky and soda, Nicholson," said his master, "and then take that chair. You'll find that one the most comfortable."

"Thank you, sir."

With an air which he had unconsciously copied from his first prime minister, Nicholson mixed a fairly stiff whisky and soda and then seated himself at a slightly pontifical leisure.

"I am open to correction," said his master, "but I regard you as a Centre man with a rather pronounced bias toward the Right."

Nicholson's confirmation of this acute prognosis was both wary and austere. The circumstances made it necessary that not a fibre of the official dignity should be relaxed. At the same time the innate urbanity of the accomplished clubman craved for free play.

"Yes, sir," said Nicholson, achieving a blend of deportment which seemed exactly to meet the case. "I think you are pretty correct. Except, perhaps, sir, that since the Marquis's time, as you might say,

I really belong more to the Right than I do to the Centre."

"Yes, I ought to have known that," said Mr. Draper. "At heart you are the born aristocrat. It is merely your professional instincts that bring you anywhere near the Centre at all. You belong to a significant type — a type which has got a very important part to play just now."

"I hope, sir, we shall be able to rise to our responsibilities," said Nicholson, filling his pipe after having been invited to do so.

"Yes, that is the all-important question for all of us. You see, Nicholson, the classes that have a natural and instinctive reverence for the established order of things are now right up against a proletariat which is developing too quickly to be healthy. A succession of ministries has pampered it quite regardless of the mischief they have been doing. The proletariat, as an inevitable consequence, has waxed insolent and become a bully. Don't you rather agree?"

"Yes, sir, I do. I always tell them that at our little society which meets every Thursday evening, of which I have the honour to be a vice-president. What I say is, sir, Democracy will have to be taken down a peg unless the whole thing is going to burst up altogether."

Mr. Draper nodded his approval.

"For the last twenty years, sir," continued
Nicholson, "the masses, in my opinion, have had
a great deal too much given to them. Enlarged
franchise, which lies at the root of all the mischief,
free food, free doctoring, free insurance, free education for their children, pensions for their old age,
have put them right above themselves, in my opinion.
It is a case of all masters and no servants nowadays."

"You would say that they have not been able to
assimilate all the blessings that have been showered
upon them?"

"Yes, sir; assimilate, that is the word. And the
more they get the more discontented they become.
They simply cry out for more instead of learning to
make use of what they have already."

"I am much interested, Nicholson, in your point
of view," said the Minister. "Something has certainly given rise to a terribly difficult and extremely
complex situation."

"The demands of Labour, sir, are outrageous at
the present time, in my opinion."

"I am inclined to agree with you, Nicholson.
But unhappily there seems to be a consensus of
opinion in the country that at this stage Capital
has no alternative but to continue to yield to them."

"Well, if it does, sir, there will soon be no capital
left in the country to yield to anything. I know for
a fact, sir, that if this Bill had gone through,

which you, sir, were wise enough to overthrow at
the eleventh hour, the masters had arranged to close
down all the mills in Lancashire."

"That is interesting. How did you acquire the
information?"

"My brother, sir, is in the service of Sir Samuel
Cooper of Preston. The Lancashire mill-owners
held a meeting at his house the other night."

"That is important. I rather wish you had seen
fit to communicate your knowledge a little sooner."

"I didn't like to presume, sir. Besides, sir, I felt
sure you would know about it."

"No; as a matter of fact it is the first I have
heard of it. It shows the point we have reached, it
shows the kind of political atmosphere we are living
in at present. The group to which the Lancashire
mill-owners belong will have nothing to do with the
Coalition Government. They have boycotted it
persistently. They prefer to keep their plans a
secret and work in the dark. And of course that
enormously increases the difficulty of the task of
government."

"Yes, sir, that I quite understand. In fact, sir,
to quote your great speech the other night, to which
I had the pleasure of listening, 'a great chasm has
opened in the economic life of the nation, and has
left Capital on one side and Labour on the other.'"

The Minister nodded his head.

"I shall never forget that speech, sir. No one who heard it, sir, will ever forget it. When I was a young man it was my privilege to hear Mr. Bright deliver his 'Angel-of-death-has-been-abroad-in-the-land' speech from that very gallery. Your speech on Tuesday night, sir, if you will allow me to say so, belonged to the same class. Those who heard it, sir, will never forget it to their dying day."

As Nicholson spoke his voice grew lower and lower, until his last words were almost inaudible. With a gesture of reverence he folded his hands in front of him.

The Minister was moved.

"It is the finest compliment that has ever been paid to me, Nicholson," he said quite simply. "I felt the occasion very deeply. I wanted to drive it home to the nation."

"And you did, sir. You turned over eighty votes in the Centre and threw out the Government. It was a very great performance, sir, if you will allow me to say so. I never expected to hear the equal of Mr. Bright, sir, but I heard him on Tuesday night — and if you'll excuse the freedom, sir, I think your mind is deeper and more practical."

"You honestly think that, Nicholson?" said the Minister, with a simplicity that was almost boyish.

"I do, sir — honestly."

"You pay me a very high compliment," said the

Minister naïvely. "It is so difficult for an emotional mind to be also practical."

"That is so, sir," said Nicholson, concurring gravely. "Mr. Gladstone and Mr. Morgan and Mr. Collins were emotional men, and all of them fine orators — not *quite* in *your* class, and Mr. Bright's you know, sir — but to my mind they were not practical men. They could always see the beginning, but they couldn't always see the end. . . . That, sir, if you will excuse the freedom, is why I admired you so much last night. You were looking ahead all the time."

"I always try to do that," said the Minister modestly.

"Mr. Hendry and the Marquis always used to do it too, sir, although, of course, you couldn't call either of them orators. But that's how they got their power in the country. They were far-seeing, practical men. They made mistakes, sir, but they could see into the future. And they never allowed the enemy to outflank them, like some other prime ministers I could name. They never gave back an inch to gain a temporary advantage, when it was presently going to cost them the whole position. I'm quoting your speech again, sir, begging your pardon. What I say is, sir, it is a merciful thing for the country that you were inspired to throw out that Bill."

The Minister, engaged in his characteristic occupation of walking up and down the room, paused to search the face of the old butler with an eager and a glowing eye.

"That is your honest conviction, Nicholson? I hope you don't say it merely to give me pleasure."

"No, sir," said, the butler gravely. "It is not my custom to speak to please anybody — when it comes to national affairs. They know that at our little society which meets every Thursday, and that's why they respect me. Please God, sir, I say what I mean and I mean what I say, when it comes to national affairs."

"I am sure of it, Nicholson," said the Minister. "I am honoured by your approval."

"Thank you, sir," said Nicholson gravely; "I am glad to be able to return the compliment. If you'll pardon the freedom, sir, there was just one man I should like to have been present in the House last night."

"Who?"

"The King, sir. I said to my friend Hawksley — butler to the Duke of Flamborough, sir, and a fellow vice-president of our little society, who was sitting next to me in the gallery — I said to my friend Hawksley, 'It is a great pity his Majesty is not here. It would be a great help to him in the present crisis.'"

"And what said your friend Hawksley to that?"

"Hawksley, sir, agreed with me. And if you'll excuse the freedom, sir, it meant a very great deal for Hawksley to do that, because up till then he had always considered you quite a second-rate man."

"You think the speech ought to strengthen my position?"

"I do indeed, sir. In fact it has done so already. To-morrow night, sir, I am going to move a resolution, that 'in the opinion of this society the Right Honourable James Draper should be invited to form a Ministry.'"

"What is the name of your society?"

"The Butlers' Union, sir, of which Mr. Hawksley and I have the honour to be vice-presidents, and of which his Majesty's senior butler is the president."

"Yes," said the Minister thoughtfully, "I appear to have made ground. But it is rather surprising, Nicholson, isn't it, that your society is political?"

"Strictly non-political, sir," said Nicholson. "That is to say, we all think alike. We all belong to the Right, sir, as our little society is confined to men of the highest social standing. Why! would you believe, sir, I nearly had to resign my membership when I entered your service three years ago. You belonged to the Left, then, sir; you were kind of working your way up. I had to appear before the committee, and in spite of the fact, sir, that I had been in the service of three prime ministers, it was only Lady Aline that saved me."

"You appear to be a very exclusive society."

"Very exclusive, indeed! In a manner of speaking, sir, the most exclusive society in London. Birth can get in, as a rule. Ability, sometimes. Money often finds it difficult. It's really best to have a combination; then you are generally all right. Not always, sir, of course; there are exceptions to every rule. Only last year, Lord Harbury's butler — old Catholic family greatly respected in Ireland — was blackballed because his master had married an actress. We carry it to extremes sometimes, sir, I'm bound to admit, but it's a fault on the right side, to my mind."

"Well, Nicholson," said the Minister, "I am very glad to have had this talk with you. And I hope on Thursday night you will put your resolution, and, moreover, that you will be able to carry it."

"I have no doubt I shall be able to do that, sir," said the butler, rising and taking his leave. "Ours is a society of sensible men."

XI

LEFT alone the Minister selected Mill's "Constitution" from the carefully furnished shelves and began to dip at random. Somehow the familiar pages were unable to hold his attention to-night. He was in a condition of strange unrest. For once he seemed unable to concentrate his thoughts, so that presently he had recourse to that never-failing anodyne for fevered minds, the "Meditations of Marcus Aurelius."

As always, that masculine intelligence was able to compose him. Presently the inner tumult began to subside. Deep answered unto deep; his soul went out to that of the noble pagan. An hour passed, and then suddenly, with a great surge of feeling, he reawoke to the exigencies of the present. He looked up from the page with a sense of inward power. His eyes fell upon the small model in plaster in the centre of the chimneypiece.

"Ask of me my country," he murmured, as if in answer to the austere gaze that seemed to meet his own.

The thought was still in his mind, the book was

still in his hand, his eyes were still upon the plaster cast, when the butler re-entered the room.

"A gentleman wishes to see you, sir," he said, "if you can spare him five minutes."

The Minister struggled back to the world of men and things. "What is his name?"

"He would not give his name, sir."

"Has he been here before?"

"Not to my knowledge, sir."

"And you don't know who he is?"

The butler had begun to look rather embarrassed.

"I don't exactly say that, sir. At least, that is to say, I may have a strong suspicion of his identity."

"Well, whom do you take him to be?" The butler grew more embarrassed than ever.

"I beg your pardon, sir, but I feel that I wouldn't like to presume to say who I think he is, for fear I might be mistaken."

His master began to grow rather impatient. "It is all very mysterious," he said. "Do you suppose I myself know this person?"

"Oh, yes, sir. I feel quite sure you do."

"What time is it? A quarter to eleven! It's a rather strange hour. Still the times are strange." The Minister hesitated before making his decision. "Very well, bring him along and I'll try to solve the enigma of his identity."

A moment later the mysterious visitor had been

ushered into the room. He appeared to be about fifty, rather under the middle height. There was an air of simple and unaffected modesty about him as he entered, and this effect was heightened by an unpretentious-looking overcoat and an equally un-pretentious dinner jacket and black tie beneath.

"I hope I am not disturbing you, my dear Mr. Draper," said the visitor, offering his hand with a quiet air of friendliness that was charming.

The Minister was clearly taken aback. For an instant he betrayed both surprise and embarrass-ment.

"Why, sir," he said, "I feel this to be a very great honour."

"I don't want you to feel anything of the kind, said the mysterious visitor with the same quiet but charmingly urbane air, which yet made an effect of perfect sincerity. "I am very lucky to find you at home. I was afraid you might have gone into the country."

"Won't you take off your overcoat, sir?" said the Minister.

"Thanks."

The visitor removed his outer garment.

"And if you will give me a whisky and soda in exchange for a cigar that I know you won't smoke —— ?"

The visitor produced a modest-looking cigar case

and offered it, while Mr. Draper rang for the other requisites.

By the time the visitor was seated at his ease, a little out of the light, the Minister, who was observing him with covert intentness, was able to see that the genial ease of his bearing, which in itself was so pleasant as almost to be captivating, was a cloak for deeper qualities beneath. A close scrutiny of the mysterious visitor's face showed it to be deeply lined, careworn and pale. There was a fixed look of sadness in the heavy-lidded eyes.

"What is your book, Mr. Draper?"

"'Marcus Aurelius.'"

"The wisest man that ever lived, I sometimes think. He's been a true friend to me."

The quiet voice was beautiful when feeling fused it.

"And who is that — on the chimneypiece? Oh, yes."

A subtle smile hovered in the careworn eyes. Mr. Draper smiled too. He rose from his chair and turned the face of the Lord Protector to the wall.

"No, no," said the visitor, laughing. "We can't have that. Somebody has to cut off the head of a king, now and again, don't you know, *pour encourager les autres.*"

"I am very glad, sir, you are able to view the proceeding with such detachment," said the Minister.

"I am very glad, sir, to have your permission to put him back again."

And laughing heartily he reversed the bust of the Lord Protector.

"I thought I would like to have another little chat with you," said the visitor, drawing quietly at his cigar. "Our recent conversation has given me a clearer grasp of the position than I have ever had before. I have discussed it lately with all sorts of people. Upon nearly every point they are widely at variance, but upon two they are absolutely unanimous in agreement."

"And those, sir?" said the Minister, fixing his sunken eyes upon those of his visitor.

"And those, my dear Mr. Draper, are — first, that the situation is extremely grave, and, second, that you are a very dangerous man."

"I?"

"Yes — they all think that. I have had most solemn warnings against you."

"I console myself, sir, with the thought that independence of mind is always viewed with the deepest suspicion."

"It was a point I urged myself, this afternoon, with the Archbishop. But he says the Right has always doubted your loyalty to the Throne."

"Oh, yes, sir, they have always doubted me," said the Minister quietly. "I have been called a republican and other hard names. They say I aim at the first presidency of Great Britain and Ireland."

"Do you aim, my dear Mr. Draper, at that high-sounding title?" said the visitor equably.

Mr. Draper took time for his answer.

"Yes, sir, I do," he said, "if it is the will of God."

XII

A ND of the English people?" said the visitor after a pause.

"The will of the English people is the will of God, sir."

The visitor quietly smoked his cigar.

"Yes, it is!" he said. "But first let us clearly ascertain it. And how, pray, are we to do it now that our electoral machinery has broken down so lamentably?"

"By an appeal to arms, sir—the old-fashioned way."

"Yes, in the last resort. But always in the last resort."

"We are very near it, sir."

"Yes, they tell me so."

The visitor's voice fell rather suddenly.

"It's a grievous thing," he said. His face looked pinched and haggard. "The mischief is continually growing."

"I have confirmation of that, sir," said the Minister.

He unlocked a drawer in his desk and took out a letter.

"Do you care to read it, sir?"

The visitor produced a pair of eyeglasses.

"Who is John Cox?" he said, when he had finished reading the letter.

"John Cox, sir, is the General Secretary of the Workers' League, which has an affiliated membership of fifteen million persons. It is an organization that ought, in my humble judgment, to have been strangled at its birth. My Manchester speech of March five years ago advocated that course very strongly. But I was then a voice crying in the wilderness. Nobody heeded me, and that speech nearly terminated my public career."

"Oh, yes, Mr. Draper, I remember the speech. But you were then regarded, you know, as a rival of Galloway. The opinion commonly held at that time was that you were trying to spike his guns."

The Minister smiled.

"It has always pleased a certain faction to regard me as the rival of Galloway. If I have said or done a thing, it has generally been attributed to a desire to score a point with the electorate at the expense of a man for whom I have a profound contempt."

"That has been rather the case, I am afraid. One is beginning to see the injustice of it all."

"I make no complaint, sir, as far as I am concerned personally," said the Minister. "But if people who ought to know better did not allow an

unworthy partisanship to override their judgment,
I sometimes think it would give us all a better
chance."

"It was certainly very wrong not to have heeded
the warning," said the visitor.

"The League has now become a great power.
It is a secret society which practically controls the
electorate. At the present moment the ruler of
England is George John Galloway."

"That is your deliberate opinion, Mr. Draper?"

"I give it, sir, for what it is worth. But there
are two hundred seats on the Left which are the
nominees of the League. The question now at issue
is whether any legislation is to be possible without
its mandate."

"I have been given to understand that Galloway is
a very dangerous man."

"In my judgment, sir, he is a menace to society.
He has a genius for organization; moreover, he in-
spires and controls a foul Press which has carefully
studied the art of appealing to uneducated minds."

"Would you say that this man is actively disloyal?"

"I go further, sir. In my opinion he is an enemy
of society."

"You are a man of strong views, Mr. Draper."

"I hope, sir, I am. One can do nothing in this
world without them. When I see a man of this

stamp inflaming the passions of the ignorant it is more than I can endure. If I were the King of England —— "

"Yes, Mr. Draper, if you were the King of England?" said the visitor in his tranquil voice, cutting off the end of his second cigar.

"I should not rest easy in my bed, sir, until I had scotched George John Galloway."

"Is there any constitutional process by which it could be done?"

"It would be very interesting to see, sir."

"Could we impeach him for sedition?"

"At any rate, sir, it would be interesting to have the opinion of the Attorney-general."

The visitor put on his eyeglasses and read the letter again.

"I quite agree," he said, "but it seems to me that this is hardly the time to take such a decisive step, even if we were advised that it could be taken. The situation is most critical."

"The more critical the situation, sir, the greater the need for decisive action. We have had far too much of this balancing of one force against another force; we have had far too much of this parleying with the enemy in the gate. We have merely moved on from crisis to crisis; we have merely postponed the day of reckoning; and all the time the situation has got more and more out of hand, and men like

Galloway have been able to turn it to their own profit."

The visitor nodded his head in acquiescence.

"Yes, Mr. Draper," he said, almost in the manner of one thinking aloud. "You certainly hold strong views."

The Minister bowed deferentially.

"I merely give them, sir, for what they are worth."

The visitor pondered; and then he smiled his rather forlorn smile.

"I wish, Mr. Draper," he said, "you were not such a dangerous man. Everybody walks, you know, in fear of a reformed democrat. Now assuming that we proceed to extremities against this man Galloway, what, in your opinion, would be the consequences?"

"It would be the throwing down of the gage of battle. The King's enemies, if they were strong enough, would show themselves and come out into the open."

"Yes — and then?"

"I would strain the law to its limits and I would strain the constitution to its limits to crush them out of existence."

"And the country might be bathed in blood from end to end!"

"Well, sir, it seems to me that that is the path of statesmanship, wherever it may lead. We are subject to an unbridled and ever-increasing tyranny. There is no tyranny like that of selfish ignorance. Democracy is going too fast. It is time, sir, in my judgment, that somebody started in to hold it back."

"But if it can only be done by machine guns?"

"So much the worse, sir, for democracy."

The visitor's laugh was rather melancholy.

"You are putting back the clock, aren't you, my dear Mr. Draper?" he said in his musical voice. "Richelieu talked in that way to Louis XIII in the days of his particular League."

"I expect he did, sir. And, in any case, it seems to me that we shall have to go back in order to go forward."

"Yes, I am afraid you are a highly dangerous man, Mr. Draper," said his visitor with a sigh as he measured himself a second whisky and soda. "And, in any case, I know nothing more trying than to be without a Government. By the way, there is a meeting of the Privy Council to-morrow morning at eleven. Will you be able to be present?"

The Minister did not answer immediately. "I am out of sympathy, sir, with much of their recent procedure," he said at length.

"But must we not proceed under constitutional forms as far as we can?"

"Yes, sir, as far as we can. But in a crisis of this

magnitude it seems safer to act first and then refer to the constitution afterward."

"Perhaps there is something to be said for that view. In the meantime we must form a Government of some kind."

"I suppose, sir, the task will devolve upon Evan Mauleverer?"

"He is the man, certainly, of the widest political experience. He at least has a solid body of conservative opinion behind him. Personally, I hope he will yield to pressure and take office. At the present moment he seems the only possible alternative. But whether he is a strong enough man to hold things together under present conditions, that, of course, is a question that we must leave time to answer."

"Time has answered it already, sir. Evan Mauleverer has accepted office on two occasions; and on each he has contrived to bring us sensibly nearer to the Deluge."

"Well, my dear Mr. Draper, can you suggest any one else?" said the visitor, knocking the ash off his cigar.

The Minister stroked the aggressive jaw which had made him so many enemies.

"In the present crisis, sir," he said after a pause, "Galloway himself would be less dangerous than Evan Mauleverer. This is not the hour for dilettantism. Evan Mauleverer is very well here in London and the home counties. But the North has absolutely no use for him. And when all is said, sir, it is the North that is the driving power of England to-day."

"Yes, I think we are all agreed upon that. Evan Mauleverer is himself aware of it. That is why he hesitates. The ground of his objection is that to govern England to-day a man must have the North behind him. And he frankly admits that he hasn't that."

"Then, sir, let him make way for a man who has."

"But where, my dear Mr. Draper, is the man to be found?" The visitor took a long draw at his cigar.

The Minister was silent.

A long and rather tense pause ensued.

The visitor peered intently into the stern face of the Minister. Presently he rose from his chair.

"Mr. Draper," he said at last, very slowly and reluctantly, "do you know what is said? Understand, I yield to the pressure of these great exigencies."

Mr. Draper drew himself up proudly and a little haughtily.

"It is not true, sir," he said in a voice of such tense emotion that it was hardly recognizable as his own. "I know what they are saying. I have never heard it, sir, from the lips of anybody, but I feel it here." With a gesture of pain the Minister placed his hand across his heart.

Under the stress of his own deep emotion the visitor also showed signs of discomposure.

"One is glad to have such an assurance, Mr. Draper," he said. "Although I would not have you misunderstand me. I have always held myself that it is an act of impertinence to pry into the private life of a public man. But this is a peculiar country. As you are aware, the contrary view is freely held. I feel it only right to inform you that the story is told against you with great circumstance and it is very widely circulated. The greatest pressure is being brought to bear against you from every possible quarter. I accept your word gladly and unreservedly, my dear Mr. Draper; I shall lose no time in informing the Archbishop; but in these grave circumstances it is desperately unfortunate that the story has been circulated at all."

The Minister remained silent. His face was not very pleasant to look upon.

"It's a blackguardly trick," he said at last, "to strike at a man through a woman — and such a woman. I'll admit, sir, I've been indiscreet. I was born with a contempt for public opinion. I see now that I have been wrong, that I have made a serious error of judgment in giving that kind of handle to my enemies. They have used it very skilfully. But, by God, sir" — the Minister brought his hand down with a crash upon his writing-table — "I'll beat them yet!"

"Yes, Mr. Draper, I am inclined to think you will," said the visitor with courteous kindness. "But having regard to all the forces that are marshalled against you, I am sadly afraid that the time is not yet. Unless —— "

"Unless, sir?" said the Minister with a kind of sunken eagerness.

"Unless we get so deeply in the mire that we are obliged to call you in to help us out."

The Minister could not repress a rather forlorn smile at this display of candour.

"I see, sir," he said in a hollow tone.

"Would you hesitate to do it, Mr. Draper — if the circumstances arose?"

"One never quite knows what one would do, sir, in a given case, until the case presents itself. I love my country, but this is the kind of thing to make a man have doubts whether his country is worthy of his love."

"Perhaps I ought not to have mentioned it."

"I am sincerely grateful that you did, sir. My instincts told me it was there all the time. I have heard whispers; I've seen eyebrows raised and shoulders shrugged. But I didn't realize that it had gone so far as this."

The voice of the Minister died suddenly in his throat. In his agitation he began to pace the room. It was clear to his visitor that he was rather badly hit.

XIII

THE Minister was still engaged in walking up and down the room in an effort to cope with a stress of mind which he made no attempt to disguise when the butler entered.

He gave his master a somewhat grimy-looking card.

Mr. Draper glanced at it, and then after a moment's hesitation handed it to his visitor. On the card was printed the following:

JOSEPH BRIGGS
President of the Engine Drivers' Association
14 Pym Street, Derby

"Yes, why not?" said the visitor in response to the Minister's look of inquiry.

"I will see him, Nicholson," said Mr. Draper.

The President of the Engine Drivers' Association proved to be a burly specimen of British manhood. He was large and hearty and not overclean; his voice was like a megaphone and his gait had a nautical roll.

"Pleased to meet you, sir," said Joseph Briggs, shaking hands warmly with the Minister. "I've been wanting to give myself the pleasure a long time."

"I am very glad to make your acquaintance, Mr. Briggs," said the Minister, shaking hands cordially. "What can I do for you?"

"Well, sir, it's a rather ticklish matter." Briggs cast a glance in the direction of the visitor, who still remained seated somewhat in the shadow.

"You can speak quite freely before my friend," said the Minister.

"Well, sir, I'm sadly afraid there is black mischief brewing at Derby."

"So I understand," said the Minister. "The Home Office, I believe, has information to that effect."

"Well, sir, my mates and I think if you would come to Derby and address a meeting as soon as possible you might do a power of good. You've got a big influence at Derby, sir, among all grades."

"I am very glad to enjoy the confidence of Derby."

"It's no idle compliment, sir; at Derby we know a man's worth. We remember your speech last year, sir, on the eve of the election. You've a good backing at Derby, sir, but unfortunately these young fellows have got out of hand."

"Yes, Mr. Briggs, so I believe," said the Minister. "And how do you account for their being out of hand?"

"Things is made too easy for 'em nowadays, sir. They want to get on too fast. I put it down to free education and free libraries partly. Instead of being satisfied with a can of ale and a pipe of 'bacca they go and overread themselves on socialism and the Galloway press. The consequence is, sir, they get right above themselves. They are all wanting to be masters nowadays."

"Can you suggest any remedy for this state of things?" the visitor interposed.

"In the first place, sir, we want a strong Government who won't stand nonsense from anybody. My own opinion is, sir, we want a Government that will put Galloway in gaol."

"You think he is a menace to the country?" the visitor quietly interposed.

"There is no doubt about that, sir. He's put all the locomotive shops and the porters and the plate-layers right above themselves. They talk of their grievances. What are their grievances? They ought to have joined the company forty years ago and then they might have had some grievances to talk about. No, sir, things are too easy for 'em nowadays. We hadn't the time in those days to trouble about this syndicalism, as they call it, and that sort of nonsense."

"You would say, Mr. Briggs, the state of things is very serious?" said the Minister.

"That is my opinion, sir."

"And you think I might do some good at Derby?"

"I am convinced of it, sir. At Derby we older men believe in you, and we should very much like to see you Prime Minister. What we say is, that if the King is a sensible gentleman he'll put you in the place of Mr. Grundy without delay."

"Tell me, Mr. Briggs," said the visitor, "do you consider the King to be a sensible gentleman?"

"Very, sir, I should say. At least that was the impression I formed of him when I had the honour of meeting him."

"When did you meet him?"

"It would be the best part of ten years ago now, sir. He gave me this."

The President of the Engine Drivers' Association indicated a small gold medal that was suspended from his watch chain.

"Oh, yes, I remember," said the visitor, keeping well in the shadow. "There was an accident; an express was derailed and you saved the lives of three of the passengers at great personal risk. You were severely scalded, Mr. Briggs, in rendering assistance, were you not?"

"Yes, sir. I was in the hospital the best part of a year after it, but the company behaved very handsome and I'm promoted now to a higher grade. These young chaps often abuse the King and say he

is no use at all, and he costs the country a great deal
too much, and so on, but when he shook hands with
me and pinned this medal on to my coat, and said,
'You are a very brave man, Mr. Briggs, and I'm
proud to make your acquaintance,' I didn't think he
was no good, I'll give you my word."

"Is it that the younger men think the King ought
to take a more active part in public affairs?" said the
visitor.   "Or is it that they think he is a luxury who
is rather too expensive?"

"I don't think they know what they do think, sir,
if you ask my opinion.   But they are so full of book
learning, sir, nowadays, that they must always be
growling at something."

"It is very mischievous for the country all the
same," said the Minister.

"Of course it is, sir.   And that's why we want a
strong Government that won't give in to them.
But the situation is very serious, sir.   They are all
ready to come out as soon as the League gives the
signal; and I also hear that the miners, the dockers,
the postmen, and the police are only waiting for the
signal."

"In other words," said the Minister, "we stand
upon the verge of civil war."

"Yes, sir, I am afraid that is so."

"Well, Mr. Briggs, if I come to Derby and address a
meeting, what is it going to profit the country now?"

"It will strengthen the hands of us Centre men, who are doing all we can to hold the hotheads back a bit."

"I see!"

"Suppose you promise to go, my dear Mr. Draper," said the visitor. "Derby seems to need you rather badly."

The Minister pondered.

"Yes, sir," he said at length, "I will go to Derby if it is your wish. You would like me to come soon?" he said to Briggs.

"Yes, sir, the sooner you come the better for everybody."

"Very well. I will address a meeting this day week."

"Thank you very much, sir," said Briggs. "You will help Derby and you will help England too."

As Briggs was about to withdraw he took a very shrewd look at the third person in the room.

"We have met before, sir," he said.

"Yes, Mr. Briggs," said the visitor, rising and offering his hand cordially, "and I am proud to meet you again. You are a very brave man and I rejoice that you have the welfare of your country at heart. But I want you to forget that you have met me here. A King, you know, is not allowed to have any politics."

"I can't do that, sir," said Briggs. "I shall

never be able to forget having met such a good and true gentleman. But I shall not speak of it, sir, to anybody, I'll promise you that."

"Thank you, Mr. Briggs. You will be rendering both Mr. Draper and myself a service."

"I'm sure I'm very proud, sir. But I'd just like to say one thing, if you don't think I'm taking too much on myself."

"Pray speak without reserve, Mr. Briggs. Mr. Draper, I feel sure, will treat your opinion with the highest respect."

"Thank you very much, sir. What I would like to say is this: Mr. Grundy and Mr. Mauleverer are good men no doubt, but this is the man the country wants and it won't be happy till it gets him."

The brawny hand of the President of the Engine Drivers' Association descended somewhat heavily upon the shoulder of the Minister. And then with a robust, "Good evening, gentlemen," Joseph Briggs affected a rolling exit from the room.

Monarch and Minister were left not a little amused. It was the latter, however, who spoke first.

"When people say to me, sir," he said, "that there is no good manhood left in the country I think at once of the number of Joseph Briggs it contains. One is always meeting them. And they are not confined, sir, to any particular class."

"Yes, my dear Mr. Draper, there is still good

manhood left in the country. And, as you say, it is to be found in all ranks of life. What we want at this moment is some co-ordinating power which will close up its ranks, which will weld it with some common purpose into a common bond."

"That is the country's need, sir." The Minister's deep voice had a throb of enthusiasm. "It is calling for a man it can follow. It is calling for a man who can rally all the Joseph Briggs in the land."

A deep sadness came upon the worn face of the visitor.

"How I wish, my dear Mr. Draper," he said, "such powerful and irreconcilable forces had not been raised against you!"

The Minister laughed rather bitterly.

"It is a dreadfully unfortunate business for the country at a time like this," said the visitor with a look of pain. "But may I venture to hope you will see your way to attend this momentous meeting of the Privy Council to-morrow morning at eleven o'clock?"

The Minister's face grew tense.

"May I exercise my own discretion, sir?" he said after a pause that was somewhat trying.

"By all means. I would make no suggestion to the contrary. But I am sure there are those who will value your presence."

"Thank you, sir," said the Minister, who was

touched by the tone. "But I feel that my presence there to-morrow will merely serve to embarrass discourse. This intrigue is bound to go on. Nothing can stop it now. It will have to run its course."

"Yes, one quite feels that. But if you could see your way to attend I should contrive to let it be known that you were present at my desire. Moreover, I shall do all in my power to arrest this calumny. But there are unscrupulous tongues at work. It has gone very far. Still one is bound to realize, and I shall hope indirectly to make others realize, that this intrigue is most perilous to the country."

The Minister stood in silence, his head upthrown.

"Thank you, sir," he said at last.

The visitor offered his hand very simply. The Minister took it gratefully.

"You will go to Derby?"

"Yes, sir, I will — at your desire. And I will go on to Leeds and Newcastle, and the North. It shall be my aim to keep things going until a decision of some kind has been arrived at."

"If you do that, my dear Mr. Draper, you will lay your country under a very deep obligation. And in the meantime I will have a talk with the Archbishop, and I will also see Rockingham."

"Rockingham?"

"Yes; he is a man of the world. Also, he is very able, and of course a man of the highest probity."

The Minister smiled darkly. There was a kind of innocence for which his visitor was famous.

"In fact, my dear Mr. Draper — I tell you this in confidence — there is a growing disposition in some quarters to persuade Rockingham to take office in the last resort."

"Is he likely to attempt the task, sir?"

"He might, but unfortunately he is devoid of all personal initiative.

Again the Minister smiled his dark smile.

XIV

"WHY aren't you at the Privy Council?" asked Evelyn Rockingham.

She had met Mr. Draper by chance in Piccadilly, while she was giving her toy pomeranians an airing. It was the morning of the third day of the crisis.

"I'm not wanted there," said the Minister bluntly.

"You oughtn't to say that," said Evelyn, rebuking him with a grave smile.

"Oughtn't one?" said the Minister, with ill-assumed indifference. "Perhaps you don't know the line they are taking."

Evelyn Rockingham knew perfectly well the line they were taking, but she was far too expert in her own particular genre to betray her knowledge.

"They?" she said innocently.

"Yes — the whole pharisaical crowd of them."

"A sweeping generalization, my friend."

"They are trying to hound me out of public life by the usual Chadband methods, as they did Horrocks and Bulstrode, and Graham, and a dozen other men."

The face of Evelyn Rockingham had become suddenly suffused with interest.

"And She — who is She? *Do* tell me."

She placed a hand charmingly imperious and daintily gloved on the sleeve of Mr. Draper's overcoat.

"You can't guess! No, of course you can't. Why should you — of all people! It's all so contemptible."

"Don't keep me on the rack any longer," she said piteously.

She turned aside suddenly to hide the laughter in her eyes.

"You are She," said the Minister quietly.

The large and expressive mouth had grown very mobile, but not a word escaped her.

"Well, what do you think of it?" said the Minister.

"What do I think of it?"

"Yes, what do you think of it?"

"Why, I think" — somehow her tone seemed to change with the oddest abruptness — "I think it is the cleverest, the most dangerous card they could have played."

"I admire you, my dear Evelyn, for being able to look at the thing like that," said the Minister with that curious simplicity which baffled friends and enemies alike. "I admire your splendid superiority to the personal equation. I wish I could look at it in that way. To me it is the damnable ruse of a cur and a coward. I would that I knew who had put it about."

"What would you do, my dear James?"

"I would punish him. I would punish him even if it were that self-righteous parson-pedagogue himself."

"I am afraid it is somebody much deeper than he. It is somebody who knows the ropes perfectly; somebody who has spent his life in pulling the strings at the psychological moment."

"Evelyn," said the Minister hoarsely, "you had better not tell me. My God, I'm capable of murder."

Evelyn Rockingham in all essentials was a finished woman of the world, but this volcanic outburst made her profoundly uncomfortable. She was bold and quite fearless, but she had far too much intelligence to toy with these elemental forces.

"My dear James," she said, "I don't know. And if I knew, I couldn't tell you."

"You would have to tell me — if you knew."

"Well — perhaps."

The answer was soft and charmingly given; the tone was almost careless, but there was a challenge in every line of the fine personality.

Mr. Draper read the challenge. With a rather awkward laugh he took it up.

"Yes, Evelyn, if you knew I'd have it out of you."

"But I don't, you see," she said quickly.

"No, of course. And I'm glad."

She noted that it never occurred to him to doubt her.

"It's lucky for everybody. In the meantime, on the strength of this despicable calumny, they are going to put me out of public life. And, my God, I'm inclined to let them."

The duchess gathered her little dogs to her arms to prevent them impeding the passers-by.

"My dear James," she said, "aren't you taking it all a little too seriously?"

"How *can* you say that!"

His stern surprise caused her to avert her face quickly. She almost wanted to laugh in spite of the chill that was in her veins.

"I'm not such an egotistical ass as to think that I matter particularly, when I know I'm innocent. But when they drag a woman I reverence through the mud in order to collect some for me, they are up against a pretty tough proposition in James Draper."

"Yes, I see." She no longer found it difficult not to laugh at his seriousness. "That's very chivalrous. That's the side that hadn't occurred to me."

"Naturally. And that's very chivalrous of you."

"So that's a 'wash-out,' my dear James." She

forced a laugh now. "And it simply amounts to this, that we are a pair of extraordinarily chivalrous people."

However, he was in no mood to suffer a diversion.

"It doesn't matter what we are," he said. "But if they can't carry on this unpleasant game of politics like gentlemen I've a great mind to make an end at once."

"No, not now," she said. "You can't do it now. There's the country to consider; you can't leave that in the lurch."

"No, of course one can't do that — not if they have still a use for me. But they mayn't have, you know, now this card's been played."

Her laugh was a little contemptuous. "Before very long they are going bitterly to repent that they've ever played it. Look there!"

"Where?"

"Across the road!"

A long procession, composed in the main of unemployables and the humbler grades of wage-earners, carrying banners, was walking slowly along the street. Emblazoned on the banners in the too-familiar yellow of the Galloway Press was on one side the legend, "Refer It to the People," and on the other side, "What's a Referendum For?"

"I'd soon put a stop to that if I could rule," said the Minister with a face of scorn.

"What, you reactionary, you would interfere with the free-born English citizen's right of public demonstration! Have you forgotten the Burgess Bill already? Have you forgotten the blood your public-spirited countrymen shed over it?"

"Yes — to tell the truth, I had forgotten that monumental blunder."

"By no means a blunder from their point of view. They never struck a shrewder blow for the cause of anarchy."

"You are quite right. And if they referred it to the people, George John Galloway would be elected Prime Minister by a three to one majority."

"Well, the sands are running out in the glass. If they don't get to know their own minds pretty soon they will be obliged to refer it to the people."

"You are quite right," said the Minister. "And, after all, it is our time-honoured Saxon way. But somehow that spectacle makes my gorge rise. Upon my soul, I'd like to put a charge of grapeshot into that procession!"

"A true democrat!" laughed his companion. "A true friend of the people! Do you forget that your name would be an easy second in the People's Referendum?"

"Don't remind me of it. There they go, holding up the traffic at every point! And marshalled by mounted police! And if that obscene thing in the middle doesn't bear the effigy of Galloway!"

"The people's champion, my friend, the noblest Roman of them all."

"Oh, it turns me sick," said the Minister. "Come on, let us walk in the opposite direction."

XV

SO they walked, but not many yards before their attention was arrested by a further affront to the established order, of which they felt themselves to be a part. The eye of the Minister was caught by a newsbill displayed at the corner of Piccadilly Circus. Its legend was large, black and ominous.

THE CRISIS
SERIOUS RIOTING IN MANCHESTER
GRAVE SITUATION

Mr. Draper drew the attention of his companion to the news.

"In Manchester, too!" was her comment; "the home of culture — moral, artistic, and sociological."

Mr. Draper hoped the comment was not ironical.

"As though one could be ironical at the expense of anything that takes itself so seriously!" she said.

"Manchester is the touchstone of the country, they always say," said the Minister, whose tone echoed none of his companion's lightness.

He bought a newspaper.

"They've started to burn warehouses. It's shameful. My God!" he said grimly, "if they burn warehouses at Manchester to-day, we shall be seeing those tumbrils along Piccadilly to-morrow."

"And if we do," said his companion with glowing eyes, "it must all be laid to the door of a mean intrigue. If the country is drenched in blood from end to end it is the price she will have to pay for St. John Becher."

"Oh, him!" the Minister snorted. "It's the other canting hypocrite who carries most of the weight in that crew. Still, 'canting hypocrite' is not véry just perhaps," he added, striving for a justness he so often found hard to attain. "I dare say they are all sincere enough, according to their lights. It is part of a bad old tradition, handed down from the bad old Victorian epoch, and, like all bad old things, it dies very hard."

By this time they had strayed round the corner into Regent Street.

"Come on to lunch," said Evelyn Rockingham.

"There's no particular reason why I shouldn't," said Mr. Draper after a little reflection. "That is, unless you are expecting a lot of people. Somehow I don't feel in the mood to face a crowd."

"There will be just ourselves and one other."

"Who is the other?"

"Ha!" She grew arch as well as cryptic.

"You must play fair. It might be Stephen Cantuar or St. John Becher."

"Oh, it's somebody much more interesting than either."

"It might be Galloway himself."

The duchess laughed.

"It's a very good shot," she admitted.

Mr. Draper was completely lost for a moment in the heavy mantle of reflection which so often enveloped him.

"Well, what do you say?" she asked at last.

"He is the most important man in the country just now." Mr. Draper chose each word as though it was a thing of value. "But I hardly see on what grounds I can meet him, or on what grounds he can meet me at present."

"*He'll* have no scruples. Besides, ought one to torment one's self with the fine shades at such a time as this?"

Mr. Draper continued to ponder.

"I think you are right," he said finally. "The needs of the hour should stand first. I believe the man to be an enemy of the country. To my mind he would look remarkably well on a convenient lamp-post. But there is no mistaking the grip he's got on things — on the masses. Yes, I'll meet him — that is, if you feel inclined, my dear Evelyn, to risk a breach of the peace."

"Oh, yes, I'll risk it," said Evelyn Rockingham, "like the true patriot I am. It is quite a happy idea. If you are able to control your feelings, no harm can be done by your meeting, and good may come of it."

"I'm afraid that's impossible. What is there to hope from such a knave? Frankly, Evelyn, at no other time would I have consented to meet him socially."

"Why, in your own way, you are as bad as the Archbishop and St. John Becher. It is exactly the same thing, except that it presents itself at a slightly different angle. James, I'm ashamed of you."

"Yes," said the Minister, "perhaps I'm rather ashamed of myself."

They walked slowly up the street, lost in talk and heeding none. Their portraits and their platform appearance were familiar to the larger half of England. From among the morning crowd of the congested thoroughfare full many a glance was levelled at them. But profoundly unconscious of the attention they excited they kept steadily upon their course. An undercurrent of excitement seemed to flow all about them; the very atmosphere seemed to thrill with a kind of tense expectancy. Sullen eyes and mischievous, brooding faces were on every side; there was an electricity generated by their progress which could be felt. But so completely were they engrossed in talk that they might have been alone.

Presently they sauntered along a by-street, crossed Bond Street and found themselves before the cheerless and ugly portals of Rockingham House at five minutes past one.

Mr. Galloway, who had been invited for one o'clock, had arrived already. His greeting of his hostess was confident and effusive; it was that of a man almost aggressively at home in his rarefied surroundings.

Mr. Galloway's reception of Mr. Draper was equally confident but not so cordial. He offered his hand to the Minister with an air that was merely ill-bred, although a sensitive person might have seen a calculated rudeness in it. It was as if he would say, "Oh, yes, I know all about you. I know where you started from. You mustn't try to impress *me*."

Women are apt to notice these little *nuances* if they are in possession of the *clou* of the comedy. The duchess watched them with a sincere, if artfully dissembled, feminine enjoyment. The meeting of two such doughty champions, strangely alike in the external aspect of their careers, would well repay a little feminine observation.

They were neither of them "gentlemen" in the purview of the beholder. But one of them at least implied so much more than falls within the scope of that rather narrow conventional term.   In describing them to a person of her own caste she would have said that "neither of them had an aitch in his composition," a rough and ready description which had the merit of being glaringly inaccurate yet at the same time hitting off what she wished to convey. Indeed, both men used the King's English in quite an educated way.   But both of them were so obviously men of the people; and in this spacious interior, "all white marble and precedence," redolent of gold plate and powdered menials, the fact was declared in the one case with a sharpness that was almost cruel, and in the other, if by no means so obvious, in the eyes of Caste was always there.

Comparing the two, however, as the feminine observer did so relentlessly, the one rose immeasurably superior to the other.   Galloway jarred every fibre of her aristocratic composition.   He had not been two minutes in her presence before she would have loved dearly to have had him flung out of doors, his subtle Cockney impertinence was so insufferable.   He gave himself airs, he peered into her face, all that he said — mordant good sense expressed in banal terms — was pitched in entirely the wrong key.   The agitator, journalist, and publicist was a cad to the marrow, and he had the subtle power of making a woman feel it in her bones.

Draper, on the other hand, made a very different

showing. He had started life at a far humbler level than Galloway. Up till the age of thirteen he had been a "half-timer" at a board school. He had begun life as an errand boy, and had acquired culture at a free library, so that presently he was able to "better himself" by becoming a shop assistant. That additional measure of refinement had brought further opportunities in its train. He had gone up the social ladder step by step, adjusting himself automatically to his surroundings as he went. If he could never be "a gentleman," as Evelyn Rockingham understood the term, in all its mystic complexity, her clear, practical intelligence allowed her to see that his genius lifted him to a plane which rendered such distinctions idle and frivolous.

Draper had none of the superficial faults of Galloway. Nature had cast him in a noble mould. Moreover, he had "manners of the heart," and they showed almost beautifully in comparison with the arrogance and the assumption of the minor public school and university product who gave him of his patronage.

"Well, Draper, how are you *these* days? We don't see quite so much of each other now."

The Minister accepted the almost disdainfully offered hand with a reluctance that he did not try to conceal.

"No, we haven't seen much of each other lately?" he said, speaking easily and lightly.

"Well, I'm very glad anyhow to meet you again," said Mr. Galloway. "In fact, I've rather been wanting to see you."

At this point her Grace was informed that luncheon awaited them.

They had the table to themselves.

"Have you been with the Privy Council this morning?" said Mr. Galloway. "It's still sitting, I suppose?"

"Yes, it is still sitting I believe, but I've not been there."

"It's a shocking tangle, eh? Really, myself, I can only see one way out."

"What way is that?" asked Evelyn Rockingham, since the Minister did not seem inclined to put the question.

"They'll have to send for me."

"For what purpose, Mr. Galloway?" asked Mr. Draper.

"To be P. M.," said that gentleman, exploding in a loud laugh which startled the butler and his satellites considerably.

"No, Mr. Galloway, I don't think they will do that," said Evelyn Rockingham with nicely calculated frankness.

"Well, I shouldn't be surprised," said he. "Who else is there?"

"Evan Mauleverer."

"He daren't take office. And if he did, the country wouldn't stand him a fortnight."

"How do you know that?" inquired Evelyn blandly.

"I know everything. Conscription settled Mauleverer's hash."

"But your loathsome paper — the *Daily Argus* — set them on to it, surely?"

"Oh, yes, we did," said Mr. Galloway calmly, "until we saw which way the cat was going to jump and then we ratted."

"As you always do, of course?"

"Yes, of course. It's no use swimming against the tide. You can't become a power in the newspaper world on those lines, can you Draper?"

"I'm afraid I'm without knowledge of the subject," said Mr. Draper dryly.

"Why, you were on the staff of the *Daily Argus* at one time."

"Never on the staff, Mr. Galloway," said the Minister with careful politeness. "I wrote a series of articles for you on the Labour question shortly after I entered Parliament."

"It's nothing to be ashamed of anyhow. We've the picked brains of the country on the *Daily Argus*, and we pay top prices for them."

"I was certainly well paid."

"Well, leaving out Evan Mauleverer," said

Evelyn Rockingham, "and leaving out you, Mr. Galloway, because between ourselves I really don't think the premiership is your line of country, it seems to become clearer every day that they will be bound to ask one man in the end."

"Shafto?"

"No, he's too weak. Besides, he hasn't the ability."

"Pollen?"

"A brilliant lawyer, but he's never really made a mark in the House."

"Well, there's no one else except myself."

"Yes, there is one other."

"Tell me his name."

"He is sitting opposite to you."

"By Jove, Duchess, that's an idea."

Mr. Galloway exploded again.

"It's odd that Draper, here, hadn't occurred to me. The very man!"

The eyes of Mr. Galloway shone with a sudden radiance. The fact that the suggestion presented itself to him in the light of an inspiration was a sufficient refutation, if any were needed, of his vaunt that he knew everything. The people who knew everything politically were only too familiar with the name of the dark horse. Such an exhibition of *naïveté* considerably lowered Mr. Galloway's reputation for omniscience in the eyes of his hostess.

"Why, yes," he said, "the very man! Draper, I've a great mind to run you for the premiership."

"Thank you, Mr. Galloway," said Mr. Draper in his dry voice.

"By Jove, Duchess, you've given me an idea. I've half a mind to run Draper for the premiership."

"You had better make it a whole one, Mr. Galloway," said his hostess.

"Yes, why not! We must see if we can't strike a bargain."

"A bargain, Mr. Galloway?"

"Yes, certainly. The Left will want to dictate the terms if they run him."

"I can make no bargain with anybody, let me say that at once," said Mr. Draper with unstatesmanlike candour, and in spite of the fact that his hostess went to the length of frowning at him.

"Don't be a fool, Draper," said Mr. Galloway with the directness of speech which in certain quarters conferred a reputation upon him of consummate ability. "This is going to be the chance of your life. The Right won't touch you with a bargepole, you know that. The Centre is frightened to death of you, so if you are not too big a man socially nowadays" — Mr. Galloway's sneering laugh was not pleasant — "to take up with your old friends, you had better come to us and see what we can do for you. Don't you think so, Duchess?"

"I think the idea is worth consideration," said she.

The idea certainly had the merit of stirring Mr. Galloway's acute brain into action. As his habit was, he began to think aloud, independent of time or place.

"Of course the Conciliation Bill is the crux of the whole matter. If you will promise to reintroduce it immediately there should be no reason, as far as I can see at the moment, why the Left shouldn't forgive your indiscretions."

"Reintroduce the Bill as it stands?" Evelyn asked.

"Substantially as it stands. It would have to remain essentially the same, although with the dangerous places nicely glossed over."

"Including Clause Nine?"

"Yes, decidedly. What's the use of the Bill without Clause Nine?"

"But he threw out the Government on Clause Nine."

"Yes, he did. And if he puts himself in on it it will be a master stroke."

Mr. Galloway laughed loudly and heartily.

"By Jove," he said, "it's a brilliant idea."

"But what about his principles, Mr. Galloway?"

"He'll have to swallow 'em, of course. There never was a man yet who grasped at power who hadn't to swallow his principles. Of course, he must swallow 'em as delicately as possible. The

G. P. will help him there. A man can do most things if he's got *us* at the back of him."

"Except remain honest," said Mr. Draper without acrimony.

"That's taken for granted, of course," said Mr. Galloway with the air of one rebuking a rather flagrant provincialism. "What use have politicians and journalists for honesty? You might as well bring up a Thomas cat on the Ten Commandments."

"Port wine, sir?" said the butler.

"Please!" said Mr. Galloway.

"Mr. Galloway," said Evelyn Rockingham, "you have a Machiavellian subtlety."

"Oh, no, Duchess, that's mere common sense. If you were in politics or journalism for your health it would be a different matter. They are dirty games, both of 'em — I don't know which is the dirtier. Of course, the thing is to make your pile as soon as you can and quit, unless, that is, you are cursed like I am with a love of power and then you remain."

"I see," said his hostess, a little aghast. She had rubbed shoulders with most of the types which had floated to the surface of her world. None realized more fully than she that it took all sorts of people to make it. But this was the first time she had enjoyed the privilege of coming to close quarters with this particular ingredient.

"I know what you think, Duchess," he said. "You think I've got a mind like a sewer. So I have. And so must any man have who knows his way about Fleet Street as I do. Politics and journalism are two of the meanest games going, and any man who lives by both of 'em, like Draper and myself, and pretends they are not, is a humbug, and that's all about it."

The hostess made a tactful remark. Under cover of it Mr. Draper was able to keep a hold upon his self-control, which was in jeopardy. His stern, deeply marked face had grown tawny. But he was content to answer in a tone of conversational lightness, and honourably maintained his share of the talk upon the same note.

"I like the scheme," said Mr. Galloway. "All the morning journals shall sing together — provided, that is, we can arrange the terms. Pledge yourself, my dear Draper, to a Conciliation Bill with the present Clause Nine retained in spirit if not in form, and then see what the G. P. can do for you."

"Why do you insist on Clause Nine?" said Evelyn Rockingham.

"It's the keystone of the arch. It's the ace of trumps."

"It secures the supremacy of Labour for the next hundred years," said Mr. Draper gravely.

"Exactly."

"The trap was very skilfully baited," said the Minister.

"Yes, the silly fools in the Centre couldn't see what was behind it," said Mr. Galloway, "until you, my dear Draper, pointed it out. By the way, why did you point it out? But I know, of course."

"Why did I point it out?" the Minister asked, reining himself in very tight.

"It was the cleverest move you've ever made, my dear Draper. I always knew in the old days that you had a pretty good head, but I didn't think it was quite equal to that. You had merely to get rid of Grundy to open the door to yourself. And you've managed to do it, by God!"

"Suppose one doesn't choose to enter the door now that it is open?"

"That would be merely Quixotic. Wouldn't it, Duchess?"

The hostess appeared not to hear the question.

"Yes, of course, it would. But you will have to play the game, my dear Draper. Give us a private assent to Clause Nine, not necessarily for publication, and we will blazon your name forth to the country."

"You control the Left, Mr. Galloway," said the duchess. "But what of the Centre, which is composed in the main of respectable people? They hold the balance, and your papers have not much weight with them, I believe."

"True," said Mr. Galloway, "but he's got his own following there. His speech in the House the other night has increased it enormously. That's where he is beginning to count."

"And you can control the Left?"

"I think I am entitled to say that I can control it absolutely."

The Minister looked the publicist straight in the eyes.

"Mr. Galloway," he said, "I make terms with none. If it is the clearly expressed wish of the King's advisers that I should undertake the task of forming a Government it will be my duty to give the matter earnest consideration. But not otherwise. I don't court office for the love of office. In fact, in these days, a wise man would prefer to be without it in any circumstances. Still, the imperative duty must devolve upon somebody. If by any mischance it should devolve upon me, I pray God that it be given to me to prove worthy of my trust."

The expressive countenance of the person to whom this speech was addressed connoted an odd mingling of amusement and disgust. His respect for the manes of good-breeding prevented his saying "Pecksniff" in a voice louder than could reach the receptive ear of his neighbour. But his manner was less discreet.

"You are taking a rather high tone aren't, you,

Draper?" he said. What his tone implied was, "Is it really necessary, my dear fellow, to play out this comedy between old friends? What's the use of trying to humbug a confrère who has watched every phase of your rise from *very* humble beginnings? It is hopeless, my friend, to attempt to deceive a man as acute as I am."

"I hope I am taking a high tone, Mr. Galloway," said the Minister quite simply. "The subject at least should demand it."

"But, my dear Draper, you are quite Gladstonian. Nay, more than Gladstonian. The Old Man, even in his heyday — but I beg your pardon. Forgive my levity."

Mr. Galloway did not actually wink at his hostess, but he came perilously near to doing so. Mr. Draper withstood all this with unruffled patience. "I hope I am sincere in desiring to serve the true interests of the country," was all he said.

Before framing his reply, Mr. Galloway looked steadily at Evelyn Rockingham, but received no answering look in return. This non-success, how-ever, did not defeat him.

"Oh, yes, Draper," he said a little impatiently, "we none of us doubt your sincerity, but isn't the form of it just a *leetle* out of date. Queen Victoria's dead. Suppose, for a moment, we drop the high moral tone altogether. Let us have a homely,

heart-to-heart talk.   You've a chance of being
Prime Minister of England — an extraordinarily
good chance, it seems to me.   And I, George John
Galloway, am prepared to go 'nap' on you if you
will give me some assurance that you are prepared
to play the game."

"Mr. Galloway," said the Minister with a gravity
that incensed his hearer, "I can enter into no compact with any representative of a political section or
party organization."

"Oh, but that's nonsense."

"It may be, in the present phase of opinion, but
I make so bold as to think that we are about to see
a change.   It is not unlikely that the country is
thoroughly tired of the party game."

"We are always hearing of that sort of thing,"
said Mr. Galloway, suppressing a yawn, "but the
party game goes on just the same."

"At any rate we are in the midst of a serious crisis
now," said Evelyn Rockingham.   "And the ablest
man in the country is needed."

"Yes, it's pretty serious," said Mr. Galloway.
"A shocking muddle in fact.   There is a wonderful
opportunity for an able and ambitious man.   If
Draper goes the right way to work he ought to play
a very big part."

"And you think the right way is to promise the
Left that he will reintroduce the Bill?"

"I do, undoubtedly. I can answer for the Left if he will give a guarantee. They are well drilled and will go solid. And in the Centre, if my information is correct, and it is as a rule, he has now a big enough following of his own to turn the scale."

"You may be right, Mr. Galloway, or you may not be right," said Mr. Draper bluntly, "but in any circumstances I cannot listen to the proposal."

"Then you are throwing away an opportunity that can never occur again," said Mr. Galloway, with an air of finality.

In accordance with his scheme of life, which consisted in parcelling out every moment for some particular purpose, this remarkable man left almost immediately luncheon was over. No sooner was the Minister alone with his hostess than she drew a long sigh of relief.

"The place will have to be disinfected," she said.

"The poisonous blackguard!" said Mr. Draper, sombrely.

"Well, he's shown you a short cut to power at any rate."

"The poisonous blackguard! And somehow he's so much cruder and so much more limited than one's recollection of him."

"When did you meet last?"

"It must be nearly ten years ago."

"You have grown since those days."

"I hope so," said the Minister with the simplicity that always touched a chord in her. "Life must be a vain business if one hasn't, after all that one's been through. But those days seem very far off just now. That poisonous blackguard, how he brings them back to me! I don't think *he's* changed much, unless it is that success has made him more unwary."

"You mustn't speak of such shallow arrogance as success."

"Oh, but it is, you know. He is the most completely successful man in the country, hence this painful exhibition of himself."

"Yes, I suppose he is. And if you feel inclined to play a coup against the noble army of the Pharisees, you have to your hand a ready and valuable tool."

"God forbid that I should make use of it."

"Amen!" said his counsellor.

But she averted her eyes.

XVI

THE country continued to pass through a period of grave tension. The wise met in council, dissolved, then met again. But no decision could they reach. It seemed beyond the wit of man to bridge the chasm that had opened in the life of the nation.

Every day that passed, with the King's Government still in abeyance, strengthened the forces of unrest and gave them boldness. Sedition was openly talked. On every hand the parasites who wax on industrial strife were making the most of their great opportunity. They were beginning boldly to ask the question, If the King cannot carry on his Government, what's the use of the King?

The deadlock seemed hopeless and complete. It was now known that the Left had nominated Galloway, that the Right had nominated Mauleverer, and that the Centre, the real brain of the Empire, acutely realized the sheer impossibility of both. By a grievous mischance it had no nominee of its own to run. Grundy, in spite of a year of heroic effort, had proved unequal to the task imposed upon him; Bryant, its next ablest man, had no longer the physical vigour; but before the next grave week had passed another name was heard upon the lips of those who were praying for their country.

The President of the Board of Conciliation went to the headquarters of the railway workers at Derby and made his speech. The next day he spoke at Sheffield, and the following day at Manchester, successfully braving bitter hostility and the threat of bloodshed. Thence he went to Leeds and to his native Newcastle, and Sunday found him addressing a hundred thousand people on a Glasgow football ground.

Thus it was during that week of suspense, which witnessed the paralysis of trade and the slow gathering of the forces of disorder, the country at large came to realize that one man at least was capable of decisive, fearless, and unselfish action. It was a week of noble labour; his magical phrases were flashed from one end of the country to the other; and it was felt in many quarters that one had arisen capable of grasping the tiller of the crazy ship of state.

For one week at least, in his own simple words, "he had done his best to tide things over." While the heads of the three parties were manuœvring for position, confounding issues and poisoning the wells of controversy, he had passed from city to city, imploring the workers not to be led aside from the path of sanity.

It was a great week's work.   He spoke at all hours; and he spoke until his throat gave out and he could speak no more.   Such sincerity, such force, such a grasp of the situation, in all its complexity, made their appeal to all sections of the community who were not drunk with passion or blinded by prejudice.

He returned from his tour in the North about midday on Tuesday, having travelled throughout the night from Scotland, and when he reached his home in Queen Anne's Gate he was in a state of mental and physical collapse.

Nicholson the butler welcomed him.   The old man's hands trembled as he helped his master off with his overcoat.

"You've saved the country, sir," he whispered. "God bless you, sir."

In his overwrought condition the sudden tears sprang to the eyes of the Minister.

"Thank you, my dear fellow.   I hope you may be right.   But it's touch and go, you know; it's touch and go."

"Yes, sir, it is.   I beg your pardon, sir, but if I have a fire lit in your bedroom, perhaps you will take a few hours' rest after luncheon?"

Mr. Draper could not forbear to smile at this solicitude.

"Oh, thank you," said he, "but I am afraid there can be no rest for me at present."

"Well, sir," said the old man, "if you'll forgive the liberty, I hope you will not overtax your strength. Everything depends on you."

"No, my dear Nicholson, everything depends on God." The odd humility of the tone was very characteristic

Hearing his deep tones, the private secretary came out into the hall to greet him.

"Well, Renshaw," said the Minister, "what of it here?"

The private secretary pursed his lips and shook his head. The Minister linked his arm through the younger man's affectionately and led him into his room.

"Tell me all the news," he said as he flung himself on to a sofa. "Are they any nearer to a decision?"

The private secretary hesitated a little before he answered.

"Yes, sir, perhaps they are. They have had an inspiration." There was an ironical note in the voice of the young man that somehow made an effect of tragedy. "You'll never guess, sir, what it is?"

The Minister flung back his head among the sofa cushions with a gesture of utter weariness.

"Rockingham, I expect."

"You are wonderful, sir — and at the first shot!"

"Oh, one kind of felt him in the upper atmosphere." The Minister closed his eyes and breathed heavily. "Oh, it's dreadful, dreadful," he said.

"Is it the beginning of the end, sir?"

"Can they persuade him to accept? that is the question. He is by no means a fool. What is the amount of his backing?"

"He can count on the Right to a man; it is said to be Mr. Mauleverer's suggestion. And the Centre has always respected him, sir, as it does respect a duke. But it is the fact that he made friends with the coal miners, by finding work for a few of them during the coal strike last year, that is thought likely to turn the scale."

"But do they seriously consider him to be capable of governing the country?"

"I think, sir, they regard him as a desperate remedy. The cabal now goes about saying that you, sir, have forgotten Rockingham."

The Minister sat up on the sofa with a face of anger and scorn.

"They say I have forgotten Rockingham! Do they, indeed? What incredible meanness and what incredible madness!" He rose from the sofa. His legs were unsteady and his face was haggard. "Renshaw, I think you had better find out if the duchess is in town.   And if she is, ask her to be kind enough to call this afternoon and I will wait in for her."

The private secretary went to the telephone, and presently returned with the information that the duchess was expected from the country at four o'clock.

"Where is Lady Aline?" asked the Minister. "Is she in the country too?"

"She went to Lady Loring's, I believe, sir, on Friday evening," said the private secretary.

"Do you know when she is returning?"

"No, sir, I do not."

The Minister touched the bell, and Nicholson promptly answered the summons.

"Can you tell me, Nicholson, when your mistress returns?"

"No, sir, I cannot," said the butler, looking very white and old.   "She left no word, sir."

"Thank you.   And by the way, Nicholson, I am going to take your advice.   I will have a little luncheon, and then I'll go to bed for a couple of hours."

"Thank you, sir."   The tone of the old man was paternal.   "I will have a fire lit at once in your room."

"There is no need to do that."

"Oh, but I will, sir.   I would very much like to, sir, if I may."

"Oh, very well."

The butler withdrew.

"Dear old fellow," said the Minister. "He at least appreciates the gravity of it all."

The private secretary, whose mind was cast in a more conventional mould, was inclined to smile.

XVII

THE Minister had declared his intention of sleeping for a couple of hours. Overwrought nature, however, took him in hand, so that the two hours grew into four, and it was six o'clock when Nicholson roused him. He was informed that the Duchess of Rockingham had called, and awaited him in the library.

He dressed in haste and then descended to greet her in his usual impulsive fashion.

"It *is* good of you," he said.

She received him with her frank and charming smile.

"I am so glad you were snatching a little rest," she said. "You must be worn out."

"Very nearly," he admitted. "Another such week would kill me."

"Well, you have done nobly."

She offered both her hands. He took only one, and this he bore to his lips with a gesture of homage.

"And now I am hungry for the news," he said. "Give me all there is. Renshaw says they have actually decided to run my lord duke."

He watched her stiffen. There was something other than malice, something other than contempt, in the narrowing of the eyes.

"Yes," she said, "the incredible happens sometimes."

"It would be a farce, my dear Evelyn," was his comment, "if we were not on the brink of an almost unrealizable tragedy. Tell me, what are his chances?"

"His chances are unexpectedly good if he cares to take them."

"Yes, one feels that. The Right will go solid. He is one of themselves, although they know his value. And he has always had a curious, an inexplicable fascination for the Centre. It's his rank, I suppose. Well, it will be a fitting requiem for Britain if the slavish snobbery of her middle class contrives her ruin. A sublime act of poetic justice at any rate. But the question is, Will the Left be able to swallow him? Tell me, Evelyn, how do you feel about that?"

"Opinions are much divided at present. But, quite frankly, my dear James, I am afraid they might. You see he found employment for some of the miners during the recent coal strike, and he's won the Derby twice. At a pinch they might accept him as a stopgap, provided there is nobody better."

"Can he keep the ship off the rocks, do you think?"

"No."

"Does he realize that?"

"Oh, yes, one would say he does. He is very clear-sighted in most things."

"Do you think he will accept office?"

"It is most difficult to say. He is such an enigma. We none of us know our Rockingham."

"No, I suppose not. By the way, they say that Cæsar is not ambitious. It that your view of Cæsar?"

"I don't think he is ambitious in the way that — shall we say that Evan Mauleverer is, for instance? Our poor dear Robert is always *grand seigneur*."

The Minister smiled.

"The point is, my dear Evelyn, is such an aristocrat capable of soiling his lily-white soul with the base cares of office in order to spike the guns of a 'Haberdasher'?"

"I won't answer your question offhand, my dear James. *Noblesse oblige* is one of those queer diseases that take a man in unexpected ways. We none of us know our Rockingham, and that is all the comfort I can give you at present."

"Well, the man is by no means a fool in whatever way his malady may take him. And if we allow a man is not a fool, we have then to hope piously that he is not a knave."

"That is to say, my dear James, that poor Robert,

being neither a fool nor a knave, is bound to realize that in this pass a Rockingham administration spells ruin for the country."

"Stark ruin."

"Can poor dear Robert be expected to realize that, especially as his backing is likely to be solid and extensive?"

The worn and haggard look grew more intense on the Minister's face.

"A Rockingham ministry is madness," he said in a hollow tone, "whatever the amount of its backing with the country in its present state. It is sheer criminal lunacy. Have they all completely lost touch with the North?"

"What it amounts to is this, my friend: the pious advisers of your Sovereign are prepared to risk Robert rather than risk you."

"Then curse their eyes!" The Minister yielded suddenly to an uncontrollable and rather hysterical gust of anger that brought him to the verge of tears.

She gave an adroit turn to the conversation.

"Where is Aline, by the way?" she asked.

"At her Aunt Loring's, I believe," said the Minister, recovering his self-possession. "She went there on Friday."

"When does she return?"

"I don't know. She has not written to me."

A faint shadow of embarrassment had crept over the face of Lady Aline's husband.

"Evelyn," he said in a rather odd tone, "I am going to make you a little confidence."

His look of pain made her heart beat quickly.

"Aline and I seem to have been drifting apart lately. Something seems to have come between us. I am afraid we didn't part friends."

Her eyes were unfathomable

"I was strongly opposed to her going to the Lorings'. They and their set are quite out of sympathy with me. I told Aline that it wasn't loyal, and I particularly hoped she wouldn't go."

'And she took it ill?"

"Yes, she took it ill."

His voice was that of a man who had been cut to the heart. "She said some cruel things. In fact, I didn't quite realize how cruel they were at first." His voice broke rather queerly. "My head was full of the Derby speech at the time. But after all, my dear Evelyn, why should I bore you with all this?"

"Please tell me, James, just what you said to her."

"I merely said it was disloyal to accept the Lorings' invitation when all England knew how contemptuously they judged me."

"And what was her answer to that?"

"Her answer was to accept the invitation." The voice of the Minister failed suddenly.

"Well, don't judge her too harshly," she said. "It is only pretty Fanny's way, although it is a very naughty way, and she deserves to be whipped. At any rate, we must hope she will return before the end of the week."

"Why must we hope that?"

"Loring has called a week-end meeting of the cabal to consider Robert's nomination."

"Ha!"

"She certainly ought not to be there then, don't you think?"

"I quite agree."

"You say she went down on Friday to the Lorings'?"

"So I am informed."

"And I am informed that my wicked husband went there on Friday also."

"Oh, yes, he is always at Cloudesley."

The tone of indifference rather took her aback.

XVIII

MY DEAR LAURA: I sit down at midnight, as usual, to bore you to tears with a mind distraught. Let it stand this time for my excuse that within the last hour I have passed through a very strange experience. It has left me breathless and rather bruised. It is not like "life" at all as you and I understand it. The whole thing seems to belong to the boards of a theatre or the pages of a very second-rate novel.

Odd and unnatural as the matter is, however, there is a something about the whole affair which has shaken me as I have never been shaken before. I am going to try to give you the thing exactly as it occurred, not so much, my dear, for your information as for my own ease of mind. It is a very strange and, to me, rather terrible matter.

Let me write down the incident in detail exactly as it came to me.

It was about a quarter to eleven. I was sitting

here in this room which we both love so well, and
instead of giving thoughts to bed I had allowed
myself to become absorbed by B.'s latest novel.
I was thinking what a wonderful power the man had;
I was thinking how the times were changing; I was
thinking, my dear, how little "the frills" of life —
from which you and I have suffered all our born days
— really matter when one comes down to the bed-
rock. Human nature seems to amount to just about
the same in a slum in the Midlands as it does at
Rockingham House or Glen Iver, N. B.

Well, who should disturb this profound thought
but Harpole. You know the man I mean —
wooden, stupid, pompous, the archetype of a ducal
servant. He came in more wooden, stupid and
pompous than usual; and after a certain amount
of hesitation and circumlocution he was able to
inform me that "a Mr. Nicholson in the service
of Lady Aline Draper would take it as a most particular favour if I would consent to see him in
private."

"Certainly," I said. "Show him up here."

Somehow I felt impregnated with the spirit of a
B. novel; a delicious sense of romance seemed to
possess me.

Well, my dear, as soon as Mr. Nicholson entered
I recognized him at once. It was my old friend —
Mr. D.'s butler; the old man with whom I have

continual skirmishes in order to get access to the Presence.

But as soon as the old fellow came in, twisting his hat nervously in his hands, and with his shabby overcoat buttoned up to the throat, there was something about him that seemed to send a shock right through me. If I have ever beheld a lost soul this was he.

I took pity at once on the poor old thing's strained face and white hairs and asked him to sit down.

"I couldn't think of presuming, your Grace," he said in a voice that I didn't seem to remember.

But I was firm, and he sat.

"Now tell me your trouble," I said, with a sincere desire to help him, for he was certainly suffering horribly.

Of course, I hadn't a thought as to what his trouble might be, and when I learned it it rather took my breath away.

He was tormented by a dreadful secret. His mistress A., it seemed, had left her husband for good and he alone knew the fact. She had gone to her Aunt Lady Loring's the Friday previous, while Mr. D. was conducting his campaign in the North. She had taken away all her clothes and her jewels, and had left a note for Mr. D. to apprise him of the fact.

"And this note was left in your care," I asked, "to give to Mr. D. upon his return from Scotland?"

He admitted it.

"And you have not done so?"

He admitted that also. And then I asked him why he had not, and he said that Mr. D. was so over-wrought when he returned that he was afraid of the effect upon him while he was in that state, and he made use of these prophetic words: "If anything happens to him *now* there will be an end of everything."

"But are you not taking a great deal too much upon yourself in withholding that letter?" I said.

He burst into tears. He was like a man beside himself.

"I didn't dare to risk it, knowing the state he was in," he said. "He is a man of strong feelings, as your Grace would know. And I feel bound to consider the country."

I pointed out to him as kindly as I could that it was hardly his place to consider the country. He replied very gently and politely that he felt it to be his duty to consider the country.

I was forced to differ; but he bowed his noble gray head — it *is* a noble head — in dissent, and he looked so piteous that I felt near to tears myself.

"You have withheld the letter," I said. "And what, pray, do you propose to do with it? Do you intend to destroy it?"

He spread out his hands — long, thin, beautiful, the hands of a poet.

"No, whatever happens I shall not destroy it. It is not mine to destroy."

"Nor is it yours to withhold," I said.

He allowed it was not. "But I hope God will forgive me," he said. "I have withheld it in the hope of saving the country."

He sat like one transfigured, his face furrowed with tears.

"But your master is bound to find out the truth."

"Yes," he said, "but I feel that if we can only tide over the next few days, while this great crisis passes, he will be able to deal with this matter as those who love England, as those who love him, would have him deal with it."

I think I have never felt so touched in my life as by those simple words and the way in which they were spoken.

"Then it is not fear of the consequences of your action that has brought you to me?"

"No," he said. "I do not think about myself. If my master, Mr. D., can save the monarchy I would gladly die to-night."

"You think it has come to that?"

"Yes," he said, "I do. I have watched this thing growing year by year. I have been in the service of three prime ministers; my life has been spent, as it were, in the inner circle. A knowledge of many things has been granted to me. A power above myself has compelled me to withhold this letter from my master until this week is out, and — and —— "

His voice broke hysterically.

"What is the power that has compelled you?"

"It is God," he said. "At least it is what I understand by God. But I have never been a really deeply religious man. And now to-night all of a sudden, something seems to have snapped inside me and — and —— "

He swayed to and fro in a kind of torment.

"And I want the help of some one who is stronger and better and wiser than myself." He buried his face in his hands. "To-night, I feel if I once let go I shall go mad."

I was too shattered to speak. Somehow I felt I was being dragged into psychical regions which wise people keep as far away from as they can.

"Has something happened to-night which has taken away your nerve?" I asked at last.

He confessed that such was the case. His master had written a letter to his wife in the country and had given it to him to post.

"What have you done with the letter? Did you post it?"

"No," he said. "I did not post it. A voice seemed to tell me not to do so. I have it here in my pocket along with the other one."

"To whom do you ascribe the voice?"

"If I were a deeply religious man, I should take it to be the voice of the Most High."

"Are you not deeply religious?"

"I am religious in a manner of speaking, but deeply religious, I am not. If I were deeply religious I should not be afraid of going too far."

"That is to say, that had you been a deeply religious man you would still have acted as you did, but you would have kept your own counsel until you felt the time had come to make a full confession to your master?"

"Yes, that is what I should have done **had** I been able to walk close with my God."

"Is it, then, that you are afraid of what you have done?"

"Yes, I am afraid. Not for myself or not because I have done wrong. But not having enough strength within me I feel that I am being pressed beyond my limit, and in the name of the country I ask you to help me."

I, too, had the sensation then of being pressed beyond my limit; I, too, at that moment felt an acuter need of a vital, personal religion than I had ever felt before.

"But how can I help you?" I said at last, feebly. "What can I do? I understand your motive, but I dare express no opinion upon it. You have acted as you think right in the circumstances. I dare not say you have done wrong."

He rocked his frail body to and fro in a way that was painful to see.

"If you can say I have done right," he said, "I can go on."

"And if I cannot say it?" And I felt a sudden, terrible tightening of the throat as I asked the question.

"Well!" He closed his eyes piteously and spread out his hands. "I feel that everything will go."

"That is to say, you will confess to your master?"

"No, I don't mean that," he said. "But what I feel is that unless you can sustain me a little I — I —— "

He covered his face.

"Haven't you been sleeping lately?" I asked.

He said he had not.

"Since when?"

"My head has not touched a pillow since last Thursday morning."

I asked the reason. With great reluctance he confessed that a certain person, whom I did not ask him to name, had spoken words to his mistress in his hearing which had prepared him for that which was about to happen.

"What steps did you take?"

"I could do nothing."

"No, of course you couldn't."

"Beyond imploring her upon my knees to reflect upon her action."

"And that had no effect?"

"No, but I could see she thought I was mad. And I almost thought I was myself, except that when a man thinks he's mad they say he isn't."

"But you tried by every means in your power to restrain her — out of love for your master, and out of love for your country?"

"Yes, your Grace. But I was only a servant, and my prayers were not heard."

"And on Friday morning she left the house fully determined never to return?"

"Yes."

"At the instance of the person whom you have had occasion to mention already?"

"I would prefer to express no opinion upon that, if you will permit me." He spoke as only a gentleman could have done.

Somehow I felt quite unnerved. This was a poor lost soul. He seemed beyond human aid. His eyes haunt me as I write. As he himself expressed it, when his master gave him the letter to post he had been pressed beyond his limit; and there he sat, bereft of his will.

"Tell me," I said, "is it that you feel that your master is not strong enough to meet this crisis in his own life, while the fate of the country hangs in the balance?"

"That is what I feel."

"But may you not be mistaken?"

"Perhaps I may. But I dare not take the risk. A man can only judge by his own strength when he acts in the place of another."

"That is to say, you would be unequal to the task of coping with such a crisis in your own life at such a moment in the life of the nation?"

"I think no man would have the strength. And I believe that is a fact that might weigh with his enemies."

"You think this business of your mistress is part of a plot to ruin him politically?"

"I am not entitled to say that."

"But you fear it?"

"I hope you will not insist on an answer to the question."

I did not. And I felt bound to respect him the more.

As I sat facing him a tragic helplessness seemed to numb me. What could I do? What advice could I give? He had made me see that his conduct was based on a high instinct, which I had neither the strength nor the courage to deny. Had my life depended on it, as I sat watching his emotion, I could not have said whether he had acted rightly or wrongly.

"You have come to me," I said, "because you want somebody to share the responsibility of your action?"

"Yes," he said. "I ask you to help me to pass through this terrible crisis in the life of the nation."

"Is it that there is any specific thing you would ask me?"

"Yes, there is one thing," he said. "If you approve of my action I ask you to take charge of these letters."

He unbuttoned his overcoat and produced the two letters from an inner pocket. Then he rose and put them on the table.

I hope I have no superfluity of copybook morality. I hope I am neither a prig nor a coward, but when thus he asked me to bear a part in his crime I felt a sudden nausea. He may have been right, he may have been wrong; I do not judge him, nor shall I ever be able to judge him, but somehow the sight of those letters seemed to show me the way for us both.

"Nicholson," I said, "it is reasonably clear that your God has imposed a task upon you beyond your present strength. Had you been equal to the task you would have kept your own counsel, you would not have come to me for countenance. But since you have sought my advice, I will give it as far as I am capable, by the light of that reason which is no more than the counterpart of your own. We are the

creatures of Fate. We must be content to be the
creatures of Fate. If it be the will of Providence
that an instrument has been appointed to deliver
our beloved country from its peril, it lies neither in
your power nor mine to retard or advance its design.
Neither you nor I can know what reserves of strength
your master may possess. God alone can know that.
But if He has chosen him to deliver our country,
whatever his enemies may do to him, He will see him
through."

I don't know that my words had any particular
wisdom; I don't think they were the fruit of any
particular faith — alas! I am no nearer to God
than the majority of my generation — they simply
shaped themselves on my lips without any conscious
volition, but their effect was greater than I could
have hoped or foreseen. The poor old man sprang
from his chair as though some secret spring had been
pressed in his heart.

"My faith has not been great enough," he said.
"When Mr. D. has recovered a little I will give him
the letters. I thank you from the bottom of my
heart."

He took up the letters and buttoned them inside
his coat, and then he prepared to leave. But I felt
that I could not let him go without some attempt at
a consolation it was not in my power to give. I
assured him that whatever happened to him, or to

his master, or to the country, he would always have
my respect.   That seemed to comfort him; and then
very shyly and humbly he asked me if I would mind
praying with him a little — and I did!

    .   .   .   Yes, my dear Laura, it has been by far
the strangest experience I have ever passed through.
It has also been a rather harrowing experience.
As I write this for the relief of an overwrought mind
— and it is all so horribly intimate that I don't
suppose this letter will go to the post, although we
have shared almost every thought we have had in
our lives — the feeling uppermost in my heart, now
that I am left alone with my emotions, is, that after
all, I may not have acted right.   Some high power
may have possessed the noble soul enclosed in that
frail vessel; some divine instinct may have inspired
him to find the way out for us all.

    The episode has shattered me for the time being.
I, too, am horribly tormented.   But in these kinds
of crises we act automatically; and whether we do
right, or whether we do wrong, we cannot go against
our natures.

    Mr. D. was much overdone when I saw him this
evening.   His week's labour for the country would
have taxed a Hercules.   A quarter of a million
people have learned the sound of his voice.   He is
completely worn out.   I am wofully afraid of the
consequences, yet for good or ill the die is cast.

Never have I felt such a need of strength as now.
I, too, am being driven beyond my limit.

We all feel this need of God: poor Nicholson and
I, the humble servants of the chosen instrument,
and he, the God-appointed one, yet more than any.
Perhaps our country would not have been brought
to this pass had she walked with Him lately as of old.
Are we to be one with Nineveh and Tyre? Has it
been left for one woman as weak and frail as myself
to undo all? No, I cannot think so. O ye of little
faith! Those five precious little words are now my
only stay. The cabal has now fixed upon R. It
meets at Cloudesley this week-end. It is a bitter
and tragic irony. I refuse to believe that such a
makeshift Government can be called into being.
Still, those whom the gods would destroy ——— !

XIX

MR. DRAPER rose late on the morning after his return. Noon was approaching by the time he was seated at his writing-table in his room.

The eyes of the butler had already carefully noted his appearance. Had he slept? The old man taking his courage in his hands, had already ventured to ask the question, and had met with a cordial and reassuring answer.

With the servant it was far otherwise. He had not slept, nor had he attempted to do so. He was still overborne by a sense of destiny. But this morning he was calm and fixed of purpose. In whatever light his action was viewed he was now secure of soul.

His master had had a good night — that was the determining factor. Compared with yesterday he was looking braced and alert this morning. Nicholson decided that twelve o'clock must be the hour.

Man proposes! At five minutes to twelve the dethroned Prime Minister called to see his late colleague.

Mr. Grundy was a man about sixty. He was of the middle height, inclining a little to stoutness, presenting no very striking point in his personality beyond a rather fine head and a calm, paternal smile which lent him an appearance of great wisdom.

It must be allowed that his habit of mind did no injustice to this outward portent. By many he was thought to be the wisest man in the kingdom. He was cautious, calculating, impartial, a little sophistical perhaps on occasion, but subject to fine flashes of candour, superbly accessible to all sorts and conditions of men, and with the rare gift of pleasing all with whom he was brought in contact. He had earned the respect of all sections of the community. As a leader he was lacking in inspiration and authenticity, but he was a man who had deserved well of his country, and his country was by no means insensible of its obligation. Had he only possessed a little more courage, a little more initiative, that dual endowment without which all leadership is vain, the present state of chaos might not have arisen.

It was the first meeting since the tragic event of the dethroned leader and the man who had wrecked his second administration.

Mr. Draper rose from his writing-table as soon as his visitor was announced and sprang forward with hand outstretched to greet him. The older statesman accepted the hand without the slightest reserve or *arrière-pensée*.

"I feel it to be so kind, so *good* of you to call upon

me," said the younger man with the impulsiveness which endeared him to his friends. Moreover, there was a ring of genuine affection in the tone. It was a quality his chief had always inspired in those who had worked with him.

"Business, business, my dear fellow," said Mr. Grundy with a charming air of brusquerie — another of his assets. "Last night we dined in high places, my wife and I. Naturally the conversation turned upon you and your wonderful week's work. The Fountain of Honour desires to thank you personally. I said I would bring you along this morning if you were available. But don't come unless you feel equal to it, because I am afraid we shall be expected to stay to lunch."

"I consider it in the light of a great honour," said the younger man.

Mr. Grundy's comically quizzical face denoted resignation.

"Well, he's easier to talk to than his father was. He can see a joke — at least, that is to say, there are traces of an incipient sense of humour in a rudimentary state. And, of course, a Christian gentleman — always a Christian gentleman. He's a dear fellow, really, I always think."

"I am glad you think he is a Christian gentleman," said Mr. Draper. "That is always the impression he makes on me."

"Yes, always that — to me. The type is not extinct as long as we have him. I wish people could be made to realize it. And a rather shrewd fellow withal in some ways."

"I am so glad you think that."

"I am not here to flatter you, Draper, but he's profoundly grateful for what you have done."

"For throwing us over the precipice?"

"No, not for that. For your splendid effort to pull the thing to rights. He has read your speeches and marked your progress, and under the guidance of Heaven he thinks you may save us yet."

The younger man was touched by the elder statesman's generosity.

"Thank you, Grundy," he said. "You don't know what it means to me that *you* should come and tell me this."

"I think we can all rejoice, my dear fellow, that he is such a good and sensible man. And my feeling is this, if those inflated fools on the Right who are so devilish full of themselves can only be persuaded to let him alone, his own instinct — and, after all, it ought to be a pretty sound one — can be trusted to find the way out."

"Grundy," said the other, his deep voice vibrating with emotion, "I am more than rejoiced to hear you say that."

"I may be mistaken, of course. But that is the

impression he gave me last night.   He is quite able
to do a little thinking for himself; and of course he
has the inestimable advantage of being outside it all."

" You feel that he may have a mind of his own?"

" I hope and pray that he has."

" By the way, is there any ground for this rumour
in respect of the cabal?"

"Rockingham?   Yes, I'm afraid."

"Is it conceivable?"

"He's won the Derby twice, you know."

"Well, he's no fool, that must be said for him.
And if only he had sincerity, upon my soul we might
do worse."

"The ' if ' is too big, my dear fellow. The thing has
been played up so high on both sides, that it is only
absolute good faith that can save the whole bag of
tricks from being blown up to the moon."

"Do you think he could play straight for once —
in an emergency?"

"Not he!   A man can't go against his blood.   It
is the ablest and the foulest blood in England.   You
never knew his father, old R.?   He was the sort of
man you wouldn't care to meet in a lonely lane on a
dark night if you had a fiver on you — and his rent-
roll was two hundred thousand a year."

"I suppose if one is born crooked one is bound to
go crooked."

"It would appear to be so in his case at any rate.

Having wearied of every other form of human pleasure, scoring a dubious point against an adversary seems to be the only recreation that never fails him."

"Well, he always seems to convey the impression of being one of the ablest men in the country — that is, if he cared to be."

"Outside his Majesty's gaols," said Mr. Grundy, who was without illusions on the subject of human nature. "The old Lord Chief always used to say that the best brains of the kingdom were kept securely under lock and key. By the way — forgive me for calling your attention to it if you haven't seen it, but I rather feel that I ought — I am sorry to see that you have had the misfortune to make an enemy of another kind of blackguard. Have you seen the *Daily Argus* this morning?"

"I never read it."

"Well, break your rule. See if they have a copy in the servants' hall."

The *Daily Argus* was sent for.

"There you are," said Mr. Grundy. "In the largest type, if you please, in the form of a leading article: 'The Great Lady and the Democrat: a Parable for the Period.'"

The Democrat read the article with an ashen face and eyes blazing with fury.

"I wish you hadn't shown it to me," he said.

The elder man laid a paternal hand on his shoulder.

"Don't be weak, my dear fellow," he said. "Weakness of any kind can't be allowed in *you*. It is nothing; the bite of a gadfly. Forget it until the time comes — and then you can bear it in mind."

"You are right," said the other, setting his teeth, "I mustn't be weak. At any rate, I'll try not to be. It is worded with skill," he added in a calmer tone.

"Yes, it is the work of a practised hand. And it comes at the psychological moment. The whole thing is very nicely calculated."

"Do you think it will do harm?"

"It is bound to do a certain amount of harm. This is a nation of Pharisees. It gives your enemies an enormous pull just at the time when they can use it best."

"Do you see the finger of Rockingham in it?"

"No, let us do him that justice. He is not the man to fraternize with the scum. He has his own private code of *friponnerie*, but he never forgets that by birth he is a gentleman."

"I am glad you think that," said the other. "One has rather felt of late that he was not a man likely to be troubled by any kind of scruple."

"He would draw the line at the G.P., at any rate."

Mr. Grundy looked at his watch.

"A quarter to one! A five minutes' walk! I'm afraid that won't give us much of an appetite for our luncheon."

XX

IT was four o'clock when Mr. Draper returned to his house. His step sounded light in the hall; there was a slight look of defiance in him, as of a man on terms with life. When he entered his room to complete a half-written letter which the arrival of his late colleague had interrupted, he found Evelyn Rockingham there. She was smoking a cigarette and reading the *Daily Argus*.

Nicholson in receiving her had not thought fit to enlighten her as to whether the secret had yet been divulged. One glance at the Minister as he entered told her that it had not.

She held up the newspaper.

"Will it do harm?" she asked. As she spoke she watched his face with covert but anxious eyes.

"Grundy thinks it may do a little," he answered, almost in a tone of indifference. "Personally, I don't."

She drew a deep sigh of relief.

"I am glad you take that view."

"One may be wrong, of course, but the whole thing seems to be keyed up far too high for a matter of that kind to take any hold on events."

"I feel sure of it. Is there any fresh development?"

The Minister did not reply immediately.

"Several," he said at last. "Grave developments. Grundy and I have been talking things over with a certain person the last three hours."

"Grundy — and you!"

"Yes, the lion and the lamb. Misfortune, you know, makes strange bedfellows."

The gravity of the Minister began to oppress her.

"Tell me what has happened?" she said.

"Well, in the first place, Rockingham has been asked to form a Government."

She blanched a little. But her self-control was complete.

"When was he asked — do you know?"

"On Saturday, I believe."

"Has he accepted?"

"No; he has asked for a week in which to consider his decision. He has been given until Monday at noon."

"After the week-end meeting of the cabal?"

"Yes, I suppose. They meet, I understand, at the King's suggestion."

"But isn't the whole scheme impracticable? On what basis can Robert form a Government?"

"Well, the scheme is this — it is the King's own, and he accepts full responsibility for it — Rockingham to be Prime Minister in a new coalition, which is to include Fern and Bayliss of the Left, and also Grundy, Bryant, and myself."

"But on the face of it, isn't it impossible?"

"Well, I don't know. There may be something in it. Fern and Bayliss, it seems, are willing to come in, provided a guarantee is given that the first act of the new Government will be to pass the Conciliation Bill, although not necessarily in the precise form in which it stands at present."

"It seems incredible that Fern and Bayliss can have any place in a Rockingham ministry."

"Well, it is the King's own idea. He has worked nobly to make it possible, and he has earned respect all round."

"And Grundy and Bryant and yourself?"

"Grundy doesn't approve, but if no better scheme can be devised he will not stand in the way. Bryant doesn't see why is shouldn't be tried. Of course the whole thing is a palpable makeshift. But no alternative has appeared on the horizon at present."

"And you?" The question was asked eagerly. "How do you feel about it?"

"Well, I told him bluntly that I didn't see how it was possible for two men to work together each of whom had a profound contempt for the other."

"Wasn't the good man a little shocked?"

"Very shocked, I'm afraid. It seemed to come to him like a blow. But it had to be said. It is no use trying to mince matters, even if Rome happens to be burning.   Still, as I said, my one desire was to keep the thing going, and to that end I would do my best to put my private feelings in my pocket for the time being."

"What did he say to that?"

"Both he and Grundy were rather discomposed. It occurred to me that it was perhaps rather selfish and egotistical to feel so strongly when everthing was hanging in the balance.   But it is the way I am made. I can't conceal my wound."

"Is it that you hold Rockingham responsible for this?"

Her reference was to the *Daily Argus*, which was still in her hand.

"Yes, indirectly.   And if one day I can punish him without punishing others I intend to do it."

"But in the meantime you consent to sink the personal equation in the common good?"

"As far as it may be possible to do so.   I said I would do my best.   Thereupon Grundy and I were asked to do down on Sunday to confer with the cabal."

"You — at Cloudesley!"

"Yes — by command.   It all seems rather ironical. By the way, Aline is still there and I've had no word as to when she intends to return."

"When did you see her or hear from her last?"

"I last saw her ten days ago, when I set out for the North. And I've heard no word of her since. But to return to this proposal that we should go down to Cloudesley on Sunday. I should have much preferred a meeting here in London; but every hour counts, and the thing is to be kept as secret as possible until all the details are adjusted, so that the whole scheme can be laid dramatically before the country."

"Why dramatically?"

"In order to drive home, I suppose, its far-reaching significance to the bosoms and the businesses of men."

"Then it is *fait accompli?*"

"Yes, I fear, unless there is a hitch at the eleventh hour."

"Have you actually given your decision?"

"No, I have not. I have asked for forty-eight hours in which fully to consider the proposal. I found it impossible to decide at once. In fact, I was not asked to do so. It may be, after all, that the old Adam will prove too much for my patriotism."

As the conversation proceeded Evelyn Rockingham had become increasingly perplexed, increasingly unhappy. And now she gave expression to the thought that was dominating her mind.

"There is one thing I see clearly," she said. "It is that you have broken through their defences.

They have done all in their power to keep you out, but it has now been brought home to them that you are indispensable to any Government that may be formed. That being the case, why not dictate your own terms instead of accepting theirs."

The Minister pondered.

"The point is an important one," he said. "And you are very probably right. At any rate I have given no definite answer; I stand pledged to nothing. Certainly I don't intend to enter a Rockingham ministry unless I am thoroughly convinced that there is no alternative which can avail the country."

"But there *is* an alternative. This is their method of confessing the unpalatable fact that you are indispensable. Why not form your own Government on your own terms?"

The Minister shook his head and smiled rather sadly.

"That is a large order. This thing must be thought out. In the meantime every hour counts. There are a number of alarming developments in the country. There are all kinds of rumours in circulation. It is said that the League has carefully prepared its plans for a great coup, and that it may play it at any moment. We may be in the throes of civil war by the end of the week."

"Well, poor dear Robert, as I read his character, is not the man to cope with it."

"No, but the point is that the blow has not yet fallen. If we can only contrive to patch up an honourable truce before it does, so much the better for us and so much the worse for the League."

"Yes, but the blow has been predicted any time these two years."

"Well, here is its opportunity. And we can't afford to delay."

Evelyn Rockingham rose from her chair. Her face was vivid with excitement.

"Yes, one quite sees that. One respects your scruples. One understands that you don't play for yourself. But the point I want to urge is, that if you do play for yourself you play for the country."

Again he shook his head.

"That is where I am by no means so clear. Splendid work has been done during the past week. The King has shown himself to be a statesman of a high order. He has made his wishes clearly known and if it is possible to respect them one feels that sacrifices should be made to that end."

"Yes, I quite see that," she said tensely. "But the point is, who can help the country most — you or Robert?"

"They evidently think Robert."

"*They,*" she said contemptuously. "They know they are beaten and are now playing to save their faces. Robert means nothing to any one; he stands

for nothing; he has never done a hand's turn for the
country; he hasn't a constructive idea in his head.
Don't be magnanimous! You have forced them to
call you in to help them; you are in a position to
exact your own terms, and your terms must be that
you are Prime Minister."

Again Mr. Draper shook his head.

"Forgive me, my dear Evelyn, but isn't that the
reasoning of an ambitious woman?"

"It is the reasoning of a woman, certainly," she
allowed, her face alive with emotion, "and of a
woman ambitious for her country. I am Robert's
wife, and I know his worth compared with yours.
I don't wish to pay you a vain compliment, but as
an Englishwoman — unenfranchised though I am
— I desire that the strongest and ablest man
in the kingdom should take charge and have a
free hand in one of the darkest hours we have ever
known."

The Minister began to pace the room uneasily.

"But assuming all that," he said, "may I not still
be able to assert myself?"

"In time, no doubt. But you will find it so much
more difficult if you yield to them now. And you
must not forget that they will always be intriguing
against you. They will use you to serve their turn,
but they will always be looking out for the moment
when they can cast you off. They only invite you to

come in because at the present moment no form of government is possible without you. You have got the whip-hand. It will be sheer unwisdom lightly to forego your advantage."

"I have no intention of doing that," said the Minister. "But I mustn't use it immorally. Whatever happens, the country must come first; we are none of us more than pawns in the game. Moreover, time is all-important; and I hardly feel equal to incurring the responsibility of overthrowing a well-thought-out scheme unless I can be quite sure that the whole thing rests on a fallacy."

"How would you define 'a fallacy' in this particular instance?"

"I should consider the scheme to be based on a fallacy if clear proof could be adduced that such heterogeneous elements would find it impossible to work together."

"Do you doubt it for one moment?"

The Minister passed his hand across his forehead, like one who suffers almost intolerable pain.

"Please don't press the point too hard," he said with a rather pathetic anxiety. "Nobody realizes more fully than I do how nearly hopeless it is. But there is always the chance that we may find some common ground on which to stand."

"Impossible! Consider, to begin with, two such men as Robert and yourself. Is there any common ground on which you can stand? You know him to be false right through."

"Yes, I feel all that. But he has earned the respect and the confidence of better men than I."

"No, I won't allow you to be magnanimous. A great mistake is about to be made by a very admirable and well-meaning person, but you must be no party to it. Whatever happens you cannot join a Rockingham ministry."

"Cannot?"

"Cannot."

"Isn't it too big a word?"

Her face had grown white and set.

"Suppose I justify it?" she said breathing hard. "Suppose I put the proof in your hand?"

"Impossible!"

"Isn't it too big a word?" she retorted. "Besides, does it really need proving?"

"Yes, I think it does," he said very gravely. "I make no secret of the fact that I distrust Rockingham, that I despise him, but I think proof is needed that it is impossible for us to sit round the same table."

Now she was as white as death.

"Are you so blind that you have no suspicions?"

"A wise man never indulges in suspicions," he said.

"A very dangerous doctrine, my friend," was her answer.

The Minister shook his head.

"Evelyn," he said very gravely, "please under-stand that I never let myself deal in such things as suspicions. The estimate I have formed of Rocking-ham's character is not flattering, but I don't go beyond that. What, pray, have I to be suspicious of?"

"Well, since you don't deal in suspicions," she said with a touch of rather venomous irony, "there is, perhaps, no need to answer the question."

"Precisely," he said, with an air of indifference.

But the air of indifference whipped up all the woman in her.

"Well," she said slowly, with biting emphasis, perhaps you will prefer to deal with hard facts."

"Certainly," he said. Her tone had aroused his curiosity, but he kept it well in hand. "One always prefers to deal with hard facts if they happen to be available. We cannot have too many of those."

"That is to say, you are never afraid of them?"

"No," he said; "one is never afraid of hard facts. Why should one be?"

"Doesn't it rather depend on the nature of them?"

"Doesn't it depend, my dear Evelyn, rather upon the nature of the person to whom they are addressed?"

"Perhaps — it may be so."

In spite of her iron will she was terribly excited

now. But he was too obtuse to perceive how hard emotion was driving her.

"Evelyn," he said, "why play with words? Rome is burning. There is more than work enough for every one of her citizens. If you are in a position to adduce any fact — mind, I say *fact* — why it is impossible for Rockingham and myself to work together, in the name of the country I call upon you to adduce it."

For a little time she was silent. Then she tried to speak, and her voice failed.

"Well, my dear Evelyn?"

He was still imperturbable, still perfectly self-secure.

"You invite me to lay the facts on the table before you?" she said in a voice strangely thin and high.

"Nay," he said with a calm smile, "I do more than that. If you possess any proof of your assertion that it is impossible for Rockingham and myself to work together for the common good, I do more than ask for it. I demand it."

By now she was trembling violently.

"Very well," she said, "please ring that bell."

XXI

MR. DRAPER touched the bell. Nicholson entered in answer to the summons. Something in the aspect of Evelyn Rockingham caused the servant to close the door behind him. He then stood in a kind of proud humility, his face averted from his master.

"Is it Nicholson you wish to see?" asked the Minister, breaking a silence that was painful.

She nodded, not trusting herself to speak. After a further moment of silence, the butler plunged his hand into the breast-pocket of his coat. He drew out two letters and handed them to his master.

"Sir," he said, speaking with a self-control that was remarkable, "one of these is a note that was left for you by my mistress when she went away last Friday week. I did not forward it to you, nor did I give it to you immediately upon your return. The time did not seem favourable. The other letter is the one you gave me to post last evening. In the circumstances I thought it right not to post it. I may say, sir, that in both cases I accept full responsibility for my action."

The Minister did not say anything in reply, but stood holding the letters, an odd look upon his face.

The butler left the room.

"Was it by your advice," the Minister asked Evelyn when they were left together, "that Nicholson has done as he has done?"

"In withholding these letters, do you mean?"

"Yes."

"I will tell you what happened. I did not know of the existence of either of these letters until last night about eleven o'clock when he came to me for advice."

"What advice did you give?"

"I advised him to give them to you at the first favourable opportunity."

"What was his reason for withholding them?"

"His fear of the consequences. He realizes that all depends on you. Yesterday, upon your return, worn out and overwrought, he could not trust you with Aline's letter?"

"That is to say, he knows its contents?"

"I think he has made a guess."

"Which he has communicated to you?"

"No, not in so many words. But having regard to all the circumstances I have been obliged to infer certain things."

"How long have you been cognizant of these circumstances?"

"For some little time past, but I allowed myself to draw no inferences until last night."

"I see," he said in a musing tone.

He still held the letter unopened in his hand. She calmly watched the working of the powerful will behind the unimpassioned mask that was presented to her. She felt it to be a wonderful exhibition of self-control.

"I would like to ask you one more question, Evelyn," he said gently, with a perceptible lightening of tone. "You must forgive my asking so many, but do you approve of Nicholson's action?"

"I have lain awake all night to consider it," she said. "And I have come to the conclusion that, taking all the circumstances into consideration, special and peculiar as they are and having regard to the man himself and the kind of man he is, his action is to be defended."

"That is to say, that had you been in Nicholson's place, you would have felt justified in acting as he has done?"

"Yes — had I been Nicholson."

He looked at her searchingly.

"You would have been tempted to think so meanly of me?"

"No," she answered; "it is hardly fair to put it that way. Nicholson, as I understand him, is a man obsessed by an idea. In his eyes you are the instru-

ment chosen by Providence to save his country. At
the most crucial of all moments he is called upon
suddenly, by a set of perverse and untoward circumstances, to imperil the efficiency of that instrument,
and wisely and rightly, and I think even nobly, he
declines to do it."

"How admirably you play *advocatus diaboli*."

As the Minister spoke, almost in a tone of jest-
ing, he slipped both the letters into his pocket,
unopened.

His self-restraint amazed her. She had the wit to
take her own cue from it.

"By the way, you got my card for Friday evening?" she said.

"What is the object?" he asked. His tone was
one of polite interest. "Is it meant for a kind of
counter-demonstration?"

"Well, hardly — at Rockingham House! Cards
were sent out, you know, before these things came to
pass. And there really seems no reason why we
should cancel a perfectly innocent function."

"But think of the amount of water that has lately
flowed under London Bridge."

"I know. But my prophetic soul seems to tell me
that we of the faith ought all to keep in touch."

"Who are the faithful?"

"Grundy and Bryant have promised to come.
The Centre will be well represented. And I think

Diplomacy, the Services, and the Army Council will be there in force."

"Quite a representative gathering, eh, of the professional interests?   A meeting of business men."

"Yes — 'To meet the Right Honourable James Draper.' "

"Did you put that on your cards?"

"No, it hardly seemed wise — at Rockingham House!   But it will be Hamlet without the Prince if you don't show up."

The Minister laughed rather wryly.

"We may all be blown up sky-high by Friday evening," he said. "Those who are the most familiar with the signs and portents predict that Friday has been chosen as the Judgment Day."

"Well, my dear James," she said, "if you are alive and well, if we are all alive and well, I want you to promise to attend my party on Friday evening, not later then eleven o'clock."

He did not reply immediately, and then he said: "I think perhaps it would be rash to make any promises for Friday.   There is no saying what will have happened by then."

The almost imperceptible change in the tone seemed somehow to strike into her.   She looked at him rather wanly.   But the impassive face was still as it was.

"At any rate," she said, "I shall expect you.   I depend upon you.   I demand a promise."

"Very well," he said. And now there was a subtle quality in his tone that struck right through her. "Very well, Evelyn — if I am alive and well."

Nothing further passed. Perhaps it was that she felt her nerve to be failing. He escorted her to the hall door, where her car awaited her, and in the fading light of the February afternoon he remained a sombre, ghostlike figure watching her drive away.

An hour later she returned, but did not penetrate farther than the entrance hall, where she held a brief colloquy with Nicholson.

"I want you to keep me informed," she said, "of anything that may happen. My number on the telephone is 049 Mayfair."

The butler promised to do so.

"Where is Mr. Draper now?" she asked.

"He is locked in his study, your Grace. He has given strict instructions that no one, not even Mr. Renshaw, is to disturb him. He is at home to no one."

The face of the butler was livid. His emotion threatened to overmaster him.

As Evelyn Rockingham was about to return to her brougham, with a sudden impulse of feminine kindness she offered her hand to the old man.

He kissed it reverently. A single tear stained her glove.

XXII

THE next afternoon about five o'clock Evelyn Rockingham came to Queen Anne's Gate for the third time that day. She was received in the morning-room by Mr. Renshaw, the private secretary.

He was an able, matter-of-fact young man with that definite, assured, persistently mundane outlook upon the world that is in itself a guarantee of success in any sphere of action in which its possessor may engage.

"Does he still keep his room?" she asked. The private secretary answered rather curtly in the affirmative.

"And the door is still locked?"

"It was when I tried it half an hour ago," said the young man.

"Did you speak to him?"

"Yes, I knocked upon the door, and asked him whether he would not take some food."

"And he answered you?"

"Yes; he said when he required food he would ring for it."

"In what manner did he answer?"

"In quite a normal, ordinary voice, I thought."

Evelyn seemed to be reassured a little.

"I would like to ask you one question, Mr. Renshaw," she said. "As a detached observer, in what light does Mr. Draper's behaviour appear to you? Knowing him intimately as you do, is there anything in especial you are able to deduce from it?"

The young man did not answer the quest on until he had spent some little time in reflection. And then he said with a melancholy smile: "I confess I am utterly defeated by it."

"Nicholson, by any chance, has not spoken to you on the subject?"

"Nicholson? Oh, no."

His surprised tone convicted her of unwariness. She hastened to cover her indiscretion as well as she could.

" He seems very upset, poor old thing."

"Nicholson?"

The tone of surprise had grown more positive. She beat a retreat, hasty and perhaps a little ignominious.

"Has the King sent again?"

"Yes, a quarter of an hour ago."

"And you communicated the fact to him through the locked door?"

"Yes."

"And his answer?"

Mr. Renshaw's own answer was to look his visitor steadily in the eyes. He had a decidedly resolute and determined mouth.

"I hope you don't think I'm impertinent," she said.

"Not at all," said the young man, summoning a very well-bred air to his assistance.

A red spot appeared in the centre of her cheek. She was keenly chagrined by the feeling that she had been taking a little too much for granted.

"You see I am a very old friend," she said.

The young man inclined his head slightly and very stiffly.

"A very old friend, Mr. Renshaw. I cannot bear the thought of anything happening to him, particularly at a time like this."

The young man again inclined his head.

"Believe me," she said upon a note of the sweetest humility, "I would not appear impertinent for the world. I would not appear in any way officious, but I realize as few people can the awful importance of all this. I hope I make myself clear?"

"Admirably clear," said the young man with an aloofness of manner equally admirable.

"Do you feel disposed to tell me what Mr. Draper's answer was to the King's second summons."

"Certainly," said the young man. "Mr. Draper's answer was that he much regretted that he was not sufficiently well to leave his room."

"Could you have told that anything was amiss from the tone or the manner in which the answer was given?"

"There was nothing as far as one could judge to suggest any kind of mental disturbance," said the private secretary, gravely measuring his words.

"Tell me, Mr. Renshaw — if you will forgive my terrible anxiety — do you yourself feel, as one who knows Mr. Draper intimately, that he is undergoing some process of mental disturbance?"

Mr. Renshaw took time for his answer.

"I undoubtedly do," he said.

"You would say his behaviour within the past twenty-four hours is inconsistent with a perfectly normal mind?"

Again Mr. Renshaw took time for his answer.

"As I envisage a perfectly normal mind," he said, "I feel bound to say yes."

"Has he ever acted in this way before within your knowledge of him?"

"Never, within my knowledge."

"Is there anything to which you can ascribe this present condition? — if you will forgive this seeming impertinence."

"I would be inclined to say, myself," said the young man, speaking slowly and with hesitation, "that it is the result of overwork. The strain last week must have been fearful."

"By the way, you didn't accompany him upon his tour?"

"Only to Derby and Sheffield."

"And he made wonderful speeches?"

"The two that I heard will always stand out as the most wonderful in my recollection. I don't say that merely because they are the freshest." The official manner was losing a little of its chill at last. "It was as old Sir George Rose, who took the chair at Sheffield, said, he spoke like an evangel of righteousness. It sounds rather like cant, I dare say, but somehow it seems exactly to describe the effect that he made."

"And you feel that nature has been overdriven, and that he is now suffering a very severe reaction?"

Once more the young man took time for his answer.

"Yes," he said, "it seems to be the only explanation that can meet the case."

As he answered slowly and deliberately their eyes met. Hers, softly luminous in spite of the tears they had sought in vain to shed, seemed to pierce right through those of the young man and to enter the hard, limited and secure soul that lay behind.

She was more than a little afraid. He was a man with whom no sort of liberty could be taken. But desperation and an intolerable anguish of mind forced her to accept the risk.

"Mr. Renshaw," she said, "there is just one other question I beg to be allowed to ask."

The clear gray eyes looked at her unfalteringly.

"I merely ask it because — because I must. If we are to save him — if we are to save England — there must be no secrets between us.   I hope you understand."

He remained motionless.

"The question I ask is this: When his wife left this house for Cloudesley last Friday week, were you aware that she had left it never to return?"

The young man kept a tight hold upon his composure.

"Having regard to the answers I have already given," he said icily, "it hardly seems necessary that I should answer the question."

"Forgive me," she said quickly, "I ought not to have asked it."

He stood tense in every line.   But a moment afterward her note of appeal had conquered him.

"Perhaps you ought not," he said, "but I'm glad you did.   That is, if it is right that you should."

"I hope it is.   It may not be, but I think if we are to help him we must both fully realize our task."

He, in his turn, now became the questioner.

"He was informed yesterday afternoon about five o'clock," she said in answer.

"By whom?"

She briefly told the story of Nicholson coming to her with the letters.

"It was really at my instigation, you see, that Nicholson divulged the secret when he did. And now the grievous problem that haunts me is, was Nicholson's first instinct after all the right one in the circumstances, and ought things to have been left as they were?"

They looked steadily at one another through the fading light of the room. The breath of each was coming quickly.

"Is that the question you ask *me?*" he said at last.

She turned aside swiftly, with a little cry.

"No, it is not. Because — because I don't think I could bear the answer."

XXIII

FOR some little time they stood looking at one another in an embarrassed silence. Neither knew what to say to the other. Each had a sense of futility, a sense of impotence, that was overwhelming.

In crises of this kind it is the woman as a rule who speaks first.

"Is there any single thing we can do?" asked Evelyn Rockingham, and she seemed a little overcome by the futility of the question.

"I don't in the least know," said the private secretary, equally conscious of impotence.

"It is too early to consult a doctor? Do you think he could help us if we did?"

The young man shook his head sadly.

"I am out of my depth," he said. "I have no advice to give."

Fear seemed to take possession of her.

"Oh, I hope he has not let go!" she said.

"That is just what one doesn't know," said the private secretary, "and it is just what no one can tell us."

Urged by a sudden impulse she left the room.

She crossed the dimly lighted hall, making her way stealthily into a dark recess in one of its distant corners in which was a curtained door.

She knocked gently upon the panel. She called the name of the Minister softly.

There was no answer.

"James, it is I! — Evelyn!"

There was still no answer.

She pressed her ear to the panel. Strain her senses as she might she could not detect a sound within.

She struck the door harder. She raised her voice louder. Again she spoke his name.

There was not a sound.

A kind of nausea came suddenly upon her.

"James! It is I — Evelyn!"

The silence gripped her strangely. She felt herself to be turning a little faint.

Involuntarily she grasped the door-handle and turned it. With a thrill almost akin to terror she discovered that the door had yielded.

Half dazed with a sudden unreasoning dread of the unknown she discovered that the door had come open and that she stood on the threshold of a room completely dark.

Again she cried his name, and now with a sob.

There was no response.

Quivering from head to foot she groped her way in. She fumbled for the wall and for the button of the

electric light, but could find neither. She stumbled
forward through the darkness, and knocked over a
chair. The fire was out in the grate. No ray of
light penetrated the curtained window or the curtained doorway through which she had entered.

It was like entering a tomb. Even her hand was
not visible when she held it before her face. She was
almost overmastered by a desire to scream.

She stood to listen. There was a dead silence
except for the ticking of her nerves. These formed
the only living presence — of that she was sure.

Cold and faint with a terror she had never known
before, she turned to grope her way out of the room.
A chair fell to the carpet with a thud. By now all her
bearings were lost. There was nothing to guide her.
She could not tell in which direction lay the door, the
window, the walls, or the fireplace.

Straining every nerve she stood in the darkness to
listen, but could only hear the beating of her heart.
Then she grew aware of the loud insistent ticking of
a clock on the chimneypiece.

"James !" she cried

At the sound of her own voice she darted forward.
She fell headlong across a sofa. Here she lay help-
less, struggling as if in the clutch of a nightmare for
the vague, intangible thread of the light of reason.

How long she lay prone she didn't know. The
clock near at hand on the chimneypiece continued

to tick, and her fluttered nerves in a sort of desperate orgy were in unison with it.   And then, just as the will began to totter, there was the sound of a curtained door opening quite near to her.   It revolved stealthily; there were muffled groping footfalls; there was a faint blur of light, and then a heavy shadow; and then the door closed again, and all again was darkness.

As she lay in a huddle on the sofa she was overwhelmed by the sense of a presence in the room.

"Turn up the light, please, whoever you are," she had the presence of mind to gasp.

There was a click — and then the light.

Nicholson, a figure of horror and consternation, was seen to be leaning against the wall.

"Oh, it is you, Nicholson," she said, rather hysterically.   "I have done such a stupid thing.   I groped my way in, couldn't find the light, lost my bearings completely, and fell over this."

"I am very sorry, your Grace," said the old servant in a rather shattered voice.   "I — I didn't expect to find your Grace.   I — I beg your pardon."

"Do you know where Mr. Draper is?" she asked. "I had expected to find him here."

"He left the house a quarter of an hour ago, your Grace, while you were in conversation with Mr. Renshaw."

"Do you know where he has gone?"

"I do not, your Grace."

"Or when he is likely to return?"

"I do not, your Grace. He left no message of any kind."

"How did he seem?"

"That I cannot say, your Grace. I had only just a glimpse of him as he went out of the hall door."

She had already noticed a mysterious implement in the hand of the butler. Her curiosity was aroused, particularly as he was at pains to conceal the implement by holding it behind his back. She asked him what it was. It proved, however, to be nothing more formidable than a screwdriver.

Prosaic as was the nature of the tool, it had the power further to stimulate her curiosity.

"What are you going to do with it?" she asked.

The question disconcerted the old man completely.

"Let there be no secrets between us. Nicholson," she said in a tone of grave gentleness.

"There shall be none, your Grace," said the old man very simply. "The truth is there is something locked up in that bureau that I feel ought to come out. And I have come here for the purpose of getting it out."

"Tell me what it is?"

"A revolver and some cartridges, your Grace."

"Why are they there?"

"We were troubled with burglars along the street about a year ago, and Mr. Draper thought it to be his duty as a householder to take precautions."

"Well, I agree with you that it would be wise to get them out."

Nicholson was of opinion that they were in the bottom drawer of the bureau, which was locked. He knelt and began to ply the screw-driver. In a short time the drawer was open, and there at the top lay the weapon beside a cardboard box.

While the servant was still on his knees holding these sinister trophies in his hands, and while Evelyn Rockingham was bending over him intently, the door of the room opened, and the Minister entered in his usual quiet manner. So completely were the two conspirators absorbed in their task that for a moment they remained wholly unconscious of his entrance.

XXIV

THEY discovered his presence with a surprise
that was almost painful. It was impossible to
conceal what they were doing. The butler rose to
his feet with the revolver and the box of cartridges in
his hands.

Mr. Draper smiled a little.

"I think you are quite right," he said gently. "It
is very well thought of, my dear fellow, although " —
he smiled gravely —"the peril is hardly so acute as
all that."

The old man was sustained by the tone, which was
calm and full of kindness.

"Forgive me, sir," he said. "Perhaps I am over-
anxious. But I couldn't bear the thought of these
things being here."

The Minister laid a hand on his shoulder.

"Quite right, my dear fellow, quite right. Pray, take
charge of them. They will be better in your care."

The butler seized the moment to effect an escape
with his trophies.

"Dear old fellow!" said the Minister to his other
friend, when they were left together.

His speech was perfectly well ordered. Everything about him pointed to the fact that his mind was under control. Fearful as was the soul of Evelyn Rockingham, she was able to take courage from his bearing. Beyond the fact that he had the air and look of a very tired man there was hardly a suggestion of strain.

"I hope I have not frightened you all too much," he said with a penitent sweetness which she had never heard before in his voice. "I am afraid it was selfish and thoughtless and rather cruel to shut one's self up like that. I am truly sorry for any alarm I may have caused —but, you see, it was necessary that I should be alone with my God."

"Yes, that I quite understand," she said brokenly.

"He has been very good to me," said the Minister musingly, almost as though he was thinking aloud.

"Very, very good to me. I am almost daring to hope He has given me that for which I crave."

"The strength to do right?"

"Yes — just that. He has been with me here in this little room." The voice and look were those of a seer. "He came to me when I sought Him. I am very grateful." The sudden tears glistened in his eyes. "Very grateful — for myself and for the country."

"Is it that you see the way out?"

"Not yet. It is too early for that. But I have a ray of hope."

"You know that you were twice sent for yesterday?"

"Oh, yes. I am quite cognizant of all that has passed. I hope the King will not think me discourteous. I have just posted a letter to inform him that for the present I am not able to attend to any public business."

"You feel, in the circumstances, that some such statement was expedient?"

"Expedient is hardly the word. But I felt it to be due to us both. As a Christian gentleman he is not likely to misconstrue what I have written."

"Is it that you have asked for an extension of the forty-eight hours in order to arrive at a decision?"

The Minister closed his eyes as one overcome with weariness.

"I have asked for nothing. I can make no decision. God will decide. It must be left in His hands. He will decide for us all."

"Has He decided?"

She put the question almost breathlessly.

"He has not yet made known His will."

"And is it that you cannot see the King until the will of God is made known?"

"Even as you say, my dear friend. The case has

been submitted to the High Court. We must now possess our souls in patience and abide the issue."

Again she felt that tightening of the throat and breast that of late had afflicted her.

"Do you seem to have any knowledge of when His will will be made known?"

"I feel it will not be long delayed," said the Minister.

XXV

ROCKINGHAM HOUSE on the night of "a crush" was a rather imposing spectacle. A string of vehicles encumbered half the purlieus of Mayfair. Wealth, rank, distinction of many kinds, charming dresses and interesting personalities in an almost endless profusion entered the courtyard, passed under the awning and found their way up the famous white marble staircase, garnished with the genius of Lely, Kneller, Gainsborough, Reynolds, Romney, and Lawrence. And at the head of the stairs the company was received by a personage who shone that evening with a genius more vital than ever canvas was endowed with, by even the greatest painter that ever existed.

The hostess presented a stiking contrast to her guests. A very tall, animated woman with a remarkable freedom of pose, she wore a plain black gown. Neither head nor neck was embellished by a single ornament. The hair was drawn straight back from the large, noble, rather masculine features; and there was some subtle quality in the whole bearing which seemed to dominate the crowded rooms.

This was a strong-spirited, remarkable woman, an *esprit fort*, with whose name at that particular moment rumour was more than a little busy. The real cause for the protracted deliberations of the Privy Council was now known to the town.

The facts as they had begun to percolate through to the gossips of the metropolis were that in the country the pendulum of public opinion had already swung very decisively in the direction of the President of the Board of Conciliation, and that a clique of intriguers and placemen, making morality their watchword, had been able up till the present to freeze him out.

To-night, as soon as the guests began to assemble, a strange tense undercurrent of excitement was present in the spaciously beautiful rooms. As minute by minute they filled up, the atmosphere became increasingly electrical. The sands in the hour-glass were running out. The country had been twelve days now without a Government; and it was realized on every hand that the nation was passing through the gravest crisis it had known for nearly three hundred years.

There were many strained and anxious faces in that oddly assorted assembly. It was of a political rather than social cast. Little intimate groups were conversing apart in low tones. Shortly after eleven o'clock the rooms were crowded, and in a vague, indefinite way it was felt that something decisive was about to occur.

"Where is Draper?" asked a member of the late Government as he made his way with an authoritative air to a group at the far end of the larger room.

"I thought we were to have the pleasure of meeting him this evening."

"I hear he has been all day with the King," said the central figure of the group, a fine looking, elderly man who wore a star.

"Things must be pretty bad, then. Has the Rockingham faction given its answer?"

"It had not up till five o'clock. Of course they have till Monday."

"And they are conferring at Cloudesley?"

"One hears so."

"Why at Cloudesley? One would have thought they would have kept on the spot."

"They can do nothing wherever they are until the decision is made. And one understands their chief object at present is to keep clear of the Press. By the way, all the world is saying that Draper has broken with his wife."

"So one hears; but one hesitates to say how true it is."

"She has been at Cloudesley a fortnight at any rate, whatever that may mean."

"Well, it was always an utterly incomprehensible marriage."

This fragment of conversation was but one among many of a similar kind. The name of Draper was upon every lip. From the midst of the slough of apathy and indecision of the last twelve days this man of will and purpose had begun clearly to emerge. It was now known that the country at large was calling for him. The solid body of common sense which has ever been at the core of the nation, that phalanx of moderate opinion which in a supreme crisis can rise above faction, was beginning now to make its voice plainly heard.

That Rockingham had been asked by the King to form a ministry, and that he had till the following Monday at noon in which to make up his mind, was known to the few. It was also known that Rockingham and his friends and advisers were conferring together during that week-end in the seclusion of a famous Tory country-house, forty miles from London. This withdrawal from the metropolis at such an hour had been much commented upon by those who were aware of what was taking place; but having regard to the electrical state of the atmosphere, the secrecy which was being rigorously maintained in respect of the negotiations, and the almost certain prospect of their leaking out had they been conducted in London, the wisdom of such a course of action until a decision had been reached was recognized by those best qualified to judge.

The events of the past week had made it clear to all that at the moment no Government of any kind would be acceptable to the nation at large unless it included the President of the Board of Conciliation. His tour of the North, which had checked the rising tide of disorder and lawlessness, had also had the effect of forcing the hand of the Sovereign, and rendering the Minister indispensable to the country's governance. It was felt that it would be worse than futile for Rockingham to accept office without coming to terms with the remarkable man to whom politically and socially he was bitterly opposed.

Apart, however, from these salient facts all sorts of sinister rumours were rife this evening at Rockingham House. It had turned half-past eleven, and the man about whose complex personality the situation crystallized had not yet appeared. For some reason, vague and hard to define, his absence was taken by many as a grave omen.

Fresh arrivals swelled the throng continually. It became increasingly difficult to move about the crowded rooms. The buzz of conversation rose higher and more insistent, and every few minutes, in the train of the latest representative person's arrival, some new and startling rumour was bruited.

The appearance at twenty minutes to twelve of

two grave and reverend members of the Army Council brought the sinister information that martial law had been proclaimed at Manchester. The statement was also made, not however by those who were in a position to confirm it, that the troops had refused to fire upon the mob. All the same, the intelligence spread like wildfire from group to group. Many there were who bluntly refused to accept the news as true; others set themselves stoutly to minimize its significance.

At ten minutes to twelve the entrance of the suavely dignified figure of the Commissioner of Police gave rise to further ominous speculations. They were supported by the fact that the Commissioner steered a straight course through the throng to a solemn-looking group which had formed apart from all the others and was composed of important public officials.

Almost immediately afterward a hush fell upon the crowded rooms. Mr. Draper had appeared at last.

"Upon my soul, the man looks like a death's-head," said a former colleague of the Minister.

Every detail of his bearing and demeanour was noted with an eager curiosity. Yet beyond the fact that he was as pale as death little could be gained from the outward man. There was seen to be an aloofness about him, an air of detachment as if at the moment he moved upon some other plane of being.

Keen, even anxious, eyes were directed upon him,

noting to whom he talked, marking him closely in all he did. It was remarked, however, by some acute observers, who also were the most closely in touch with the trend of affairs, that the man bore no trace of consciousness of that signal triumph which he must have known to be his already.

As a matter of fact he looked so ghastly that he might have met a ghost on the stairs. And as he moved among the throng exchanging a few perfunctory sentences with this person and that, it was as though this critical but heterogeneous crowd had neither meaning nor interest for him, and that his mind was away elsewhere.

The Minister, however, lost no time in making his way to what was known as the Vandyck room, where, surrounded by effigies of the historic past, was assembled a number of those who were responsible for the maintenance of law and order. In the midst of these stood the hostess in earnest conversation with the Commissioner of Police. The appearance of Mr. Draper with his ghostlike countenance had the effect in some strange way of increasing the tension that was felt by all.

Every moment now seemed to add to the volume of wild speculation. By twelve o'clock all in the crowded rooms appeared to realize that the floodgates had opened, and that the surging tide of popular unrest had broken loose.

Precisely the form in which organized hostility to the established order had manifested itself none seemed to know. But somehow, in a subtle and indefinable manner, it was realized that the country was in the grip of a cataclysm. And then quite suddenly, a few minutes after midnight had passed, there came, in as strikingly effective and dramatic a fashion as the wit of man could devise, an evidence, a potent and irrefragable evidence, that the forces of industrial anarchy had declared war against society.

A T a few minutes after midnight, on the morning of the fourteenth of February, without any sort of warning, the brilliantly lighted rooms of Rocking-ham House were plunged in darkness. No omen more startling or disturbing could have been devised. Coming at such a time, as the climax to those sinister fears in which the minds of all were engulfed, it struck a chill into every heart.

There was not the least sign of panic. The good sense, the instinctive restraint and self-possession with which educated English people are generally able to arm themselves in a crisis were remarkably displayed. Darkness, sudden and complete, had descended upon the crowded assembly, but every person in it supported the calamity and the hint of untold ones to follow with a stoicism that was wonderful.

Matches were struck in various parts of the rooms. In a very short time the servants, aided by a number of the guests, were able to procure a tolerably efficient supply of candles.

Presently, by the orders of the hostess, a table was

moved into the centre of the largest of the rooms. She then mounted it, and in a clear, steady, and penetrating voice addressed her guests.

"I am afraid," said Evelyn Rockingham, "that a very grievous thing has happened, but a thing which I am sure, as Englishmen and Englishwomen, we shall all know how to bear with calmness and fortitude. As perhaps some of you have surmised already, the nightmare which for a number of years past has been a phantom in our minds has at last taken shape. The news has been brought to us, and this sudden darkness has confirmed it, that a wicked war has been declared against society at large by those whom we can only regard as its enemies. I grieve to tell you that the Workers' League has declared a universal strike throughout the country. This sudden darkness into which we are plunged is the confirmation of the fact. The Bishop of London, whom by the grace of God we have here in our midst, will offer a short prayer of intercession."

The hostess descended from the table, and the plaintive but sweetly impressive tones of the clergyman stole over the curious hush that now enveloped the rooms. Those who witnessed the company, which had assembled for a very different purpose, kneeling in prayer never forgot the spectacle. The candles shone fitfully upon the darkened scene. Many of the choicest spirits of the time humbly invoked the aid of One in whom some of them had not a very profound belief. There was a deep silence while the Bishop, a snow-white patriarch, bent with years, interceded for the country, and begged that the lives of the innocent might not be sacrificed.

When the Bishop had concluded his prayer, Evelyn Rockingham mounted the table and once more addressed her guests. "The President of the Board of Conciliation," she said, "desires to address you. He has been throughout the day in consultation with our beloved Sovereign. He wishes to lay before you a scheme which has been formulated in this dire emergency, almost on the spur of the moment, for the maintenance of law and order, and for the security of the Throne. In the absence of a Government he is only able to speak to you as a private citizen. But he begs you to give him the courtesy of a hearing. It is a matter of the gravest urgency he wishes to lay before you, since not a moment is to be lost if an appalling sacrifice of life and property is to be averted."

Good manners prevented any dissent being audibly expressed while the hostess was making her proposal. But as soon as she had yielded her place to the President of the Board of Conciliation, who in the fitful and uncertain light looked more like a ghost than ever, the silence was broken by a storm of hisses and cries of "Traitor!"

It was then seen that there were many present in that assembly who were still bitterly hostile to the Minister. In many hearts there was a deep-rooted dislike. There were those who held that the blame for the present catastrophe must be laid to his door. Their minds were obsessed by what they considered to be his ill-considered action in throwing out the Coalition Government on a minor point of detail.

At first it seemed that Mr. Draper would be refused a hearing. A storm of angry voices was raised all around him. Many were the gestures of protest. But as the austere figure stood there confronting them with a calmness that seemed to transcend the passions of men, the look of a seer upon his face, all who had eyes to see were overawed.

For a time the ascetic figure stood there, deadly pale, head bent in patience, not attempting to utter a word. The gesture was one of pain almost too great to be borne. Something seemed to have happened to the aggressively indomitable personality. His attitude as he stood dumbly confronting this hostility was completely passive, completely submissive, as of one walking close with his God.

When at last he opened his lips, every voice was hushed.

"My countrymen and countrywomen" — the wonderful voice floated clear and dominant throughout the room — "I ask you in the name of God to forget your politics."

The appeal was not in vain. The noble simplicity which could never fail of its effect in the ears of those accustomed to judge men spoke to every heart. In the lineaments of that ghostlike presence was embodied that rare and precious thing for lack of which the country was like to bleed to death.

The bitter enemies of James Draper, and the room held many who hated and distrusted him, were forced to listen to his words. The power of his personality, fused into action by a grave crisis, was all-compelling. And having heard those words, few, plain, and fitful, broken by the deep emotion of the speaker, which at times threatened to conquer him, the dullest and most prejudiced heart thrilled in response.

In the eyes of many, the rather strange figure mounted upon the table was a little grotesque. But those who heard his words, slowly and painfully uttered, and so charged with emotion that they could hardly be induced to leave his lips, seemed to recognize that it was the voice of God speaking to the people of England.

Every heart was uplifted by an austerity which by some inward grace that few had suspected to be there was raised to the highest power. Here was no oratorical trickery. It was the unstudied expression of a humble-minded citizen who loved his country.

This was no political phrasemonger bemusing his hearers with insincerity and claptrap, but a spritual-minded man accustomed to fear his God, and to walk with Him on occasion.

An old peer at the far end of the room, with the tears streaming down his face, whispered to his wife, "This man is a Cromwell."

In a sense it was true.   In some such manner must the Lord Protector have addressed his countrymen.

"I would to God," said the great, deep, vibrant tones, full of an odd kind of harmony, "that we had not tarried so long in the gate.   Incalculable mischief has been done.   The King has been twelve days without a Government.   And now that this long-predicted blow has fallen upon us with awful suddenness there is none to advise him.   This is an hour when the King does not know which are his friends and which are his enemies.   But I have to inform you that he proposes to take immediate steps to find out.   A Royal Proclamation is in the course of preparation and will be issued at daybreak.   It will call upon every able-bodied man in the kingdom between the ages of sixteen and seventy, irrespective of creed or class, to enroll himself immediately as a special constable pledged and empowered to maintain law and order, and to protect life and property to the utmost of his power.   A special badge, or insignia, has already been devised, whereby it will be possible to distinguish the sheep from the goats. But as it will not be possible to prepare one specially for the purpose, it it proposed that every loyalist when he has been sworn should wear a white band round the left arm."

Loud cries of assent greeted the suggestion.

"The scheme is, of course, both hasty and imperfect, designed under pressure to meet a special case which does not admit of a moment's delay. May I ask all present who approve the scheme to hold up their right hands."

Every right hand in the room was raised instantly.

"It will strengthen the hands of the Sovereign," said Mr. Draper, "that this hastily designed scheme has met with the unanimous approval of this distinguished and representative assembly. Within a few hours from now every loyal man in the country will know what measures to take in order to protect and uphold the State. There is not an instant to be lost. By daybreak the King will have empowered every magistrate within the precincts of his kingdom to administer the special constable's oath. And in the meantime I will bear to him the assurance of your unanimous approval."

The President of the Board of Conciliation stepped down from the elevation on which he had poised himself. Murmurs of gratitude, reverence, and admiration accompanied him as he made his way out of the room.

PART TWO

CUTTING THE KNOT

I

CLOUDESLEY was one of the great Tory houses of England. It had long cherished political power. But of late years it had found it increasingly difficult to keep a hold upon affairs.

In the golden days before democracy had begun to realize itself, the Lorings in common with the Stanhopes, the Howards, the Russells, and other well-placed families had been accustomed to shape affairs as a matter of course, and to legislate in accordance with the interests of a particular class. But these days had passed. Very reluctantly the few had had to yield to the many. Here and there a clan such as the Lorings fought tenaciously for a semblance of power. Politics was in its blood. Moreover, it had an intense appreciation of the usefulness of certain things.

But now it was felt by all that class interest had come to its Armageddon. Indeed, to many the fact that a Rockingham ministry had only been made possible by the inclusion of James Draper was a confession that already the battle had been fought and lost.

Loring himself made a perfectly charming host. There was abundant evidence of the fact in the appearance of the Cloudesley breakfast table on the morning of Saturday, the historic fifteenth of February. As one by one his guests reached the dining-room, and after a brief interchange of pleasantries with those already at the table, which suggested that such a gathering was more in the nature of a family party than a momentous political conclave, they found their way to the heavily laden sideboard, it needed little in the way of observation to tell that these were the best of their kind.

Each had the air, the manner, the indefinable but superficial grace of those who have lived soft for several generations. Each had the look of race and the peculiar timbre of voice that accompanies it. Fastidious to a degree they were yet frankness itself in the company of each other.

There was only one exception to this pervasive air of "thoroughbredness." This was provided by a Yorkshire manufacturer who had enjoyed wealth for a comparatively short time, whose voice in consequence was pitched slightly too loud for such an assembly, whose air, moreover, was a little too confident, and whose opinions were a shade too unqualified. For that reason, perhaps, he sat next to the host and remained perpetually under his ægis.

Loring himself had always been *persona gratissima* in his own sphere, and indeed in any other in which he had ever chosen to mingle. He was not a profound man in any sense of the word —mere depth does not win general acceptance in any society — all his opinions were plain and unvarnished, but he had a most agreeable faculty of expressing the obvious with a half-comic air of conviction. He conveyed an impression of being perfectly straightforward. One somehow felt that in spite of a commonplaceness of mind that was a little painful at times, and a homely method of expressing it that verged upon the vulgar, beyond all things the man was sound at the core.

It would have been difficult to tell from the manner of the guests at the breakfast table that they had been and still were preoccupied with the making of history. There was no affectation of weight. Even Rockingham, buttering his toast, and wondering what sort of a year it was likely to be for birds, conveyed no suggestion that he was face to face with the gravest decision that any man could have been called upon to make.

A discussion of birds became general. Even in the middle of February they are better worth discussing than politics; that is, to members of the

Right. There was an exception even to this rule, and it was the Yorkshire manufacturer who provided it. He presented the curious anomaly of a member of the Right who actually preferred politics to sport.

"I say, Loring," he said in a voice a little louder than was necessary, since his host sat next to him, "when do you expect Grundy?"

"To-morrow afternoon."

"And is Draper coming?"

"I believe so."

Smith-ffolliott had had three bad years running. This year he felt inclined to let his moor.

"What'll you do with Draper?" said the undefeated Mr. Ansell, in his insistent voice.

"Oh, I expect we shall be able to find a mat for the dirty dog to lie on," said the host with an opulent chuckle.

"On the servants' side, I hope," said the mincing tones of a neighbouring marquis.

"Or at the bailiff's cottage."

"But he's too important, ain't he —nowadays?" said the undefeated Mr. Ansell, whose long suit was a literal precision of language in all things, hence his immense reputation for hard-headed clear-thinking among the journalists of his country. "I shouldn't advise going out of our way to insult him."

"Wouldn't you, by Gad!" said Rockingham, who was seated opposite the member for South East

Leeds, with a rather formidable air. "Wouldn't you, by Gad!"

Smith-ffolliott felt obliged to snigger furtively into his coffee cup.

"No, I wouldn't," said Mr. Ansell with statesman-like decision.

"We mustn't then," lisped a quizzical person very softly.

Mr. Ansell rose from the table with the air of one who has once again saved the empire and exchanged the remains of a sole for some delightfully cooked kidneys and bacon.

"Does Lady Aline know that Draper is expected?" he asked, as he resumed his place at the table.

"I am afraid I have no information I can place at your disposal," said the host with a dryness he seldom achieved.

II

BEFORE the morning was far advanced com-
plaints were general that neither letters nor
newspapers had arrived. Moreover, it was impossible to get a London call on the telephone. Inquiry
at the post-office in the village threw no light on these
matters. The postmaster merely knew that the
trains were not running to Deighton, the nearest
railway station, three miles off, and that for some
mysterious reason it was impossible to get into any
sort of communication with the metropolis.

A rather sinister feeling of uneasiness descended
upon the Cloudesley house-party. The members of
it were in a position to know that the fate of the
nation was hanging upon a thread. Had the blow
fallen? Had revolution, had civil war, broken out?
These questions were asked freely, and for a time
none was able to give an answer.

About eleven o'clock, however, news came. At
that hour a King's messenger arrived in a motor car.
He brought an urgent request from the King that
Loring should go up to London at once. In the letter
which the King had sent to the master of Cloudesley

he stated that the events of the last twelve hours had made it imperative that a committee of public safety should be formed without a moment's delay.   Such a committee had been called into being already, and Mr. Draper had been temporarily appointed president.

It was the King's desire that Rockingham, Maul-everer, Ansell, and the other distinguished members of the Right at present in conclave at Cloudesley, should remain where they were until such a time as they had been able to reach a definite decision respecting the formation of a Government.   They had until the following Monday at noon in which to promulgate it.   The King hoped that in spite of the exceedingly perilous state of the country it would be possible for Grundy and Draper to leave the metropolis for a few hours on Sunday in order to meet the Duke and his advisers at Cloudesley.

The messenger, whose name was Brandreth, was able to supply a number of details which had been omitted from the royal communication.   It seemed that a general strike had been declared.   It embraced all the lower grades of wage-earners, with the ex-ception of the Navy, the Army, and the Police.   And in Wales and in the North even among the two latter classes there was said to be a grave fear of disaffec-tion.   Sedition was reported to be rife on every hand. The whole country was in imminent peril.   The

Workers' League, with its anti-social propaganda, and its millions of subscribers pledged to advance it by every means in their power, had brought the life of the nation to a standstill.

The members of the Cloudesley house-party were without exception the bulwarks of the class which had all to lose. They did not need to be told what lay behind the declaration of war on the part of the League. The gauge of battle had been thrown down because in the opinion of its leaders the hour was favourable in which to wage the bitterest civil strife since the terrible days of 1642. The land of England for the People of England was the motto emblazoned on the banners of the League.

In the eyes of God and the Law, said the chief spokesman of the League, all men are equal. The hour is here, my brothers, in which to make an end forever of a vain, pretentious, idle, and corrupt plutocracy. These people who do nothing but pursue their worthless and ridiculous pleasures, who enclose all the fairest and noblest portions of the island for their own private playgrounds, must show cause and make good, else they will not be allowed to continue. Great Britain is the gift of God to the people of Great Britain, it is not the perquisite of a handful of commercial adventurers mainly cosmopolitan in their origin, however subtly they may in some cases have concealed the sources of their wealth.

Rockingham, the owner of one half an English county and about one twelfth of Scotland, seemed less perturbed by the news than anybody. He was an extremely clear-sighted man, and on occasion he had the habit of expressing his mind with a cynicism which even his closest friends found repellent.

"I wonder that the fools have let us go on so long," had been his historic comment on the propaganda of the League. And he took the declaration of war with equal coolness.

Loring, less developed mentally, yet with almost as much to lose, was hardly equal to this philosophical aloofness. More famous as a sportsman than as a politician, it was in his capacity of an honest, forthright, rather rough but decidedly shrewd fellow that he bore his part in public affairs. It is always good for a nation that men of this type, with a wide if superficial knowledge of the world, should be called to its councils in a time of crisis. Loring was not actively a politician, but his tremendous *Britishness* made him a person of considerable weight in any assembly of his countrymen. He was the incarnation of the average man; a good fellow to boot; one whose animal passions and fighting instincts had been dulled by hyperculture.

"If the dirty dogs are out for a fight," said Loring, "I expect we can give 'em their bellyful at that game. Eh, Evan, what say you?"

Mr. Evan Mauleverer, that prince of reactionaries who was never visible until noon, had just sauntered down into the hall.

"Why, cert'nly, my dear fellow," lisped the silver-haired leader of the Right with the rather obvious and carefully cultivated charm of manner which he sometimes put to infamous uses. "A whiff of grape-shot. There's nothing like it."

Evan Mauleverer adjusted his pince-nez with a languor it would have been easy to mistake for indifference. Gazing coolly around the circle of gravely anxious faces his eye fell on Brandreth, the King's messenger, who was known to him.

"Hulloa, Brandreth," he said, "what's the matter now?"

Loring explained. There was considerable fervour in the recital. It was terminated by the appearance of a servant with his master's fur travelling coat and soft felt hat.

"I shall be back to dinner, I hope," said the host. "In any case I shall be here by lunch-time to-morrow. And I shall try to induce Grundy and Draper to come with me."

Evan Mauleverer laughed ironically. "I'll bet you a sovereign you don't get Draper," he said.

"I'll bet you a sovereign I do," said Loring with an air of conviction. "That is, of course, if he can be spared."

"He'll not come down here, you'll see," said the leader of the Right. "Why should he?"

"Why shouldn't he?"

"Why shouldn't he?" Evan Mauleverer gathered himself in the slow and calm manner that made him so formidable in all kinds of debate. "My dear fellow, do you ask the question seriously?"

"Yes, I do." Loring stood his ground with the tenacity of the plain man who is rather proud of his limitations.

"Well, I'll tell you" — Evan Mauleverer slowly readjusted his pince-nez for no obvious reason beyond "a sense of the theatre" — "the 'Haberdasher' has now every ace in the pack. And if he plays his hand carefully he will be the first president of the new republic."

Mr. Mauleverer's unqualified opinion drew sharp cries of dissent from all save Rockingham, who was merely content to shrug his high shoulders and to smile to himself.

"Never!" rose a deep-voiced chorus.

There were several women present, and these expressed themselves more at large. The hostess, a daughter of an old governing family, grew very red in the face.

"My dear Evan," she said in a rather unpleasantly high-pitched voice, "I don't think any man who calls himself an Englishman should say that."

Mr. Mauleverer bowed a stately gray head.

"I agree, my dear Alice," he said with an assumption of humility that was absolutely disarming. "I quite agree. I beg pardon."

Rockingham, however, seemed amused.

"But why not look the facts in the face, my dear Alice?" he interposed in his rather elaborate manner.

The hostess at once joined issue with a spirit that lent a kind of beauty to her homely countenance.

"It shall not be said in this house, Robert," said she. "You must please understand that."

"Alice is quite right, my dear Robert," said Mr. Mauleverer with gallantry.

"Well, what do you say, Aline?" said the Duke, mischievously tenacious of his point.

His question was addressed to the wife of Draper. Lady Aline must have been conscious of the fact that twenty pairs of eyes were pinned upon her. She grew very white. Beyond that, however, she betrayed no visible evidence of discomposure.

"I quite agree with Aunt Alice," she said in a cold, quiet tone.

A snub was intended; but the woman was not born who could administer a snub to a man of the type of Rockingham.

He proceeded to look her down steadily from his great height.

"Don't be a little fool," he said in a tone half play-ful, half contemptuous. "We can't allow *you* to play the ostrich and bury your head in the sand. You at least ought to know that the 'Haberdasher' is *capable de tout.*"

Lady Aline made no rejoinder to this studied and slightly brutal insolence. She bit her lip and the proud face turned to the colour of snow. Rocking-ham had scored rather heavily, and in their inmost hearts the group of observers were not sorry. It was generally supposed that Lady Aline had already repented of her crime of marrying Draper, but her own world had not forgiven her, and it never would.

She stood like a small statue exquisitely wrought. Her slight form was tense, but the sensitive mouth trembled a little. Suddenly with an impulse of maternal kindness her aunt placed her arm about her waist and led her away from the others and out of the hall.

III

AS THE day wore on it seemed to generate a smouldering excitement. Certainly the atmosphere of the luncheon-table was surcharged with electricity. The other members of the proposed cabinet, one and all cast into a state of excitement they were hardly able to repress, were a little inclined to resent the supineness of Mauleverer and the cynicism of Rockingham. These were their prophets. To these they looked for bread, and both appeared to be content to offer sustenance in the form of a few carefully selected stones.

In the afternoon, over whisky and cigars, there was a discussion upon the subject of general tactics. It soon grew rather heated. The Yorkshire manufacturer was strongly in favour of *force majeure*.

"If the devils won't work I'd make 'em," said he. "We've got the finest artillery in the world, and I'd blow 'em to blazes sooner than stand their nonsense."

"That is theoretically sound, no doubt, my dear Ansell," said Mr. Mauleverer. "But are you absolutely sure of your artillery?"

"Why, of course I am," said the Patriot at Large,

"and so is every man worthy of the name of Englishman. I'll stake every penny I possess on the absolute loyalty of our troops."

"That is all right then," said Mr. Evan Mauleverer with his rather affected lisp. "That is very
reassuring. And is one entitled to suppose that
this requisition that has been signed by the non-
commissioned officers and the rank and file of
twenty-eight regiments for a considerable increase
of pay, better facilities of promotion to the commissioned ranks, a more liberal scheme of pensions, and
more humane treatment of time-expired men, really
amounts to nothing?"

"Practically nothing, I assure you, when the monarchy is in danger. I am absolutely convinced that
our soldiers are loyal to a man, and no Englishman
worthy of the name could ever bring himself to think
otherwise."

"Well, it is very reassuring," said Mr. Mauleverer,
relapsing into a condition of impending somnolence.
"One is being constantly reminded that the masses
are losing the sense of romance."

"Would you define an Englishman's loyalty to
the Throne as being based on a sense of romance?"

"Yes — for want of a more exact definition," said
Mr. Mauleverer warily.

"Oh, but surely!" Mr. Ansell spread his hands, a
gesture inherited from his chapel-going forebears.

"Take away the monarchy and you take away all that we have. An imperishable and unique tradition. Upon my word, Mauleverer, I hardly see what it has to do with a sense of romance."

"Doesn't it all rather depend, my dear Ansell, upon the angle of vision at which one happens to see things?" said the leader of the Right, who appeared to be approaching perilously near to slumber. "For example, those tin-bellied donkeys prowling up and down St. James's Street every blessed morning of their lives are part of a unique tradition, but personally I was sick to death at the sight of 'em at the age of two and twenty when I was a young chap in the Guards."

"My *dear* Mauleverer," said his colleague, shocked not a little, "I am afraid you are decadent. Satiated with every pleasure, you appear to have outlived every emotion. It is one of the griefs of my life that I have been so ill-advised as to send my boy to Eton. The atmosphere of Leeds Grammar School, where his father was educated before him, is in every way so much more wholesome."

"I doubt whether you would have got him into the Blues had Leeds Grammar School been his Alma Mater," murmured Mr. Mauleverer. "Although one has always understood that that seat of learning is in every way an admirable institution."

"That is undoubtedly the case, my dear Mauleverer," said Mr. Ansell with enthusiasm. "At Leeds Grammar School they form character. They make men. I speak from first-hand experience. It is there that I received my own early training."

"You do it the very greatest credit, my dear Ansell," said the leader of the Right, almost as one who talks in his sleep, "if I may be allowed to say so. But why, if I may ask the question, did you not let well alone? Leeds Grammar School having fulfilled its functions so admirably in the case of the father, why was it not permitted to have a chance with the son?"

"If I must confess the truth, it was simply that I allowed myself to be overruled by my wife," said Mr. Ansell, with a slight display of embarrassment.

"Then you desire that your wife should accept sole responsibility for the workings of the modern spirit, which apparently is unable to let well alone?"

"Perhaps, my dear Mauleverer, if you put it in that way I must accept a little of the responsibility myself."

"I am glad you do, my dear fellow, because that will help me to prove my point. Everything is in a state of flux. For better or for worse our ideas about everything are changing. A generation back the few governed the many. Now the many are governing the few. I don't say it is good, I don't say it is not good, but I agree with Rockingham that the time has come when we must look the facts in the face."

"Frankly, my dear Mauleverer, I am in total disagreement with Rockingham and yourself. The many have never been able to govern in this country, and they never will."

"It is rather soon to begin disagreeing with Rockingham, isn't it?" murmured the leader of the Right, himself the prince of reactionaries, "having regard to the fact that it is only last evening that he invited you into his Government."

Thereupon the leader of the Right put his feet on the sofa on which he sat, and gave himself up entirely to the slumber which he was no longer able to resist.

IV

CONTRARY to expectation, Loring returned that evening in time for dinner. He brought back grave tidings. A strong-willed, resolute man, he did not yield readily to panic, but there could be no doubt that the country was in the throes of a deep and organized revolt against the established order. Not only were the propertied classes in danger of being shorn of their possessions, but also the monarchy itself was seriously menaced. Up till five o'clock that evening, the hour at which Loring had left London, no breaches of the peace had been reported in the metropolis itself, but all shops, offices, warehouses, and public buildings were closed and barricaded; no newspapers were being issued; every form of business was at a standstill; neither telephones nor telegraphs were working; the postal service was suspended; trains and omnibuses were not running, and continual rumours were being spread of the grave condition of things in the country.

The King remained in town, but the Queen, yielding to the earnest entreaties of a hastily improvised committee of public safety, had left London during the day under a strong escort. A rumour was rife that one hundred thousand miners from the North were marching upon the metropolis. Moreover, it was certain that if the present condition of things prevailed until that day week, London and the larger towns would be in the throes of famine.

All modes of transport had broken down. Arrangements were being made for the military to take charge of the railways. Hundreds of miles, however, of permanent way were menaced by the strikers. Portions of it were said to have been torn up already at Derby and Crewe. Thus there were the gravest doubts as to whether there were enough troops in the country efficiently to police the railway system.

It was clear that almost without exception the humbler ranks of industrial workers were organized in a universal strike. The baker brought no bread, the milk-seller no milk, the postman no letters, the County Council scavenger left the streets of the metropolis unswept. There was no 'bus, tube, tram, nor taxi to be had. There was no traffic in the streets. The parks were infested with huge crowds and raucous orators. Hooligans marched in procession along barricaded thoroughfares, demanding the right to live, and displaying banners bearing such mottoes as England for the English, Down with the Plutocracy, To Hell with the Jews. Already it had been deemed necessary to station a battalion of the

Grenadier Guards round the mansion in Park Lane of one who upon a basis of illicit diamond buying had raised a fortune of many millions. And various eminent financiers domiciled in the vicinity of Grosvenor Square were having their residences guarded by companies of distinguished regiments.

At Cloudesley, Loring's return had been awaited eagerly. The leading members of the Right there assembled had come to a decision already. It was that they should urge Rockingham to carry out the King's wishes and form a Government of his own. They were content that it should include Fern and Bayliss, two moderate members of the Left; moreover, it was to include Grundy and Draper.

Still, it was now clearly realized that James Draper held the key to the whole situation. Whatever Government might be formed he was the one indispensable man. Without his loyal co-operation the scheme must fail. The power of his personality had dominated the crisis. It alone had the power to touch the imagination of the masses. Whoever aspired to carry on the business of the country during its present pass could not afford to dispense with the services of this remarkable man.

One and all, however, assembled in that house were aware that in the nature of things there must be a bitter enmity existing between Draper and Rockingham. There it was pretty clearly understood that Draper and his wife were no longer on terms. Moreover, they knew it was idle to burke the fact that in this alienation Rockingham counted as a very important factor. The question of questions was, had Draper the moral strength in the supreme hour of his country's need to rise above a private wrong? Throughout that day, so big with fate, whenever two persons found themselves together in a sequestered corner of the house, the subject was discussed in hushed yet eager tones.

Immediately dinner was over Evan Mauleverer put his arm through that of his host and led him apart. Mauleverer, a former Prime Minister and the official leader of the Right, was a man of immense ability. Unfortunately, his wilfully and rather perversely narrow mental horizon had caused him to become utterly discredited in the country. Not only was he wholly out of sympathy with the aspirations of the masses, but he was convinced that they were a menace to the country's welfare. He held the opinion that universal education was all very well as an academic theory, but that it broke down entirely as a working hypothesis. In his view it was a tragic mistake for any country to educate its proletariat. He had been the author of the Conscription Bill. In the teeth of tremendous opposition he had carried it to a third reading in the House of Commons, and by so doing had struck an almost irremediable blow at the prestige of his party. In the privacy of social intercourse, however, he was a remarkable and considerable figure.

When they were entrenched comfortably in a quiet corner with their coffee and cigars, Loring said:

"I want your advice, Evan."

Mauleverer gazed at his host with a rather quizzical air.

"Before I give it, my dear fellow," he said, "whatever the nature of it may be, I would like to ask a question. Is Draper coming down here to-morrow?"

"Yes," said Loring. "I understand that to be his intention."

The leader of the Right nodded his head.

"I'll confess," he said, "that I didn't for a moment think he would."

"Nor I," said Loring. "But, as Robert says, he's a man about whom it doesn't do to anticipate. When I got to the Palace I found the beggar installed as a kind of generalissimo. We held a kind of council of war. He sat on the King's right hand, and Richards and Mitchener on his left."

Evan Mauleverer raised his eyebrows slightly.

"The President of the Committee of Public Safety, eh?" he said. "But why a civilian? Why not Mitchener?"

"Well, I gathered that the King rather insisted on it."

"Very unwise?"

"It seems so to most people. From what one or two of the household chaps say, he seems to have got the top side of the King altogether."

"What do Richards and Mitchener say about it?"

"Well, they seem to think it is a job for a civilian at present. They say that if they have to take it in hand nothing can save bloodshed."

"Who said that?"

"Both of 'em. They think that Draper is the only man who can possibly avert civil war."

Evan Mauleverer pensively stirred his coffee.

"If that is the case," he said, speaking very slowly, "to my mind the remedy is rather worse than the disease."

"I am inclined to think you are right, Evan," said Loring, with his accustomed bluntness. "That fellow is playing a double game. He plays for the people one minute and he plays for us the next."

"And he comes down here to-morrow?"

"Yes, that's his present intention."

"To meet Robert?"

"Ostensibly to meet Robert."

"Does he know his wife is here?"

"Evelyn says he does."

"Ha! —you've seen *her*."

"Yes, I just had time to call at Rockingham

House.   I thought it just as well to get to know all
there was to be known."

"Quite so."

Mr. Mauleverer smiled.

"She is certainly the ablest woman in England,"
said he.

"And to my mind she is the most enigmatical."

"She's always been beyond me," said Loring.

"But, then, I admit I'm a dunce.   But she's made
up her mind to do what I am certain is absolutely the
unwisest thing she can do."

"What's that?" inquired Evan Mauleverer, wearing the cloak of indifference a little less effectually
than usual.

"We are now coming to the subject I want your
advice upon."

"Well, my dear fellow?"   Evan Mauleverer's
quizzical eyes were only half-veiled.

"Evelyn is coming down here some time to-night.
Alice is in a terrible rage.   She is capable of refusing
her house-room."

Evan Mauleverer pensively smoked his cigar.

"My dear Loring," he said at last, "it seems to me
that all of us are getting pretty hopelessly into the
mire.   What on earth is *she* coming *here* for?"

"She seems to think she may be able to help us
a bit."

"My God!"

Mr. Mauleverer's invocation of the Deity seemed to afford him little consolation.

"It is sheer madness, my dear fellow, for her to come down here!"

"I told her so," said the master of Cloudesley.

"And what did she say to that?"

"She seemed to think I was too big a dunce to have any opinion on the subject."

"But surely you told her, my dear fellow, that her presence here was bound to aggravate a situation that was already almost intolerable?"

"Yes, of course. But she is a very self-willed woman."

A frown knitted the intellectual front of Mr. Evan Mauleverer.

"She is not showing her usual good sense," he said.

"One is bound to admit that. What in the world can she hope to do?"

"There's no saying, my dear Evan. There's no accounting for a woman's mind. But with her coming down to-night, and her friend the 'Haberdasher' coming down to-morrow, everything seems to point to our having a pretty lively week-end."

"Yes, by Gad!" agreed Mr. Evan Mauleverer.

"What I want to know is, what's to be done about Aline? This house is going to be no place for her."

Mr. Mauleverer pondered at rather considerable length.

"Aline can be trusted to take care of herself, can't she?" he said at last.

"Ye-es, one would suppose.   But is Draper to be trusted? — that is the point."

"Trusted for what?"

"To behave like a gentleman."

"Ha, there you have me," said Mr. Evan Mauleverer.   "Hardly the horse for that course, eh? "

"You think he is capable of making himself damned unpleasant?"

"Certainly capable, but hardly likely."

"Well, he'd got a pretty queer look in his eyes when he said he was coming down here to-morrow to confer with Rockingham."

"Did he ask whether his wife was still here?"

"No, he never mentioned her."

Mr. Mauleverer grew reflective.

"Well," he said finally, "if the man is the patriot he is represented to be, he will be content to forget all domesticities at such a time as this."

Loring shook his head despondently.

"We'll hope so, at any rate," he said.   "But he's a rough devil, I'm certain.   Although, mind you, he is a big man in his way."

"The question is, my dear fellow, is he a big enough man to keep the King upon his throne, and at the same time to exact his pound of flesh from Rockingham?"

"Personally, I would say yes."

"That is to say, you think he is entitled to his pound of flesh from that quarter?"

"Do you press the question?"

"Yes, I do rather. Leaving this unpleasant game of politics out of the case, tell me what is the precise view you take of l'affaire Rockingham?"

"Well, as Robert is my guest, I think I'd prefer not to express it."

"But I particularly want your opinion, my dear fellow. This is a matter upon which I crave for guidance. Before to-morrow is out we may all have to crave it. Let me put it in this form: Has anything occurred within, shall we say, the past forty-eight hours to change your views in regard to Robert."

Loring hesitated.

"Well, Evan," he said at last, "if you press the question I am bound to say my view of Robert has changed a good bit lately."

"I feared it."

In spite of an air of detachment that never deserted him, Evan Mauleverer was visibly discomposed.

"Well, I'm sorry," he said. "I'm sincerely sorry. This poor old land of ours never had such a need of a straight man, of a man who was absolutely straight in every relation of life."

V

A PAUSE followed upon the expression of this dictum by the leader of the Right. Both men looked a little uneasy.

"You see the dilemma?" said Loring at last.

"In regard to Draper's wife?"

"Yes. I don't like to go over the mark, but I call a spade a spade. I'm convinced Robert has used Aline as his tool in order that he might score off her husband."

Evan Mauleverer stayed his host with an elegantly uplifted hand. Loring's bluntness was proverbial, but there were occasions when it was a little too much for a fastidious mind.

"My dear fellow," said the leader of the Right, "pray don't forget that we are all of us pledged to sit in a Rockingham Cabinet."

"I'm not a politician myself," said the incorrigible Loring, "and I thank my God I'm not."

Mr. Mauleverer was fain to smile, in spite of the discomposure he was suffering. But his state of mind did not allow him to stray far from the subject in hand.

"Tell me, my dear fellow," he said, "what is responsible for this rather sudden change of heart?"

"Do you mean in regard to Rockingham?"

"Yes."

"Well, partly it is due to Evelyn, whom with all her crochets I believe to be an honest woman, and partly to something that Aline said to my wife."

"At all events, my lord duke appears to have cast a considerable amount of dust in the eyes of the King."

"Not a very difficult proceeding. But by no means so much, Evan, as you'd think. Anyhow, I'm not sure that the King has not been on the right horse from the start."

"Draper?"

"Yes. He has the whole country behind him now, and with all respect to you fellows he is the only man who can keep things in hand."

"We shall see what we shall see," said Mr. Evan Mauleverer stoically. "To-morrow may tell us something."

"Yes, I think it will. But to return to the subject of Aline. I should like her to leave this house before Draper arrives."

"Why?"

"Mark my words, Evan, that's an ugly devil when he's crossed."

"But what can he do?"

"He can make himself damned unpleasant."

"In what way?"

"There are several ways open to an injured husband. I say frankly that I would give a good deal for the fellow not to be coming down here."

"But you don't think he will be such a fool as to make a public exhibition of himself! He's much too calculating, and he has himself too well in hand."

"Maybe. At any rate we'll hope so. But you can't trust a man of that type — that's my feeling. Anyhow, I'd give a good deal for him not to be coming down here to-morrow."

"I also, if it comes to that. And if your diagnosis is accurate it makes it practically impossible for him to sit in a Rockingham Cabinet?"

"Of course it does."

"Well, what's the alternative?"

"A cabinet of his own, I expect."

"Do you believe such a cabinet to be possible?"

"Don't you?"

No reply to the question was forthcoming from the Leader of the Right.

Both these men, staunch representatives of an order of things that was literally fighting for existence with its back to the wall, made no attempt to cloak their feelings. In their different ways they were both men of wide experience. But events had moved at such an alarming rate during the past few days

that they were conscious of having been carried out
of their depth by an interplay of forces they were
powerless to resist.   Not only had they completely
lost their bearings, but somehow they seemed to have
lost their foothold in the world.   Versed as they were
in many kinds of affairs, they did not know in the
least how to gauge the elements which were striking
a succession of terrible, paralyzing blows at all that
they stood for.

This sinister and deep-seated uneasiness was
common to every person under that roof.   All were
by this time aware that the fate of the country
depended on a single man — upon a man whom from
the depths of their souls they disliked and despised.
No true-blue member of the Right had ever deigned
to dissemble his feelings in regard to the President
of the Board of Conciliation, and now that their
personal interests together with those of the nation
at large were about to be given over to him they had
not the slightest reason to expect the leniency that
they themselves would have been the last to grant.

That evening, a little before eleven o'clock, Evelyn Rockingham arrived from town by motor-car.
Her entrance into the dismayed Cloudesley drawing-
room, dressed with all the careful but rather severe
simplicity she affected at an evening party, was a
splendid piece of comedy, although it called undoubtedly for an *esprit fort* to carry it off.

The hostess turned pale as she rose to receive the uninvited guest. Herself a woman of strong character, she knew well enough how to sustain the dignity of her position. Her reception of the intruder was the reverse of cordial, although only a woman could have told that cordiality was not intended. In any circumstances, however, and at whatever disadvantage she might be placed, Evelyn Rockingham was a great-spirited woman, and more than a match for any member of her own sex.

"My dear Evelyn," was the hostess's greeting in her rather high-pitched voice, "this is an unexpected pleasure."

Absolutely direct and unconventional in speech, manner, and deed, Evelyn Rockingham placed a hand on each of Alice Loring's shoulders, although she must have been aware that behind her smile of welcome the mistress of Cloudesley was seething with anger.

"I felt I must come," said Evelyn. "I felt bound to come. I can appreciate your feelings, my dear, but it simply had to be. England is more than any of us, although you'll think that's cant. But I'll risk that. I don't care what you think, my dear. I don't care what any of you think." With a high imperious gesture she suddenly flung up her fine head and met unflinchingly the circle of astonished faces that formed a background to the room. "I am beyond caring what any of you think." There was a curious, an almost perilous, quiver, in the voice. "Except" — her voice almost failed —"except you, my dear, dear Lord Peveril!"

As she spoke she strode past Alice Loring across the wide drawing-room to where a venerable white-bearded man sat very upright in a straight-backed chair. Impulsively she extended both her hands, and at the same instant the wonderful eyes set deep in the haggard cheeks brimmed tears.

The old man, very frail and ascetic looking, rose slowly to greet her. He yielded his gaunt hands in response to hers, and the gesture had in it all the tenderness of a father receiving a favourite daughter.

"Quite right, quite right, dear child," he said in a voice that was very gentle; "if you think you can help us, ever so little. I am sure we all feel that."

In his capacity of host Loring strode across the room.

"Delighted to see you, Evelyn," he said with a rough cordiality which made an effect of absolute sincerity, whether it was entitled to do so or not. "Always delighted to see you. In this house, and at any time, you are always welcome. At such a time as this you are more than welcome."

Evelyn's response was frank and immediate.

"Thank you, Loring," she said, with her noble air. "You deserve well of your country — far better than some of 'em. Yes, I mean you, Evan, for one."

Half the room was included in her brilliant sweeping gesture. "You are too much of a Briton, Loring, to misjudge me at such a time as this. But I don't intend to put Alice out. I have engaged a room at the inn in the village — the Coach and Horses — where I shall sleep."

The host was very firm, however.

"No, Evelyn, " he said, "we can't allow that. House-room is not so scarce as all that. Here you are, and here you've got to stay — that's if you'll honour us."

VI

EVELYN ROCKINGHAM'S arrival had astonished everybody. Her audacity was proverbial. In all her actions she was a law unto herself; but in the opinion of a majority of the guests a surprise visit to Cloudesley in such circumstances was merely a piece of insolent foolhardiness. But even the Evelyn Rockinghams of the world do not act entirely from caprice. What had brought her down there? was the question each person asked of his or her neighbour.

Lady Aline was seated on a distant sofa, half hidden in a recess, and Rockingham was by her side. They had hardly paused in their conversation when the unwelcome guest had entered the room, and they proceeded completely to ignore her presence. Those near to them, however, who happened to have a nose for drama, were by no means insensible of theirs. Veiled and stealthy glances were levelled in their direction from time to time. Certainly the situation was piquant; and the mask of consummate indifference presented by the chief personages in it was felt to be acting of the highest order.

Evelyn herself, accustomed by divine right of personality to dominate all assemblies in which she happened to be, was of course the cynosure of every eye. After a little tour of greeting she seated herself on a sofa by the side of the venerable Lord Peveril. He was her godfather; and if hardly a great, he was certainly a very high, type of man. He had sound judgment, high principles, and an almost passionate devotion to his country. Had he been anything of a publicist he might, without impropriety, have now stood in the place of Rockingham. His name appeared seldom in the newspapers, yet he had been the familiar friend and the chosen adviser of three sovereigns. Those who moved in the inner circles of politics and society knew that in some things he possessed an almost unique authority. He had always stood aloof from party; his voice had never been heard in "the gilded chamber," but for thirty years he had been a power behind the throne.

He had come to Cloudesley at the request of the King. The members of the Right were perhaps better able to appraise his worth than any other political section. They were not a little grateful for his presence. Of advice he had been sparing, as was his wont, for like most men of weight he was not a great talker. But he had counselled absolute loyalty to Rockingham, since Rockingham in a sense was the nominee of the Throne.

He had a real affection for his god-daughter, now seated by his side. He had been the husband of one of the most remarkable women of the time, and like all men of a high type he had known how to love and to admire. He held an exalted opinion of women without idealizing them unduly. They were essential to the human race, and they also ennobled it. Such a man was not likely to misjudge a woman of the quality of Evelyn Rockingham.

"*You* don't censure me, Lord Peveril?" she said in a very low, half-pleading voice.

"Censure you for what, my dear?"

The old man took one of the exquisitely formed hands, entirely innocent of feminine adornment, fondly into his keeping.

"For coming here to-night."

"On the contrary, I think it particularly right, if in any way you feel you can help us."

Evelyn drew a sigh of relief.

"I am so glad you have not lost your confidence in me. I hope you will always trust me."

"I will always do that," said the old man, very gently.

She placed her other hand very tenderly in his.

"You cannot think how glad I am to hear you say that, dear friend.   There is only one other person in the country for whose opinion I have an equal respect.

"You are too kind, my dear. Far, far too kind."

"There is only one other man I have met who has your perception."

"You rate me far too highly, my dear. But do you mind telling me the name of this paladin?"

"I think you ought to be able to guess."

"Robert?" There was a mischievous twinkle in the eyes of the old man.

"You mustn't trifle with me," she said.

"Well, I'm afraid it isn't Evan Mauleverer, with all his merits. Grundy always strikes one as a good and sincere man. Him do you mean?"

"No; although I am convinced he is quite a good man as far as he goes. No, I mean the President of the Committee of Public Safety."

"Ha! Well, you know him better than I do, my dear. The King certainly thinks well of him."

"And you, Lord Peveril?" The tone was not without a note of slight anxiety.

Lord Peveril was silent.

"You see," he said, "one has had so few opportunities of judging the man. I have met him only twice in my life. He impresses one with his force — the kind of force that Gladstone had. But you know, my dear, it isn't ever very easy to make a silk purse."

"Out of the wrong material? Yes, my dear lord, but isn't there a danger of jumping a little too hastily to the conclusion that it *is* the wrong material?

Appearances are apt to be deceptive, aren't they?
One expects *you* to have a bias in favour of birth.
We all have that. It is only natural. But don't
let us forget that it isn't birth that produces genius."

"What is it, then, my dear?"

"I must refer you to the Eugenists. But singularly few men of the very first rank have come out
of our class."

"I am not so sure about that, my dear," said the
old aristocrat, shaking his head rather dubiously.

"There can be no doubt of it," said his god-
daughter, with the conviction that was a part of
her charm.

"Well, even if it is so," said the old man with a
gallant refusal to contest the point, "do you put this
man Draper in absolutely the front rank?"

"Yes."

"I am interested to hear you say that. Heaven
knows, we never had a greater need of such a one."

"Well, we have him. And I think he is going to
save his country, if only his country will give him
the chance."

"What sort of a chance can she give him, my
dear?"

"She must make him her next Prime Minister."

"But that's impossible. These fellows here
wouldn't hear of it. Besides, the King has nominated Robert."

"Yes, but the country has nominated Draper."

"Then it would seem that he will have to choose between the country and the King."

"I pray not.   That way lies civil war."

"But in any case he is hardly likely to desert the Throne."

"I am sure he will not.   But the Throne must not desert him.   And I appeal to you, my dear lord, to throw the whole weight of your personal authority into the scale if you would save the country."

The old man sat gravely silent.   After all, this was only the expression of a woman's opinion, but Evelyn Rockingham was a woman whom he had learned to respect immensely.   Her opinion, moreover, confirmed others that had recently come to his his ears.

"I must confess," said the old man at length, "that it seems impossible at the eleventh hour to go back on the King's nominee."

"But if the King withdraws his nomination?"

"Ah, then!   Yet in the circumstances that is impossible too.   Robert has formed his ministry, I understand."

"Is Mr. Draper in it?"

"He is to be President of the Board of Conciliation, I understand."

"Has he accepted the office?"

"Provisionally, I believe.   At any rate he has

promised to come here to-morrow to confer with Robert."

"And that promise is held to be tantamount to acceptance of office?" she asked rather breathlessly.

"Yes," said Lord Peveril, "that is the view that is held by them all. And let us pray it is not a mistaken one."

Evelyn was visibly cast down.

" I feel sure," she said, "they are not entitled to jump to any such conclusion. And, I will go further. In my own mind I am absolutely convinced that he will decline to accept office under Robert. And if he does decline, where will the country be then?"

Lord Peveril shook his head sorrowfully.

"There you have me," he said. "That is a contingency that not a man of them appears able to face. But if Draper has the welfare of the country at heart it is hardly a contingency that is likely to arise. After all, he is in very close touch with the King."

"Yes, Lord Peveril, but he has been used so shamefully."

"By whom?"

"By the Right, and more particularly by Robert."

Lord Peveril grew silent. Somehow the directness of his god-daughter seemed to embarrass him. For her own part she did not know how to gauge the measure of his information, nor did she know how far it might be accurate.

Of one harsh fact, however, she was aware: The political enemies of Draper had not scrupled mercilessly to misrepresent the nature of her own intimacy with him. Enormous capital had been made out of it. Lord Peveril, an honest, simple, and upright man, had had no means of learning the truth.

She recognized that it was not a moment for half measures. So much might depend upon the line taken by this old man.

"There is one question I must ask you, my kind friend," she said. "Are you aware that Robert has come between this man and his wife?"

"I am not aware of it," said Lord Peveril.

"Between Aline and her husband! At the instance of Robert she has left her husband's house, never to return to it."

"I was not aware of the fact," said Lord Peveril rather coldly.

"Robert has urged the contemptible pretext that Aline is entitled to avenge herself."

"Upon whom?"

"Upon her husband, because of his alleged liaison with myself."

A look of pain overshadowed Lord Peveril's sensitive face.

"Please forgive me," said his god-daughter,

"but I have come here partly that you, upon whom so much depends, shall learn the truth. Robert's jealousy has led him to play a contemptible part. I ask you to believe me when I say that no act of mine has given him the slightest warrant for entertaining it. I swear before God that my relations with Mr. Draper have been perfectly honourable. Our friendship has been based upon an intense desire, which we have in common, for the country's welfare. In some ways I may have been a little indiscreet, but there is not the slightest foundation for the charge that has been brought against me. I feel it to be right, Lord Peveril, that you should know this. Robert's jealousy is wholly unwarranted, and he has made use of it in the most contemptible and merciless way in order to compass the ruin of a political adversary."

The look of pain deepened upon Lord Peveril's face. He remained silent.

"It is absolutely necessary, Lord Peveril, that this should be known to you. And I ask you to believe me."

She turned her fine eyes full upon her venerable companion. An acute distress was in both their faces.

"My dear, I do believe you," said the old man.

"Thank you, my kind friend." There were tears in her eyes. "And now, do you not see how im-

possible it is that Mr. Draper can sit in a Rockingham Cabinet?"

"But it is the King's desire," said Lord Peveril
in an agitated voice. "The fate of the country
depends upon Mr. Draper's loyal co-operation."

"Yes, I know."

"It is a terrible test," said the old man, "but if
the man is a true patriot I think we may still hope."

"Yes, but is it not asking too much of any man?"

"I have lived in strange times," said Lord Peveril.
"I have seen strange things happen, I have mixed
freely with all sorts of people, but the more I see and
the more I know, the greater is my faith in human
nature. If this man is all that you believe him to
be, he will not fail his country in the supreme hour."

The words were those of a seer. Evelyn, who had
a deep reverence for the speaker, was strangely
moved by them. Moreover, her courage rose.
Somehow she felt sustained in the most difficult and
hazardous course she was determined to follow.
She was daring all. A much maligned, a much
misunderstood woman, she had made up her mind
that the true facts of the case should be known.
There should be neither pretext nor excuse for un-
sympathetic or hostile action.

Lord Peveril believed her. That was clear gain.
To have him learn the truth meant much. But
others must learn it too.

VII

AS Lady Aline was lighting her bedroom candle
in the hall, she was surprised by a voice at
her side.

"Let us talk for a few minutes. May I come
to your room?"

With a slight flush of annoyance she turned to
discover Evelyn Rockingham at her elbow. Open
rudeness was against her code, but her instinct was
to escape with her candle as speedily as she could,
and entirely to ignore the presence of her rival.

It is not easy, however, to ignore the Evelyn
Rockinghams of the world.

"Let us talk, my dear child," she said with a
gentle insistence. "Your room will be best. We
can have privacy there."

Without further preface, and with perfect self-
possession, she accompanied the younger woman
to her room. Neither spoke as they passed up the
stairs. Evelyn was only too well aware of the
contemptuous hostility that was smouldering in the
other's heart.

They entered Aline's bedroom. Evelyn closed

the door. Then she seized two stone-cold hands in her own vital grasp.

"My dear child," she said, "I have come down here to-night with a particular purpose in view. You are most necessary to the fulfilment of that purpose. I insist that you hear what I have to say."

The contempt in the eyes of the younger woman was almost cruel.

"I have no wish to hear anything you may have to say to me," she said slowly, without vehemence. "I have not the slightest wish that you should speak to me."

"That I know well enough," said Evelyn. "It would be surprising if you had, since you have always judged me so mistakenly. I do not blame you for that. Wiser people have been equally at fault, and they have not had your excuse."

The younger woman had grown deadly white. The eyes, steady with the light of anger, shone cold and clear.

"I cannot, I will not, talk to you," she said.

As she spoke she moved toward the door of the bedroom for the purpose of opening it. With a swift, sudden defiance the elder woman barred her way.

"Aline," she said, "you must listen, please, to what I have to say. You are not wholly a fool. Your mind has been poisoned. You have been made the tool of one who has not scrupled to exploit you for his own ignoble ends."

The deadly pale face of the younger woman seemed suddenly to blaze with fury. Not a sound escaped her lips, yet she had to bite them to repress a cry of rage.

"I will not allow you to talk to me in this way," she said.

"Aline," said the older woman, "you of all people must be aware of the state of the country. One man only can save it, and that man is your husband. That you must realize. And if you are a woman worthy of your country it behooves you to help him and to help it in any way that may be possible in such an hour as this."

Lady Aline was wholly unmoved by the appeal.

"I decline to discuss the matter," she said. "And I must ask you to leave my room immediately."

Evelyn Rockingham, however, held her ground.

"There are certain things I am going to say to you, Aline," she said, "and you cannot choose but hear them. I well know you to be the victim of an insane jealousy. Jealousy of whom? I will tell you. Jealousy of myself, Evelyn Rockingham. No, leave the bell alone. I will not allow you to touch it." She sprang forward as she spoke and caught the slighter, more delicate woman by the wrists. "Before I leave this room, my dear Aline, it is my intention that you shall realize the truth. Evelyn Rockingham is not the base *intrigante* you take her to be. Your husband and I have worked side by side in a great national crisis. We are still working side by side in the hope of saving that precious thing to which we are devoted. But that is the beginning and the end of our intercourse. Your suspicions are entirely unfounded, that I swear before God."

The jealous wife was fully determined not to listen to the woman whom she believed to have supplanted her in her husband's affections. But her words in their burning intensity and her own situation, moreover — held firmly as she was by the wrists with a power that far surpassed her own physical strength — compelled her to do so. She rejected the appeal, however, with a contempt that was almost savage.

"You choose not to believe me, Aline," said Evelyn Rockingham. "Very well. So much the worse for us all. Nay, I don't care in the least what you may think of me" — this in answer to the immeasurable scorn that seemed to transform the eyes into those of Medusa. "You were always an inferior woman. It is the irony of things that such a man as James Draper should have made the tragic mistake of marrying you. But I intend that you shall realize the truth. I am an honest woman.

You have all your husband's love, as much as you
had it ever. You are still his idol. He is still
devoted to you. I only hope that you can say you
are an honest woman also."

The furious pride of the younger woman caused
her to become passive.

"Let go my hands, Evelyn," she said very quietly.

"Yes, when you have accepted the truth. I have
come here to-night that you should learn it. Your
husband comes down here to-morrow. It is of vital
importance that once for all you should put away
these unworthy suspicions which are ruining his life,
which are ruining your own, and, moreover, are
imperilling the safety of the country. Give me some
assurance, Aline, that you accept the statement
I have made."

Lady Aline maintained a stubborn silence.

"As God is my witness, I have spoken the truth,"
said Evelyn Rockingham. "I cannot say more.
If you choose not to believe me you will have to pay
a heavy price for your wickedness and your folly.
Perhaps we shall all have to pay it — England more
than anybody. But your husband comes down here
to-morrow, and I ask you then to remember what
I now swear before God."

"Leave my room," said the younger woman.

"Please give me some assurance that you accept
my statement, and that you will act upon it."

"The matter is not one that we can discuss."

"For heaven's sake, don't treat the matter in a merely conventional spirit. Surely we have gone beyond that. There is so much at stake. Aline, on my knees I implore you to believe me and act — if it is still possible for you to act — in accordance with your knowledge."

There was something in the sudden humility of the appeal that affected the younger woman. Only a heart of stone could have been proof against it. In spite of herself so complete a self-abasement touched the heart of Aline.

"Will you not believe me?"

There was a moment of silence.

"I implore you to believe me. For your husband's sake and for your own and for your country's, I implore you to believe me."

The younger woman was no longer proof against emotion. She averted her face, but already a subtle change had been wrought in it. Loath as she was to admit the truth, it was yet impossible to remain impervious to such an appeal. She was a woman convinced against her will, but by sheer force and sincerity Evelyn Rockingham seemed almost to have conquered.

VIII

MR. DRAPER and Mr. Grundy were expected to join the Cloudesley house-party in the course of Sunday morning. Speculation ran high among the guests. All were members of the caste to whom Draper beyond all men was intensely antipathetic. The man's whole career was an affront to those nurtured in the faith of *laissez faire*.

Neither Harrow nor Eton nor the older universities had touched this unpolished gem with their chastening hands. Nor had they touched his fathers before him. But in spite of the severe handicap nature had imposed upon him — or because of it, said the cynical — the "Haberdasher" was proving himself in the supreme hour to be great in the hearts of the people.

It was idle for any body of politicians to burke the fact that James Draper could not be dispensed with. He had taken such a hold upon the imagination of the masses that it now appeared that he alone could right the crazy ship of state. Beyond everything else this was due to a strong and inspiring personality which stood foursquare to the winds of party. But then again the man's integrity had told heavily upon those of his countrymen who set a high value upon personal character.

In the beginning his wonderful rise from a small tradesman's counter in a provincial town had been due to the fact that he had had the wit and also the luck to be the first to bring home to the masses that somebody had not been playing quite fair for several hundreds of years. His famous — or infamous? — land bill had been designed to put the matter in order. The success of that measure had imbued his early followers with the lust of triumph; they determined by the advantage they had gained to push up to the hilt. The Conciliation Bill had been the outcome of their valour. But then, to their indignant surprise, the man's deep-rooted sense of fair play asserted itself, and he cried, "Halt, you are going too fast!"

The stern admonition had shattered to pieces the Coalition Government of which he was a member. His friends were shocked and disconcerted; his enemies shouted with glee. Here at last was the long-looked-for opportunity of those whom he had shorn of their ancient privileges. He thinks he is strong enough to do without us now, said his friends; Mr. Facing-both-ways, said his enemies. Only a very small and deeply perceptive minority came near to the truth.

Had it been possible at this point for two such deadly foes as the Right and the Left to co-operate there might have been a speedy end of James Draper. But it was asking a little too much of human nature, and perhaps this he knew. He had committed an almost tragic indiscretion in the matter of his marriage, but even this was not able wholly to undo him. Nevertheless, it had exposed him to the machinations of a powerful and unscrupulous social clique which grasped eagerly at the chance of bringing off a great political coup.

Among the guests assembled at Cloudesley was more than one of those who had aided and abetted Rockingham in his well-laid scheme to put this dangerous foe forever out of public life. The attempt was made with a sure and subtle knowledge of the pharisaical British nature. For nearly three weeks the issue had hung in the balance, during which time the whole industrial life of the country had been brought to the verge of chaos. A single false step on the part of him against whom the plot was laid would have been fatal; but the man's remarkable calibre had declared itself in this crisis. It was now felt even at Cloudesley, the headquarters of the conspirators, that unless at the eleventh hour the unforeseen occurred, James Draper was bound "to come out on top."

Was it possible that even now the unforeseen was

about to happen? Sinister rumours were rife from an early hour that Sunday morning. It was known by then that a further urgent and lengthy communication from the King had been received by the master of the house. The nature of it had not been disclosed, but soon after breakfast there was a conference held in the library between the Prime Minister-elect, Evan Mauleverer, Loring, and Lord Peveril.

During the course of its progress less august persons gathered in little groups in odd corners of the house. A strange gravity seemed to envelop the place. In the very atmosphere of the old house there was a sense of something impending. Precisely what it was none could tell. On the face of things it would appear that Rockingham had been able to form a Government acceptable to King and People alike. Its heterogeneous elements had consented apparently to work together for the common weal, in order that the country might not bleed to death, yet always providing that the unforeseen did not occur at the eleventh hour.

Had the negotiations broken down? Anxious politicians, unable to possess their souls in patience for a little while longer, eagerly canvassed the question with one who was likely to have the very latest information.

Mr. Ansell in particular was importunate.

"You must tell me, Duchess," he said, "just what you think. Are we to have the honour of lunching with the 'Haberdasher,' or are we not?"

"I can only counsel you, Mr. Ansell," said Evelyn Rockingham with a rather elaborate air, "in the phrase of a great statesman of the past: you must 'wait and see.'"

"Well, I'm sure *you* would know, if anybody does," said the member for South East Leeds, not very tactfully.

"Nobody does know, except Mr. Draper himself. Personally, I am inclined to believe we *are* to have the honour of lunching with him. Last evening it was undoubtedly his intention to come down here in the course of to-day."

"Plenty of time to change his mind since then, though."

"Yes, but why should he? He is not a man much given to changing his mind."

"I don't mean without adequate reason, of course. But somehow one feels that something may have suddenly gone wrong."

"In the country, do you mean?"

"No, I don't mean in the country. Things can't go much more crooked there, unless London is already sacked and burned, and that would surprise nobody. But somehow I've taken the notion that Mr. D. may not be quite playing the game."

"I am afraid I don't understand you, Mr. Ansell."

"Well, he may, don't you know, have found it impossible to play straight, as a man of his class generally does when he's really put to it."

"In what way is it open to him not to play straight?"

"Well, he may have tried, don't you know, in a manner of speaking, to overreach the King. Anyhow, that's Loring's opinion, and he was in London up till five o'clock last evening."

"In what way, Mr. Ansell, would it be possible for Mr. Draper to overreach the King?" There was a rather amused ring in the voice of the questioner, which was wholly lost upon the earnest patriot, whose thoughts were centred solely upon the welfare of his country.

"Well, you know," said the Yorkshireman, laying a mystical finger on the centre of his forehead, "he suffers from that."

"That?" queried Evelyn.

"Megalomania. He imagines he's a Cromwell. And if a man imagines he's a Cromwell he is *capable de tout.*"

"In other words, Mr. Ansell," said Evelyn Rockingham blandly, "you are prepared to impeach his loyalty to the Throne?"

"Yes, by jove! If that man sees his chance he'll stick at nothing. Everything is at sixes and sevens:

Evan says Navy and Army and Police are out for higher pay, like the rest of 'em; a certain person — this is strictly between ourselves, mind! — is as weak as water in a crisis; this fellow has got the ear of the masses as no man has ever had it before in this country; and if he's the man we all take him to be he is not going to hold the candle to Rockingham, whom he hates like poison."

In spite of her amused air, the wife of Rockingham looked rather unhappy. The man who spoke so naïvely was himself a power in the land. Extremely rich, and a large employer of labour, he was endowed with the North countryman's power of seeing the thing immediately in front of his nose without being embarrassed by any particular mental subtlety. It was certain that when he expressed such a frank opinion it was one that was very widely held.

"I can only say, Mr. Ansell," said Evelyn at last, "that I don't agree with you in the least. There can be no question that Mr. Draper is a single-hearted man, and a pure-minded politician. He is much too highly developed to seek personal advancement at the expense of anybody — particularly at the expense of his country."

Mr. Ansell shook his head. There was the smile of the sceptic upon his not specially prepossessing features.

"Ha, you idealists!" he said. "You are one of the greatest dangers this old world has to face."

"Yes, I know." Her immense power of sympathy enabled her to put herself in the place of a man from whom she differed fundamentally, and to appraise his merits without despising him too much. "Yes, I quite see that. And he's an idealist, too, and that is why you are all so shamefully afraid of him."

"We are only afraid of him because he makes us all so damned uncomfortable," said Mr. Ansell, with an accession of luminous candour.

"As all idealists do, I suppose?"

"Yes, you are quite right there. That's a power you all have in common. And what, pray, have you done with your idealism? Raised up the Under-dog. Got him to take a pride in himself. Got him to wear a collar, and to brush his hair. Widened his horizon. Taught him how to read newspapers, and how to write 'em. Increased his scale of living. Made him very acute in minding other people's business. And what's the result of it all? Instead of an unwashed, under-paid, under-fed, but moderately contented cur, you get a sleek, well-fed, thoroughly discontented mongrel, who is determined at all hazards to get on top. Idealists like Draper have not made the world a whit better for anybody, and they've made it a much worse place for everybody to live in. I may go so far as to admit that the man is sincere, according to his lights, but it would have been far better for his country had he never been born. Let well alone was my father's motto, and the more I see of things the more I'm convinced it takes a great deal of beating. That's my opinion, Duchess, and I make so bold as to present you with it, free, gratis, and for nothing."

The outspoken Yorkshireman turned away with a satisfied laugh. He was conscious that his indictment of a dangerous heresy admitted of no defence worthy of a moment's consideration from a judicial mind.

IX

A LITTLE after midday the conference in the library came to an end. Four grave and reverend councillors emerged from their seclusion with an air sufficiently portentous to increase the curiosity of those who were burning to know the latest turn in the game. Were the negotiations on the point of collapse, even now that Rockingham had formed his Government? Could it be that, after all, Draper had declined to come in?

About a quarter to one o'clock these doubts received a rather startling confirmation. Then it was that Mr. Grundy arrived alone. His colleague, it appeared, had come down too, but he chose to remain at the inn in the village rather than invade the precincts of Cloudesley. And to the surprise of all, he had sent a formal request that Rockingham, Evan Mauleverer, and Loring should attend him at the Coach and Horses any time during the afternoon that might be convenient to them.

It was hard to understand such a line of conduct. Why take the trouble to come down at all if one was not going to have the grace to enter the house of the

279

enemy? Certainly such a scruple augured ill for the success of a Rockingham ministry. If the most important figure in it was able to display such discourtesy — the least censorious of his critics felt it amounted to that — toward the accredited leader and his friends, the entire scheme was doomed to collapse.

Luncheon was not altogether a comfortable meal. But it passed more agreeably than might have been the case had Mr. Grundy been less adroit. His personal popularity was not confined to his own political followers. His moderate and rather cautious views, tempered by the patience and sagacity of a true statesman, commended themselves equally to the members of the three parties.

The perfect plainness of speech and manner, the directness, the complete absence of "pose," and above all the genuine kindliness of the fallen leader of the Coalition had never stood him or his cause in better stead than at this moment. He was too shrewd not to realize that he was in a dangerously heated atmosphere. None saw more clearly than he that the 'rather impolite reluctance of Draper to enter that house and to sit at that board had strained these all-too-recent negotiations to the breaking-point.

Those among whom Mr. Grundy sat were beyond all things men of the world, but they found it almost impossible to conceal their chagrin. Loring himself, the squire and sportsman, trying his level best to fulfil a rôle for which nature had never designed him, was obviously piqued. He found it as much as he could do to be civil to the leader of the Centre. Such an attitude was of course unworthy of a man like Loring, but he seemed to feel the affront that was offered as a personal thing. Evan Mauleverer took it with far more philosophy. His mind was deeper, his self-command, his acquaintance with affairs much greater. He sat opposite Grundy, and while he said very little, his slow, formidable, cynical smile was trained full upon him.

Rockingham, on the other hand, seemed quite unaffected by the absence of Draper. He was much too *grand seigneur* to wear his heart upon his sleeve. Rockingham House might be burning, together with the rest of the metropolis, but the ground landlord of one fifth of Mayfair chatted equably throughout the meal to his feminine neighbours, one of whom was Lady Aline and the other his hostess, with a detachment of mind that was a little enigmatical as well as a little tragic.

As soon as the women had risen from the table Loring ordered his butler to send coffee and cigars to the library, and he invited Rockingham, Mauleverer, and Grundy to retire to that seclusion in order "that they might have a little talk." To this suggestion they assented readily, and in the course of half an hour or so Evan Mauleverer returned in search of the host, whom he found in the depths of a cosy armchair in the hall.

"We want your help, my dear fellow," said the leader of the Right, with his slow and formidable smile. "Come and help us."

"To do what?" growled Loring.

"To make up our minds. If Mahomet won't come to the Mountain, is it meet for the Mountain to go to Mahomet?"

"I'd see him damned first," said Loring, in characteristic phrase.

"Exactly my opinion." The formidable smile of the famous reactionary seemed to grow more dangerous. "But for some occult reason that doesn't seem altogether to meet the views of Robert."

"Why not?" said the host. "We've had more than enough of Draper's nonsense as it is. And to my mind this about puts the cap on."

"Exactly my view. But Robert doesn't quite see the thing like that. What is in his mind I can't fathom. For some inexplicable reason he seems to lean to the side of Grundy, and Grundy, of course, is all in favour of paying a visit to the Coach and Horses at four o'clock."

The host rose stubbornly and rather rheumatically from the depths of his armchair.

"I am bound to say," he said, "that Robert defeats me. If he's a wise man he'll keep clear. Why should he, of all people, want to go near the dirty dog. Mark my words, Evan, that swine has come down here for no good purpose. He is out for mischief."

Mr. Evan Mauleverer offered no comment. But expressions so unparliamentary seemed in nowise to offend his fastidious soul. My lord was accustomed to call a spade a spade; moreover, he seemed to have touched a responsive chord in the bosom of the leader of the Right.

"You are just the man to talk to Robert," he said, linking a fraternal arm through that of his host.

X

ARM in arm they entered the library. They found Rockingham and Grundy smoking their cigars in a silence that was a little tense.

Evan Mauleverer closed the door softly.

"Loring thinks exactly as I do," he said.

"Of course he does," said Rockingham, drawing imperturbably at his cigar. "And you are both absolutely right — absolutely right." The Prime Minister-elect repeated the phrase almost as if he was in the process of weighing it carefully — "as far as you go — both absolutely right as far as you go."

"You think we don't go far enough?" said Loring, rather sharply.

"Perhaps — perhaps," mused the Prime Minister-elect.

"You've all gone a great deal too far already, that's my opinion," was Loring's rejoinder. "And I refer to you, Mr. Grundy, as much as anybody. It's only my opinion, mind, but there it is if you want it."

Mr. Grundy's face was tinged with sly amusement.

None understood better than he the man with whom he had to deal.

"Lord Loring," he said in his suave, almost paternal manner, "I know you well enough to be aware that no man is more deeply attached to the country."

"I take no credit for that," said the forthright Briton.

"Quite so. But what I would venture to point out to you is that all four of us are passionately attached to the country. We may be at variance as to what is the immediate course to pursue, but the fact that we are at one on the main issue ought, I think, to guide us in this minor matter. Now, the point is this: The Duke and I are agreed that it is expedient to accede to Mr. Draper's request — his polite request — that we should pay him a visit at the inn in the village some time this afternoon. You and Mauleverer, I gather, are opposed to that course."

"That is so," said the leader of the Right. "In my view it is a request he is not in a position to prefer."

"I am afraid, my dear Mauleverer, I cannot agree with you," said the leader of the Centre, with all the urbanity of which he was capable. "You must be aware that an immense quantity of water has flowed under London Bridge during the past forty-eight hours."

"So I am informed," said the leader of the Right in his dryest manner.

"You mean," Loring interposed hotly, "that the King has allowed this traitor to overreach him."

"Well, no, not that exactly," said the leader of the Centre, in the soothing accents he might have used to a child. "And with all respect, my dear Lord Loring, that statement does not envisage the true facts of the situation — that is to say, as the facts of the situation present themselves to the Duke and myself."

The almost caressing note of urbanity was lost upon all save Rockingham, who smiled slightly.

"I'm a plain man," growled Loring, "and that's how it strikes me, anyhow, and that's what I told the King."

"I am aware you did," said the leader of the Centre. "But I am not aware that the King shares your opinion."

"You don't expect a man to admit he's been done in the eye, do you?" snapped my lord.

"And I think I am entitled to say," quietly countered the leader of the Centre, "that the Duke here doesn't altogether share that opinion either."

Loring turned to face Rockingham with explosive eyes.

"I can't understand what you do think, Robert,"

he said petulantly; "upon my word, I can't. I tell you plainly this man is a traitor."

"One is not yet convinced that he is," said Rockingham, whose rather fatigued air seemed in the circumstances deliciously casual. "I think that is what we have to find out."

"And you think, my dear fellow," said Evan Mauleverer, "that if we respond to his kind invitation to take tea with him at the Coach and Horses this afternoon at four o'clock, we may be able to set at rest our doubts upon the subject."

"I confess it may not be unlikely."

"I am sorry to be unable to follow your reasoning," said the leader of the Right. "It seems uncommonly like responding to a direct invitation to walk into the spider's parlour."

"Assuming that it is, what harm can the spider do us?"

"He might swallow us piecemeal."

"I don't quite understand."

"Well, I will not be more explicit at the moment," said the leader of the Right, "but my view is that it will be the height of impolicy. There is no adequate reason why he should not come here to discuss the situation. And if there is an adequate reason the situation no longer admits of discussion."

The Duke and Mr. Grundy nodded an affirmative.

"Yes, that is the crux of the whole matter,"

said the latter, after waiting courteously but in vain for Rockingham himself to frame an answer. "The question now 'to be decided is, has or has not the matter passed beyond the phase of discussion?"

"Exactly," said Loring.

"Well," said the leader of the Centre, "I can only have recourse to the King's explicit request, made this morning at ten o'clock, that Draper should confer with us four at the earliest moment, and to acquaint him with the result of our deliberations not later than to-morrow at noon."

"Was this request made personally to Draper?" inquired the leader of the Right with a light of menace in his eyes.

"Undoubtedly."

"And what was Draper's reply?"

"He promised to do so on one condition."

"Condition! Aha! makes conditions, does he?" The light in the eye of Mauleverer seemed to grow more sinister. "What, pray, was the condition?"

"That he — the King — would give his personal assurance that martial law should in no circumstances be proclaimed in London before Monday midnight."

"My God!" groaned Loring, "was he insane enough to give it?"

"Yes," said the leader of the Centre in a voice so passive that nothing could have been deduced from it.

"Just what we might have expected," gasped Loring. "Upon my soul, I believe he's undone us."

"It may be so, Lord Loring," said the leader of the Centre; "on the other hand, it may not be so. I, at least, am not prepared to prophesy. But that was the condition laid down, and upon due reflection the King saw his way to accept it."

"Was there no other condition?" asked the leader of the Right."

"None."

"Absolutely none?"

"No other condition was imposed."

"Then it appears to amount to this," said the leader of the Right. "Draper is pledged to confer with us, and it is entirely a question of his personal convenience whether the meeting takes place in this house or at the inn in the village."

"Quite so," said the leader of the Centre impassively.

"You mean to say," said Loring, "that the man has the impertinence to impose the place of meeting upon us when he has really no choice in the matter?"

"That would appear to be a not inaccurate statement of the facts," said the leader of the Centre dryly.

"But he's in a cleft stick," said Loring. "He's bound to come here whether he wants to come here or not."

"I agree," said the leader of the Centre. "But then the question of expediency arises. It cannot hurt us to accede to his request, but conceivably it might hurt him to accede to ours."

"I don't understand," said Loring bluntly. "Why shouldn't the man be made to come to this house?"

"Do you press for the reason, Lord Loring?"

"Certainly."

"His wife is a guest in this house, and I think I betray no secret if I say they are no longer on terms."

"A totally inadequate reason. Why can't he behave like a man of the world?"

"I presume to offer no opinion upon that," said the leader of the Centre with an air of grave courtliness. "But I do feel very strongly that we should keep ever before us that we have to deal with a rather abnormal personality."

"Swollen head, eh? All the more reason we should not give in to it. But one would have thought he knew enough of things by this time to behave like a man of the world."

"Your world or his, Lord Loring?" inquired the leader of the Centre in debonair accents.

"There is only one world," said Loring.

The leader of the Centre deferred in silence to this dictum, but once again there was a stealthy light in the sagacious eyes.

"Loring means there is only one world inhabited by educated people," said the leader of the Right with his rather fatigued drawl.

"Thank you, my dear Mauleverer," said the leader of the Centre. "I think we all strive to appreciate that."

Rockingham, who in all circumstances was prone to indulge the comic sense, turned aside to smile.

"Well, I see no reason at all why we should yield to him," said Loring, summoning a superb air of finality. "I don't think we need care particularly for his fine feelings. He has never cared for ours. We are here if he wants us, and are ready to receive him. It is really a matter of indifference to us whether we meet him or not."

"But it is not a matter of indifference to the country," said the leader of the Centre.

There was a pause. It was broken by Rockingham.

"Do we want him here particularly?" he said in his casual voice.

"You mean, can he be trusted to behave himself if he comes?" said Loring. "Personally, I take leave to doubt it."

"I too," said the Prime Minister-elect.

"I too," said the leader of the Right.

"One is inclined to think," said the Prime Minister-elect, "that he has shown a certain self-knowledge in not trusting himself within these precincts."

"Would you say that was his reason?" Loring inquired.

"It is not improbable, I think. He is bound to meet us in any case, but he may feel he has not got himself sufficiently in hand to meet us here. What is your view, Mr. Grundy?"

The Prime Minister-elect turned to the leader of the Centre with a rather elaborate if slightly ironical gesture, as of one seeking the light.

The leader of the Centre was not unequal to the occasion.

"I have no claim to be considered a psychological expert," he said in his dryest voice, "but if you press the point I am constrained to admit that the hypothesis may not be inconceivable."

"At all events," said the Prime Minister-elect, "I am convinced that nothing will be lost if our conference takes place at the village inn."

Like many men of limited mentality, Loring was extremely tenacious. But Rockingham's opinion carried weight. And, after all, it was to Rockingham that the affair mattered most. If he felt that the concession of this rather immaterial point did not in any way jeopardize his own strategical position there was no particular reason for his friends to be unduly sensitive.

"Well, Robert, you are going to be Prime Minister," said Loring with the best grace he could muster, "and I suppose it is right for your opinion to be paramount."

"Yes, I think it is," said Rockingham, with characteristic coolness.

"Well, I place myself in your hands," said Loring, who, like most of his kind, knew how and when to defer to authority.

"Thank you, Loring," said the Prime Minister-elect. "I am sure you will not regret your action. And, after all, the point is quite immaterial."

Evan Mauleverer found himself to be the sole representative of the minority. Therefore he expressed the stoicism upon which he was wont to pride himself by acquiescing gracefully in a course of action of which he strongly disapproved.

XI

AS THE afternoon was fine, and the Coach and Horses was within sight of the lodge gates of Cloudesley, Rockingham, Grundy, Mauleverer, and Loring set out on foot from the house a few minutes before four o'clock. There was still a fair amount of light, and Rockingham, his arm entwined confidentially within that of the leader of the Centre, led the way along the famous beech avenue to the park gates. At an interval of some fifty yards, Loring and Mauleverer followed not over-graciously in their wake.

Both the leader of the Right and his host were puzzled not a little by the demeanour of Rockingham. Always an enigma, even to his most intimate friends, trusted the least by those who knew him the best, his newly displayed respect for the opinion and personality of Grundy nonplussed them completely. An aristocrat of aristocrats, if such a phrase has a meaning, a man fastidious in all things, except in the matter of the Seventh Commandment, that such a man should be ready to dance to the piping of Solomon Grundy, was one of those contradictions for which they were at a loss to account.

"Robert is getting an enormous patriot these days," said Evan Mauleverer with one of his cynical chuckles. "Or is he meditating another of his little coups, I wonder?"

"I hope he won't let Draper get on top, that's all," said Loring sourly.

"Somehow I don't think he will do that. No man yet has ever plumbed the depths of Robert's resources. But I must say this thing has an ugly look. It has been played up far too high. Something may very easily snap. Let us hope it won't be Robert Rockingham."

"Pooh!" said Loring. "If it comes to that, he is quite able to take care of himself."

"I will tell you better in an hour's time, my dear fellow," said Mr. Evan Mauleverer.

By now the party had arrived at the Coach and Horses. Evidently they were expected. An overwhelmingly obsequious innkeeper received them at his threshold and ushered them up a flight of very dark, very narrow, and decidedly unwholesome-smelling stairs.

They were shown into a private sitting-room on the first floor. Although there was still a certain amount of daylight the lamp was already lit, and the curtains drawn across the window. A cheerful fire was burning, and the room, though antiquated and meanly furnished, was not without an aspect of comfort.

In a rather dilapidated chair next the fireplace reclined a very pale, sombre, gaunt-looking man. Spectacles on nose, he was making a show of reading the *Planet* newspaper.

Almost before his visitors had entered he had risen to receive them.

"I am so much obliged to you all for the honour you are doing me," he said.

"Not at all," said Rockingham, rather grimly.

He had been the first to enter the room. With a nonchalant air that was yet not ungenial he offered his hand.

"Please take a chair," said Draper.

He ignored the hand that was offered, yet with a tact that made the omission appear unintentional.

"I am afraid none of these chairs are very comfortable," said Draper. "How do you do, Mauleverer?" He bowed perhaps a shade elaborately to the leader of the Right. "How do you do, Lord Loring?" The bow was repeated. "I am immensely obliged to you for coming here."

"Not at all," said both of these in their deep voices.

"These chairs are the best I can do for you, so you must please make the best of them. May I offer you some little refreshment after your walk? A cup of tea, Duke? A whisky and soda?"

They were none of them in need of refreshment.

It was some little time before they could accommodate themselves with chairs. But at last they were able to do so.

"At the outset," said Draper, "may I be allowed to ask if the situation is quite clear to you? I should like your formal assurance that such is the case."

The tone was even, friendly, and almost careless.

"The situation is reasonably clear, I think," said Rockingham lightly.

"Still, perhaps you will forgive me if I rehearse it a little before I say what I have to say?"

"Pray do so by all means," said Rockingham with his courtier's air.

"This is the situation as it presents itself to me. It may not be the situation as you yourselves envisage it, but I can only accept responsibility for the workings of my own mind: The country has been without a Government for seventeen days. Some form of constitutional Government is absolutely indispensable to it. The King has invited the Duke of Rockingham to form a Government, but he has thought well to impose one vital condition. That condition is that I, myself, should hold Cabinet rank in any Government the Duke of Rockingham may form. May I ask, is that an accurate statement of the facts of the case?"

"A perfectly accurate statement of the facts of the case, Mr. Draper," said Rockingham very quietly.

"At the risk," said Draper, "of going over ground that may already be familiar to you, I may say I am here at the King's request. I have been asked to confer with the Duke of Rockingham and with certain of his friends and colleagues. I have been asked to afford any assistance that may lie within my power in order to arrive at the decision, which I understand is to be promulgated to-morrow at noon, as to whether it will be competent for the Duke of Rockingham to take office in compliance with the premises laid down by the King."

Rockingham acknowledged this résumé by a courteous inclination of the head.

"I have to thank you very much, Mr. Draper," he said, "for stating the case so clearly and succinctly. And let me say at once that your presence here and any assistance, any advice you may feel competent to give, cannot fail to be of the greatest advantage to myself, to my colleagues, and to the country."

Mr. Draper bowed in his turn.

"Duke of Rockingham," he said, "I thank you for speaking in such flattering terms of any services it may be within my power to render. But before proceeding one step further I deem it only right to inform you and your friends that for my own part I find it to be wholly impossible to accept office in any administration of which you yourself are the head or of any cabinet of which you a member."

XII

A PIN might have been heard to fall in the
room. There was a look of blank consternation in the faces of three of the emissaries. Diffi-
culties had been foreseen. But none had expected
a complete refusal in such bald and uncompromising
terms.

Rockingham, outwardly a stoic, as became his
attitude to life, did not relax a muscle. It was
impossible to read any kind of emotion into the
urbane half-smile with which he received Mr
Draper's announcement. But his three colleagues,
deeply solicitous for the country, were not able to
accept the blow with this slightly contemptuous
detachment. To them it meant total darkness and
eclipse.

The silence which followed was painful and
prolonged. The President of the Committee of
Public Safety, standing tense in every line, had
grown very pale. The deeply expressive, luminous
face was strangely drawn. The sunken eyes were
fixed upon Rockingham. None had realized until
this moment what implacable enemies they were.

At last the silence was broken. It was broken by the one among the five persons present whose voice had the least authority, by the one indeed who had the least right to be present in such an assembly.

"Why can't you?" said Loring in a rather queer, wholly ineffectual voice that was strangely different from his normal one.

A further silence ensued, and then Draper took up the question.

"I will tell you why, Lord Loring." There was a slow gathering together of the man's immense hidden reserves of power. "I will tell you why, in the fewest possible words. The Duke of Rockingham is a contemptible blackguard."

The three colleagues of the Prime Minister-elect sprang to their feet. The liveliest horror was in their faces. Rockingham, on the contrary, kept his chair and folded his arms with an air of the completest indifference. The half-smile, now tinged with a slight, almost imperceptible mockery, was still upon his face.

"He has sought my ruin by every means in his power." The accusation was made passionlessly. "He has spread and fostered a base calumny, he has perverted my wife and turned her against me. I know he has always regarded me as an enemy of the country. His hatred of me is sincere and perhaps disinterested. That justice will I render him.   But I should be less than a man or I should be more if I did not resent by all the means that are open to me the machinations of one whom I abhor from the depths of my soul."

Again came a painful silence.   The colleagues of Rockingham were too much astonished and too much distressed to intervene.

"My lord duke" — Draper moved a pace forward to where Rockingham sat — "you have done me the greatest injury that one man can do another. I should not have consented to meet you now, except with one particular and especial purpose in my mind.   My lord duke, this is the purpose for which I have met you."

As he spoke he struck Rockingham a light blow on the cheek with the palm of his hand.

Grundy, Mauleverer, and Loring stood petrified. Not one of them had dared to foresee the design that was in the mind of Draper.   They were powerless to do anything.   Indeed there was nothing they could do.

"I formally challenge you," said James Draper.

Rockingham rose slowly to his feet.   His great height and impressive personality seemed for a moment to overshadow his adversary.

"As you wish, Mr. Draper," he said almost negligently.   "I shall be most happy to give you any satisfaction that lies within my power."

"May I suggest to-morrow morning as soon as there is light enough," said Draper curtly. "There is a field here behind this inn which might suit our convenience."

"It will suit me perfectly," said Rockingham.

"You, of course, have the choice of weapons."

"I am afraid I am not up in the rules," said Rockingham with a well-considered air. "I was not even aware that people fought duels nowadays. But if you really feel I have done you a deep personal injury," he added with a courtesy that was charming, "I shall be most happy to oblige you in any way that may be open to me."

Mr. Draper bowed.

"I believe it to be usual in these somewhat difficult circumstances" — a subtle note of mockery came into Rockingham's voice — "to leave the discussion of details to third and fourth parties. Our seconds — and I hope two among our three friends here will do us the honour to represent us, unless Mr. Draper has other views — may perhaps be able to arrange the details of our meeting to-night."

"The suggestion is excellent," said Draper with a very matter-of-fact air. "I shall ask my friend Grundy to represent me if he will have the great kindness to do so."

The leader of the Centre stood visibly perturbed.

He directed a look of mingled consternation and incredulity at his two companions that in other circumstances would have been comic.

"Perhaps Lord Loring will be my man," said Rockingham, whose manner was equally to the point. "Will you be my man, Loring?"

"Hasn't this foolery gone far enough?" said the master of Cloudesley, finding his tongue at last.

"Lord Loring " — the voice of Draper had taken a curious note — "I can only say that as there is a God in heaven it is my clear and fixed intention to meet the Duke of Rockingham."

The tone no less than the words seemed to strike a chill to the heart.

"It is madness, it is worse than madness," said Loring.

"You may be right, Lord Loring," said Draper rather forlornly, "but the affair is out of my hands. A Higher Power has intervened."

"But the country, man, the country!" cried Loring aghast.

"Yes," said Draper in a falling voice, "I know, I know. But, as I say, this thing is out of my hands."

"But surely, man," said Loring, "you must realize that if anything happens to you or to Rockingham many thousands of lives may be sacrificed. It is the most colossal piece of egotism I have ever heard."

Draper was silent. It was noticed that the sweat had begun to pour down his face.

"Lord Loring," he said in a voice that almost failed him, "this matter is out of my hands. I can say no more than that."

XIII

ROCKINGHAM and his three companions filed very slowly and in a gingerly manner down the dark stairs of the inn. It was with a sense of profound relief that they found themselves at last in the open air. It now was quite dark. A moonless February night was come. There was a light fall of rain in the air.

The four men walked abreast. Not a word was spoken by one of them until they had passed through the gates of the porter's lodge and halfway up the long avenue to the house which yawned before them like a crypt.

At last the voice of Loring was heard. It sounded ghostly and hollow.

"I have always thought him a bit cracked," he said.

None of the others answered him. In a silence which seemed the deeper for having been disturbed, they walked on. There was only the muffled, rhythmical sound of their feet falling upon the gravel and the gentle patter of the rain upon the canopy of leaves overhead.

They came to the house and entered, still without speaking. Divested of their overcoats they seemed to move automatically, instinctively, in the direction of the library. Loring opened the door and held it for the others to enter. The moment they had done so, he entered too and closed the door after him.

They formed a little group upon the hearthrug before the fire. Still no word passed, but in the faces of them all, in that of Rockingham no less than that of the others, was a look of utter consternation.

Finally it was Evan Mauleverer who spoke.

"Well?" he said.

That monosyllable seemed to embody the sense of impotence that was common to them all.

"Well, what's to be done?" said Evan Mauleverer.

"Things must take their course, I think," said Rockingham quietly. "After all, the proposal is not unhonourable."

"My dear Robert," said Evan Mauleverer, "I feel very strongly that none of us can be a party to this amazing proposition."

"Why not, my dear fellow?"

"Why not?"

"Yes, my dear fellow, I repeat — why not? As I say, to my mind the proposal is quite an honourable one, and in the circumstances even a legitimate one."

"Honourable! Legitimate! Are you going to admit that it is justified?"

"Certainly," said Rockingham coolly. "No man ever tried harder to ruin another than I tried to ruin that fellow. You all know that. And I consider the state of the country to be my justification. Unfortunately I do not appear to have been able to do it, and that is my only regret."

This cynical candour seemed to intensify the strain.

"The whole house of cards is on the ground, at any rate," said Evan Mauleverer.

"Not a doubt of it."

"Well, my dear Robert, what is the next turn in the game to be?"

"I may be better able to tell you at this time to-morrow."

Thereupon Rockingham sauntered out of the room.

Left to themselves, the three others, so diverse in their natures yet fused into a kind of fraternity by the similarity of their outlook upon the world, made each his confession of impotence.

"Well, what's to be done?" asked Evan Mauleverer, repeating his futile question.

"If you want my opinion," said Loring, "they have both fully made up their minds to have it out. And in the circumstances I am by no means sure they are not right."

"It is putting back the clock a hundred years," said Evan Mauleverer.

"Yes, but the circumstances are altogether exceptional."

"I feel it to be our clear duty to avert a meeting by every means in our power. I feel sure, my dear Grundy, that you agree."

"Well, since you ask me," said the leader of the Centre, whose reputation was founded upon compromise, "I am bound to say I do. I think the proposal is altogether monstrous at this time of day, and yet the odd thing is that I am by no means clear that ethically it is not correct."

"I expect we all feel that more or less," said Evan Mauleverer sadly. "We have all of us felt from the first that this thing has been played up far too high."

"Why have you fellows played it up so high?" asked the leader of the Centre.

"Well, it is hardly necessary to tell you," said the leader of the Right, "that Draper has aroused an extraordinary personal animus against himself. I suppose it is inevitable that any man should who sets class against class."

"We in the Centre, as you know," said Grundy, adopting the suave legal manner which earlier in his career had brought him fame at the Bar, "are not prepared to admit that he has been guilty of such a crime. Still we shall always respect the *bona fides* of the duke and his friends," he added.

"In their view Draper is an enemy of the country —
I will not say because he has hit the landlords so
hard in their pockets. I will not say because of
Draper's intimacy with the duchess, which I for
one believe to be entirely innocent. I am prepared
to believe that the antagonism is even deeper and
more subtle than this. I think it is because they
are fighting with their backs to the wall. They are
menaced as they never have been menaced in this
country since the time of Cromwell. They know
they have to deal with a very powerful adversary,
who seems to have rendered them desperate. And,
to vary the metaphor and to use a candour that I
hope will be forgiven, I am afraid that Rockingham like a ruined gamester has been tempted to
use loaded dice."

"By God, you shan't say that!" said Loring hotly.

"But Rockingham has admitted the fact," said
Grundy tenaciously.

"I don't agree."

"Let us waive the point. But in any case it seems
impossible to compose the quarrel between them.
And we are still face to face with the problem of
what is the right course to pursue in these terribly
difficult circumstances."

"Yes, that is the eternal problem I grant you,"
said Evan Mauleverer. "At all events, I think
one of us should see the King to-night."

"Do you advise taking him fully into our confidence?" asked the leader of the Centre.

"Yes, I am in favour of that course myself. After all, he is a man of the world."

"But," said Grundy, "this affair will cause him the greatest distress. Indeed I feel very strongly that every means must be used to prevent them from proceeding to extremities. Should any untoward accident happen, a very grave responsibility will rest upon us all."

"Theoretically you are right," said Evan Mauleverer, "but in practice I am afraid that none of us has the power to prevent them."

"Whatever view one takes of it," said Grundy, "it is a very grievous matter. And in the present state of the country it is a very deplorable matter. And, in any case, I think before we decide to invoke the aid of the King we shall do well to take the advice of Lord Peveril."

Mauleverer and Loring saw at once the expedience of this course. Thereupon the host sought out the old man, whom he found to be engaged in writing letters, and presently returned with him to the library.

Mauleverer was deputed to tell the news. Lord Peveril was shocked and distressed when he learned what had occurred. He was strongly of opinion that no means must be neglected by which Rockingham and Draper could be prevented from proceeding to extremities.

"It will be to the lasting discredit of all concerned," said Lord Peveril, "if we permit this thing to go on. Irreparable injury to the country is bound to result. I will see this man myself. I am sure it would be the King's desire. I will go at once."

Lord Peveril displayed the capacity for prompt action of one half his years. A long lifetime's association with representative minds and an intimate knowledge of public affairs conferred a very special authority upon him. The others felt strengthened by his council and it was with a sense of gratitude and relief that they sped him to his mission to the village inn.

The master of the house ordered round a motor-car, and Lord Peveril promised to return with the least possible delay.

That return was most anxiously awaited. Was it too much to hope that the wisdom of this old and good man would prevail? As men of the world, they were fain to believe that the line taken by Draper, extreme and uncompromising as it was, reflected no moral discredit upon him. "Unto him that smiteth thee on one cheek offer also the other," was to them hardly more than an academic precept. They were content to take the world as they found it; and the man who in the right place and season could return a blow, perhaps with interest added, was he of whom the best account could be rendered.

Lord Peveril was away a full hour. He returned in a state of the deepest dejection. Not only had he found it impossible to move Draper from his purpose, but it had hardly been possible to discuss the subject with him.

XIV

THE news was kept sedulously from the other inmates of the house, but immediately after dinner, a dull and gloomy meal, Lord Peveril sought out Draper's wife. He led her apart to a quiet corner of the drawing-room. In a few brief and broken words he told her what had occurred. The old man's manner made it clear to Lady Aline that he was suffering the acutest distress of mind.

"My dear," said Lord Peveril with the tears beginning to course down his face, "if your husband perseveres in his present design, which is to kill Rockingham at daybreak to-morrow, or if by any mischance Rockingham should kill him, we shall have the deluge upon us. The floodgates will burst, the monarchy and all our most cherished institutions will be swept away, and the country will be bathed in blood from one end to the other. Do not think these are the words of an alarmist. Only too well do I know the state the country is in. Only a miracle can keep Labour from the throat of Capital as it is; your husband is the only man alive who can perform that miracle, and if by any mischance he loses his life in this insane and wicked brawl, or if by an almost equal mischance he is insane and wicked enough to take the life of Rockingham, we shall witness a thing too dreadful to contemplate."

The wife of Draper was affected deeply by such a speech. It proceeded from the lips of one for whom she had a profound and instinctive reverence. This was a known good man; moreover, an accomplished and wise man, whose habit it was on all occasions of life to express himself temperately.

She was not an emotional woman. But now her distress was very acute. Moreover, it was tinged with remorse. Whatever had been the nature of her husband's relations with Evelyn Rockingham, and until the previous evening she had had good reason to construe them in the worst possible light, she now began to realize with an almost overwhelming sense of shame and horror that she had allowed herself to be made the tool of Rockingham himself.

As the truth began to dawn upon her, she grew deadly white.

"Oh, what have I done!"

One by one the words were wrung out of her.

Lord Peveril, the slow tears still coursing down his cheeks, sat in silence by her side.

"Oh, my God, what have I done!"

The unhappy woman covered her face with her hands.

All at once her pride and her will seemed to break. The slight frame was shaken with emotion.

The old man by her side took one of the ice-cold hands in his.

"I have been mad," she moaned. "I have been base. I have been inconceivably wicked. God forgive me." Again she covered her face.

Lord Peveril was overcome with pity. Such a distress was very painful to witness.

"Ought I to see him?" she asked wildly. "Could I do any good if I went to see him to-night?"

"You yourself can be the sole judge of that," said the old man very gently.

She shivered. There was something in the words, kindly spoken as they were, that seemed to open a vein in her body.

"O God!" she cried wildly. She clasped her hands to her heart.

XV

A LITTLE later that evening the occupant of the private sitting-room at the Coach and Horses was seated on a rickety chair at a rickety table writing busily. He was completely absorbed in his task. Now and again he paused to bite the end of the penholder in order that he might grapple the better with his thoughts. They appeared neither to flow nor to be well ordered.

The face of the man was deeply lined and deadly pale. It was framed by a mass of hair which in a few weeks had grown almost white. The whole aspect was that of one who suffers an almost insupportable burden, but whose will, thrice welded in the furnace, still remains inviolate. Looking at such a face without any knowledge of its history, an observer must have felt it to be that of an indomitable fighter perilously near his overthrow.

The act of composition was a sore labour. The writer was trying to express something that was elusive, intangible, that continually declined to be expressed. Several times he wrote a sentence, crossed it out, wrote over it, and then, still unsatis-

316

fied, destroyed the page. His gloomy eyes, tinged
a little with blood, began to show a look of hope-
lessness. Every fresh attempt that he made appeared to take him a step farther from the goal of
his intention.

At last with a sigh of despair he laid down the pen.
It was as if he realized that he was overwrought and
that he did not enjoy the full use of his faculties.
His mental state could hardly have caused him
surprise. His head had not touched a pillow for
many weary hours.

Presently he closed his eyes and sought to impose
some control upon the race of his thoughts. They
were terribly insurgent. The exigencies of the hour
seemed to be pressing him to death. Fragments
of his early life began to present themselves at
intervals in this mental chimera; he heard his
mother's voice and saw her face. Then he saw the
face of one other and he felt a curious restriction of
the throat and breast.

What that other had meant to him the man of
iron will had hardly known until now. She and
his country were the supreme things in his life.
He had lost her. Was he about to lose his country?
was he about to destroy her by the dreadful step
of the morrow? It had all been referred to the God
who was so real to him; yet, alas! in spite of his
faith, to which he clung with desperate tenacity, he

was in many ways no more than the creature of his generation, a frail mortal shuddering upon the brink of the abyss.

He was trying to indite a few brief pages of counsel to the Sovereign, that true friend of the country, in case of his own death at daybreak. He was even seeking to vindicate his death in the event of its occurrence. But how was it possible to do that? What vindication was there for such a deed? It must seem an act of gross selfishness that he of all men should have deserted the ship with the rocks grinding her keel. And yet what could he do? He must go through with this thing. It was part of his destiny. The voice of reason had addressed him many remonstrances, but for some little time past he had come to feel that he had entered the region of the supra-natural. It was as if his soul had passed into the custody of some higher power.

He laid down the pen with a growing sense of dismay. There was too much to be said to him who of all men discerned his worth in the sum of things. He recalled the whispered words of their parting: "My dear Draper, if you find you can serve under Rockingham, I think you will save us; but if you find you cannot, I at least shall understand."

Suddenly a moan escaped the man in his agony.

Like an animal caught in a trap he realized that he
was taken in the coils of some unknown power.
When he had left London that morning it had been
his fixed determination to confer with Rockingham
and to enter his Cabinet if a way could be found.
But, confronted with the man in that miserable
little room, he had been suddenly possessed by some
primordial force which had made him speak and act
as he had not intended.

In the midst of the torment that was closing in
upon him, that was pinning him down, he seemed
to hear a soft footfall on the stairs. In a dim,
remote way it echoed through the chambers of his
brain. And then he began to realize that the door
of the sitting-room had opened and had closed again,
and that away beyond the lamp there was a presence
in the room.

With insurgent nerves he rose from his chair
at the table to satisfy himself that this was the fact.
There was a form in blurred outline, partly concealed
by the shadows of the door.

"Who is it?" he said hoarsely.

He had not to wait for an answer.

The reply was given in the low voice of a woman.

Without surprise he recognized it as the voice
which had been stealing through the inner purlieus
of his mind during the whole of that evening.

"Aline," he said.

"Yes — it is I."

A cloak had been thrown over her dinner gown; her shining, ordered hair was uncovered; the tiny satin slippers made not a sound as they moved toward him.

"Jim," she said, "I want you to kill me."

Limply, mutely, she sank down before him, pressing her forehead against his knees. In the next moment she had prostrated herself completely at his feet.

For a little while she lay there. Then he gathered her slowly in his arms and raised her up. With a strength easily capable of crushing out the slender exquisite life, he held the slight form before him.

She felt the labouring breaths meeting hers. She did not struggle. But one thing she desired, and that was that death should come to her swiftly.

Her eyes were wide at the level of his. All too slowly darkness was overcoming them. She lay perfectly passive, perfectly inert. She seemed to feel that her life was ebbing, and yet she had not expected death to be like this.

Quite suddenly it was borne in upon her senses that his grip had relaxed, and that the light was coming back to her eyes. There at the level of hers were the eyes with the tinge of blood in them. The face was full of an intolerable anguish; the forehead was all wrung and distended.

XVI

IN the next instant she had swooned.

She awoke presently to find arms of a familiar tenderness about her. She lay back, brushing her hair against his cheek.

All that had been their life in the past, which in the madness of anger and reprisal had been discarded, rushed back upon her. This was the love she had known and betrayed; this was the love she had spurned and forgotten. Again she asked for death, but now he smothered in kisses the lips that sought it.

In the anguish of remorse she could have screamed. But already she was growing weak again. Like a timid child afraid of the dark, she quivered against his coat. Her whole being was shaken with sobs that refused to come out of her body.

For hours she lay in his arms. In spite of all that had happened, they were still as they were. Perhaps more than they were. In their life together they had known great moments. And now they had passed through a furnace seven times heated. Their passion was raised to a higher power. Perhaps never until then had she known what depths there were in him, what a quality of mingled strength and tenderness was his. It may have been that since last they had lain in the arms of each other a cubit had been added to each of their statures. At least he meant more to her now than he had ever meant to her formerly.

Was he not so much more than the indomitable fighter, the successful politician? "I am sure you will go far," she had said to him on the night of their marriage. "Wherever I go you must be with me always," had been his answer. Again remorse overcame her. What had she done! To what uttermost Hades had she consigned him!

The hours passed. They both desired that death should come to them, as thus they lay in the arms of each other. Not a word was spoken except when now and again he bade her very gently try to sleep. But sleep was very far away. At the back of her brain was dull terror. This night of rekindled love and reconciliation must pass all too soon. Her soul shuddered when she remembered what the dawn must bring.

Some time after three o'clock by the crazy little clock on the chimneypiece he carried her over very tenderly to the sofa, and laid her there. Then he draped the gay cloak about her, and sat down again at the table, and took up the pen.

He was far better able now to order his thoughts. The words began to flow. He found it possible to draw up a sort of précis of the situation for the guidance of the Sovereign in case of his own death at daybreak. Also he wrote a score of letters to be delivered, in that event, to those who looked to him for guidance.

He worked calmly and well until about six o'clock, while the occupant of the sofa lay watching him, with wide, haunted eyes. Then his labours were disturbed by a knock on the door, and a slatternly maid-servant came into the room. She had brought the information that a gentleman was below in the coffee-room who desired to speak with him.

He descended there and on the threshold of that dismal apartment, smelling strongly of cheese and stale sauces, he was received by a burly, rubicund individual in a mackintosh with the collar turned up, and a soft hat pulled down over his eyes.

They entered the coffee-room together, closing the door after them. The visitor then removed his hat, unbuttoned his mackintosh, turned down the collar, and disclosed the homely features of the master of Cloudesley.

"The duke has asked me to act for him," he said bluntly and briefly. "Who is your own man?"

"Grundy, I hope. I know of no one else. Please try to persuade him. I sincerely hope he will, although it seems unkind to ask him, because he is beyond all things a man of peace."

"Yes, it seems hardly his line of country," said Loring, with a rather forced laugh. "But there is no one else apparently. We can try him, at any rate. Will eight o'clock suit you? There should be light enough by then."

"Eight o'clock will suit me perfectly."

"In one of the fields at the back here?"

"Yes."

"Very well. Grundy and I will choose the ground — that's if he'll act, of course. Rockingham, by the way, has chosen pistols, although I am to tell you that he is quite willing that the choice of weapons should be left to you."

"I am very much obliged to him. Pistols then."

"He thinks it would be advisable to use weapons and cartridges of a similar type. I happen to have a pair of Webleys. Will those do?"

"Yes, thanks."

"Very well. Eight o'clock. And Grundy and I will choose and mark the ground."

Lord Loring concluded the interview with a brisk and businesslike air, and marched out of the coffee-room into the mirk and the rain of a rather wild February morning.

XVII

M R. DRAPER courteously attended his visitor
to the inn door and watched him depart.
He then summoned the slatternly servant girl, and
ordered some tea to be brought up to the sitting-
room at seven o'clock. Then he returned to his
labours.

Still perfectly calm, with mind clear and well
ordered, he continued to write, while the occupant
of the sofa lay watching him. The look of horror
was still in her eyes. A little before seven his
labours were at an end, and the last packet sealed.
Then he sat by the side of his wife, gently chafing
her ice-cold hands.

Not a word did they speak. The fateful minutes
passed. Again were they experiencing that passion
of the spirit which had borne them through the night.

Suddenly, without preliminaries of any kind, a
woman came quite unexpectedly into the room.

It was Evelyn Rockingham.

The occupant of the sofa sprang to her feet as
if a blow had been dealt her. Her husband took
her in his arms and gently made her lie down again.

"Come over here, my dear Evelyn," he said. "Come and put your hand in hers. You have both to promise me that you will be friends."

Evelyn came at once to the sofa with both hands outstretched. There was a radiance in her eyes that only a true woman could have displayed.

Lady Aline shuddered in her embrace.

"You have been diligent," said Evelyn Rockingham to Draper, in a tone of carefully assumed lightness, as her eyes fell on the great pile of letters on the table.

"I have need to be," said the writer of the letters in a weary voice. "By the way, tell me, how have you passed the night over there?"

"You may well ask. Everything is in a state of inconceivable panic and turmoil."

"Has the affair leaked out?" Draper asked the question under his breath.

"Yes, I am afraid. It was known to too many, you see. Some of the women may not know. I don't believe Alice Loring does. But all the men are in the secret."

"I am sorry for that," said Draper, still in a very low tone.

"It was inevitable, I fear. And I understand they are bringing all possible pressure to bear upon Robert not to meet you."

He made no comment.

"But I feel I ought to say at once, my dear James, they will not succeed. They don't know their Rockingham. His Grace's Cabinet has been sitting all night in the library in earnest deliberation, and his Grace has been sitting all night reading Thackeray in his private room."

"What is the result of their deliberations?"

"That I don't know. The conference was still sitting at six o'clock this morning. Everything is at sixes and sevens. No two members of the Cabinet seem to think alike. One great problem has been whether they should invoke the aid of the King."

"I hope they have not been so unwise," said Draper anxiously.

"No, they have not been so unwise. They decided finally to call Lord Peveril into their councils, and pledged themselves to be guided by his advice."

"I am sure he would be dead against it," said Draper, with a sigh of relief.

"Yes, he was strongly of opinion that now was not the time for the matter to be brought to the ears of the King."

"Sensible old man."

"By the way, there is a rumour that Evan Mauleverer is in possession of a letter from the King which is only to be opened in the event of Robert being unable to complete his Cabinet."

The President of the Committee of Public Safety smiled rather dourly.

"Yes, my dear Evelyn, I think I am in a position to confirm that rumour."

Her expressive face grew flushed and startled.

"Oh, do tell me!" she said. "You are acquainted with the contents?"

"I am afraid that is rather a leading question," said Draper impassively.

"Oh, *do* tell me. I am sure you know."

"I cannot admit that I know, even if I know I do. It was very wrong to admit that I was even aware of the existence of the letter."

Pain and deep disappointment contended in the face of Evelyn.

"Forgive me," he said very gently. "Heaven knows what depends upon this letter. It may be the crux of the whole thing. Pray forget that I made such an unguarded admission, but, having made it, beyond all things I desire to know whether that letter has been opened and read to the Cabinet."

"To the best of my information it had not been opened at six o'clock. I understand that the question of opening the letter has been debated furiously for two hours, and that at six o'clock they were still unable to reach a decision on the point."

"What is their difficulty? It is abundantly clear

that Rockingham will never be able to complete his Cabinet on the lines laid down."

"Evan Mauleverer and the other extremists are, I believe, the lions in the gate. They think the time has not yet come. And they think that when the time does come the letter should be opened by Robert himself."

"Perhaps they are right there. And yet I don't think it matters particularly by whom it is opened. By the way, did I understand you to say that his Grace has taken no part in these deliberations?"

"Absolutely none. He has never left his private room all night."

"Why?"

"That's the man. He's past all understanding."

"Indifference?"

"No, I should be inclined to say pride. He must always be *grand seigneur*. He must never dismount from the high horse. He must never raise a finger openly, whatever he may do under the rose." The voice of Rockingham's wife had taken a note of bitter contempt. "It is his strength and his weakness. He is a very strange enigma."

"Well, his aloofness may undo him."

"It may, but human nature is a strange thing. All sorts of qualities have been read into him that he doesn't possess. Some of them speak of him as a man of blood and iron, but personally one would be inclined to say of him as Bismarck said of Salisbury, he is a lath painted to look like iron."

Draper shook his head rather sadly.

"I am by no means clear upon that point, my dear Evelyn," he said, "but it will be a very merciful dispensation for this country if that proves to be the case."

At this point the conversation was interrupted by the slatternly servant girl, who came in to lay the breakfast.

Draper gave a glance at the clock.

"Twenty past seven," he said. "I have until eight."

XVIII

A N EXTRA cup was sent for, and each of them
drank a cup of tea. Yielding to the maternal
solicitude of Evelyn Rockingham, Draper ate a slice
of bread and butter. His self-possession was very
remarkable. In the mind of his wife and in the
mind of his friend was a clear conviction that either
he or his adversary would lose his life. Their
antagonism was bitter, deep-rooted, intense. There
could be no doubt that each had suffered heavily
at the hands of the other. Having proceeded to
such an extremity, neither was likely to stay his
hand at the eleventh hour. Draper was not the man
to flinch from any issue, however grim it might be;
and Rockingham, slow to move, was known to have
the ruthless force of will of a historic line of warriors.

At twenty minutes to eight Draper retired to
perform a scanty toilet. When after the absence
of a few minutes he returned to the sitting-room
he found the faithful Grundy there.

"Ah, my dear Grundy," he said in his frank and
cordial way, "this is indeed noble of you."

The leader of the Centre was affected almost to

tears. Unable to reply, he averted his face from that of his colleague. It looked painfully strained and ashen white.

"It is a bad, and mad, and sad business," he said bitterly. "I should have judged myself to be a man of too much sense to bear a part in such a piece of buffoonery."

Draper placed his hand impulsively on the shoulder of the elder man.

"Somebody had to stand, my friend," he said in a low tone, "and I asked for you. It is noble of you."

"It is a piece of wicked folly," said the ex-Prime Minister. "I shall never be able to forgive myself for being a party to this transaction, and yet, as you say, some one had to be your friend."

"Mr. Grundy," said Evelyn Rockingham, coming forward from the window from which she had been looking into the dawn, "can you tell me what is the result of the deliberations of the Cabinet? What course is to be taken?"

The statesman to whom the question was addressed shook his head. "Forgive me if I reveal no secrets," he said.

"I do not ask for secrets," said she. "I was hoping you had made the result of your deliberations known to the world."

"Whatever decision may have been arrived at,"

said Mr. Grundy, with the marked kindness of tone which endeared him to so many, "I am afraid for the present the world must remain in ignorance."

"It is five minutes to eight, my dear Grundy," said Draper. "Let us pay the compliment of being on the ground at the time appointed."

"As you wish," said the ex-Prime Minister.

He turned abruptly as he spoke, and, without so much as a glance at either of the two women, or without taking any sort of leave of them, he led the way out of the room and down the stairs. Draper lingered a moment before he followed in his wake. In that moment he had kissed the ashen cheek of his wife, and had taken the two hands of Evelyn Rockingham in his own.

"Be of good courage, deliverer of my country," whispered his friend softly as his sombre eyes met hers.

When at last he was gone the two women sat forlornly apart. Evelyn sat by the window looking through the chill half-light across the inn-yard. Aline crouched shivering over the uncertain fire. For some little time each remained motionless, and in absolute silence. Not a word was spoken by either.

At last the woman at the window knelt very quietly before the chair in which she had been seated and began to pray. A little afterward the other woman slipped to her knees also, and pressing her head to the sofa began instinctively to do the same.

For a period of time that seemed to them both much longer than in point of fact it was, the two women remained upon their knees. In some subtle way of which neither was overtly conscious they seemed to derive strength from the nearness of each other. That their thoughts were centred on the same thing appeared to lend a curious intimacy to their emotion.

The clock upon the chimneypiece told the half-hour after eight. As if galvanized into life by the sound, Evelyn Rockingham sprang to her feet.

Overwhelming anguish forced her to utter a cry.

"Oh, my God!" She pressed her hands to her forehead, almost as if she was afraid that everything would go.

The sense of intolerable tension was relieved by a thud upon the carpet. It was the sound of a body falling. She turned to look at the sofa, and found Aline insensible upon the floor.

Evelyn gathered the frail form in her strong arms. She laid it on the sofa. Then she knelt and chafed the cold hands. When a little warmth had been restored to them Evelyn rose unsteadily. Her temples were throbbing as if they would burst. She seemed hardly able to breathe.

She walked across to the window and opened it,

and thrust forth her head to meet the rain. Hardly aware of what she did, her unseeing eyes roved out to the landscape. And then all at once her attention was caught by a distant object. Below and away beyond the inn-yard, at the extreme verge of the mist, perhaps a hundred yards distant, the faint and blurred outline of a sombre figure fixed her eyes.

The figure was that of a man in the act of closing a gate. Such a detached human effigy was without significance for a mind distraught, and yet in some remote way it had the power to make a direct personal appeal. Straining her eyes to meet it as it came slowly and heavily through the mire of the inn-yard, the light of the morning began imperceptibly to clothe it with a familiar aspect. The senses were too overwrought to realize what was happening. But the impact of the oncoming figure was unmistakable. It was rather tall, and had a gait that was a little ungainly, although the stride was large and free. And then a rush of blood darkened her eyes and her senses reeled.

With a cry she ran to the sofa, and with wild caresses embraced the shivering form that lay inertly upon it.

XIX

"HE IS coming back!" Evelyn whispered hoarsely.
The four simple words were too much for the
woman who loved the victor. In a surge of feeling
altogether beyond her control she strained close
to her who spoke. All was forgotten in that moment.
The long, slow, inevitable antagonism was almost as
though it had never been.

"He is coming back!" The wife repeated the words.

Gratitude had brought reaction. Almost for the
first time she was melted to tears. The proud spirit
was broken.

There came the sound of a heavy, deliberate
footfall on the stairs.

"He is here!"

Together they rose to receive him.

He entered the shabby little room with the same
air of deliberation with which he had left it. The
wet was gleaming on his overcoat. Evelyn drew back
a little in order that Aline might come forward to
help him to remove it.

Hardly any change had taken place in him. His
face had still a deadly pallor, but his eyes in lieu of

336

their inscrutable sombreness had almost the light of exaltation.

Neither woman uttered a word. Draper stood between them. He took the hand of each, but he had the look of a man who walks in his sleep.

"If it is anything we oughtn't to hear —— !" said Evelyn in a voice that emotion had rendered unrecognizable.

The sound of her voice, which was yet so remote from her own, had the effect of bringing him back to the present. He started as one in the act of emerging from a dream.

"I will tell you exactly what happened," he said, "unless —— !" He pressed gently the cold fingers of his friend.

"Unless!" she echoed, beginning to tremble.

"No, it is not that," he said quickly. "We never met at all."

"You never met at all!" She repeated the incredible phrase very slowly. "But that is not Rockingham."

"As you have always said, my dear Evelyn, we none of us know our Rockingham."

A great surge of feeling threatened to overmaster her.

"Yes, that is true at any rate," she assented a little hysterically. "We none of us know our Rockingham." She fought for composure and finally gained it. "Tell me, please, in two words, what occurred."

"It can be told in less. But no, it shall be told with circumstance." In spite of an iron control he kept upon himself he could not repress a certain ring in his voice. "Grundy and I walked through the mud across the fields to the place he and Loring had selected. Loring had been chosen by Rockingham as his second. It was three minutes after eight by the time we got there, but there was not a sign of either of our men. We took shelter under the trees of a sort of spinney near by and awaited their arrival. We filled in the time by discussing the mysteries of .38 Webleys, a pair of which Loring had undertaken to provide. I had to confess that I had never fired off a pistol in my life, whereupon I was informed that Rockingham was considered rather an expert shot. Rather tactless of my second, I thought. Well, to cut a long story short, we waited solemnly until twenty minutes past eight, then, lo and behold! Loring came alone across the fields. There was never a sign of Rockingham. 'Come, where is your man?' I asked, feeling a greater access of valour than I think I have ever experienced in my life. 'Reading the words of Thackeray, like a wise fellow,' growled poor Loring, the very picture of a discomfited sportsman. 'But he's sent you this.' He began to fumble in his mackintosh. 'That is, if I can find the damned thing.' My lord fumbled and fumbled, but he was hanged if he could find the thing. 'Upon my word, Loring,' said Grundy, looking more warlike than I ever thought him to be capable of looking, 'you are absolutely the most incompetent second I have ever had to do with in the whole course of my experience.' 'Oh, you wait a minute and be damned to you,' said Loring. 'I shall find it presently.' 'What are you looking for?' I asked. 'Wait till I've found it and then you'll know,' snapped Loring. He began to go through each one of his pockets solemnly, and then a flash of inspiration came to him and he remembered that he had put it in his cigar case. Finally he produced the document, and here it is for you to read."

Draper produced the letter in question and handed it to Evelyn Rockingham. The envelope was inscribed in the rather florid handwriting of the duke to the Right Honourable James Draper, M. P. She read as follows:

SIR: Yielding to the importunity of my colleagues, I have decided not to keep the appointment made on my behalf for this morning at eight o'clock. I may say that this step involves my withdrawal from political life. I remain, sir, your obedient servant,

ROCKINGHAM."

The wife of Rockingham made no comment upon this document. Knowing the veiled ambition of the man, knowing his sensitive dignity, she realized that this had not been an easy letter to write.

"Poor Robert!" she said at last in a rather queer voice.

"Poor Rockingham?" he echoed softly.

"Well, it was bound to happen to one of you," said Evelyn. "There would have been no room for you both in one Cabinet. But enormous pressure must have been brought to bear upon him. Your victory is swifter and more complete than your friends could have hoped."

"The victory is not mine," said Draper. "It is the victory of the day and generation. The old order changes. Rockingham stood for the past; a very brilliant, rather tragic, not inglorious past. He stood for the few against the many. And the many have prevailed, as prevail they always must, if they are only efficiently organized and efficiently led. It is my earnest prayer that the world will have no reason to regret his decision."

"I echo that prayer," said Evelyn softly. "I can only say I believe the world will be the better for his withdrawal. The few may have less in the way of cushions to lie on, but I think the many will at least be assured of a mattress or a bundle of straw. Do you agree with me, Aline?"

The wife of Draper, still wearing her dinner dress of the evening before, stood near the fire with her cloak gathered round her shoulders. In spite of an expression of joy in her face she looked very worn and pale.

"I am afraid I don't understand these things," she said. "I never have understood them. I only know that I have never liked the many."

"Yet you married one of them," said her husband.

"No," she rejoined with a wan smile, "I married one of the few."

Evelyn Rockingham loosed a peal of laughter.

"What have you to say to that, my democrat!" she cried.

The democrat had to admit that he was baffled.

XX

THE door of the sitting-room opened to admit the leader of the Centre. Mr. Grundy, urbane of countenance, entered light yet firm of step.

He bowed to the two women and then shook hands with Draper.

"Allow me," he said, "to be the first to offer congratulations to the Prime Minister of England."

Draper changed colour ever so slightly.

"I have been asked to convey to you," said the leader of the Centre, perhaps a little rhetorically, "the unanimous invitation, subject to the King's approval, of the three parties to undertake the task of forming a Government. Further, you are empowered to exercise an absolutely free hand in the formation of a Cabinet."

Mr. Draper bowed his head. They noticed how white it had become. The tall, rather ungainly figure looked bent and aged. The luminous face was strangely furrowed by suffering.

"My dear friend," he said humbly, with tears in his eyes, as he placed his hand in that of his colleague, "I rejoice that if such news had to be brought to me you are the bearer. We have fought many battles side by side. I hope you will help me now."

The elder and less emotional man was also visibly moved.

"Any little aid it may be mine to give," he said simply, "I freely bestow. I rejoice that in this dark hour the country has been visited by wisdom, I will even say visited by as great a wisdom as it has ever known. I also rejoice that it has so wise and true a friend in the Throne." He clasped the right hand of his colleague in both his own. "God be with you, my dear fellow! God bless you!"

The emotions not of the men alone, but of the women also, had been wrought to a pitch of curious intensity. A silence ensued which was broken at last by Evelyn Rockingham.

"It insures a measure of industrial peace," she said. "We can all congratulate ourselves upon that."

"Yes, I think it does," said the leader of the Centre.

"Perhaps at a great cost to some of us," said Evelyn.

"Perhaps," said the leader of the Centre. "Yet I feel we are all entitled to hope not. The situation is one of great peril and difficulty, but we all realize now with devout and thankful hearts that the hour has brought forth the man. I think it is no idle prophecy that the Prime Minister will have a united Cabinet which will prove capable of restoring order in the country."

"We will pray that it succeeds," said Evelyn Rockingham. And then she added with a rather strained laugh to cloak the unabashed curiosity of her sex, "Perhaps now, Mr. Grundy, you will kindly tell us what the sealed letter contained that was sent by the King to Evan Mauleverer."

"My dear Duchess, I wager you have guessed that long ago," said Mr. Grundy with an arch smile.

"I will hazard a guess, at all events. Was it not to inform all whom it might concern that in the event of Rockingham being unable to complete his Cabinet there was only one man in the kingdom who could insure the safety of the monarchy?"

Mr. Grundy was proof against this feminine importunity.

"The secrets of the constitution are sacred," he said with a rather mischievous smile.

"Admit, at least, that my long shot is uncomfortably near the target."

"Not a thousand miles off the target, perhaps. And perchance the shot itself is not made at quite the long range you would have us believe."

"My dear Mr. Grundy, I wish you would be a little less cryptic. Yet I have observed it to be a quality that flourishes in the hearts of all who have been Prime Ministers. Still there is one small fact that may not be without an interest for you. When the secret history of this troublous time comes to be written, the inspiration of this famous letter is not unlikely to be traced to a meddlesome female of the period."

Mr. Grundy held his hands high before his face, almost as if he would rebuke such levity.

"Duchess, you are incorrigible!" he said.

"And now that I have given away this great secret," she said, "may I in turn demand one? Tell me, was it not that letter that finally undid Rockingham?"

Mr. Grundy shook his responsible, statesmanlike head.

As Evelyn Rockingham had put the question, her air of badinage had seemed suddenly to desert her.

"There is no need for you to answer." Her voice fell. "I know that. I feel it here." She placed her hand on her heart. "Poor dear Robert! What a strange coil the gods weave about us when they set to work! Who could have foreseen that that letter involved his complete and final overthrow?"

"Evan Mauleverer foresaw it at any rate," said the leader of the Centre, almost with the air of one who speaks aside. "As soon as the letter was opened he pulled his long face and said, 'At all events, that's the end of Us.'"

"Sapient man!" said Evelyn Rockingham. "But opposition always seems to sharpen his wits for him. *Do* tell me, was Robert present when that letter was read to his Cabinet?"

"Ah, no! His Grace was in his chamber busily preparing a trout fly."

"Are you quite sure his Grace was not absorbed in the study of "Vanity Fair?" It is always well to give a touch of colour to the *histoire intime* of a really critical period."

"It may have been so," said the leader of the Centre, conceding the point gracefully. "At least it may have been sufficiently so for the matter to be debated by the well-informed in the time to come. But at all events it may be accepted beyond controversy that his Grace was in his chamber when the famous document was read aloud to the members of his Cabinet."

Evelyn laughed a little wryly.

"It is well, at least," she said, "to establish that salient fact upon a historic basis. Now please tell me this, Mr. Grundy — if you would see me the Madame Liebenstein of the future — who was it who finally bore the epoch-making document to be perused by his Grace in the sanctity of the ducal apartment? Was it poor dear Evan himself?"

"No," said the leader of the Centre, "poor dear Evan rather funked it."

"*Really* funked it?"

"Well, you see, with that letter to guide us, we ventured to draw up a round robin, which, by the way, every man of us signed, earnestly praying the duke in the name of his King and country to refrain from taking the field at eight o'clock."

"Oho! How delicious! At what hour was that?"

"A quarter past seven by the morning."

"One foresees that the memoirs will have *un succès fou*. Now tell me this, Mr. Grundy: If it was not poor dear Evan who had the courage to bear the round robin of the Cabinet together with the communication of the Sovereign to his Grace in the sanctity of the ducal apartment, who was the paladin? I demand the name of that Bayard in the sacred name of the muse of history."

"I, my dear Duchess, I was the man," said the leader of the Centre modestly.

"And alone you did it?"

"Alone I did it."

"Now tell me this, Mr. Grundy, and I promise it shall be my last question: In what manner did Robert receive his *congé?*"

Mr. Grundy smiled rather dourly.

"Well," said he, "if I must speak the truth, he took it with absolute indifference. It was really wonderful. It was as though he could hardly bring himself to be interested in the matter at all."

"Yes — but that is so like him."

"Well, it was a very remarkable exhibition considering what it must have meant to him. Poor fellow!"

There was an odd note of sympathy in the voice of the leader of the Centre. He was a man who differed fundamentally from such a man as Rockingham. There was scarcely anything they had in common unless it was a desire to conserve the resources of their country. Indeed, deep down in their characters was a very real antagonism. But the note of pity rang true and somehow it had the power to touch a responsive chord in the heart of Rockingham's wife.

Suddenly she felt a stab of remorse. Was she not rejoicing in the tents of her husband's victorious enemies, when he, utterly overthrown, lay sick of his wounds. She had never loved Rockingham, she had never understood him. If for any length of time she allowed her mind to dwell on that enigmatic personality, a sense of deep-rooted aversion was invariably aroused in it.

But remorse came upon her now. She had a subtle consciousness that more than any one she had contrived his defeat. All feeling for him was long since dead, but there was enough of the woman in her to make her suffer a vicarious pang that his overthrow should be so complete.

There and then, upon a sudden impulse, she determined to take a course that in victory would have been impossible. She would go to him. Perhaps she might be able to help him a little. It might even be given to her to staunch the grievous wound that she herself had dealt.

XXI

IT was not immediately possible for Evelyn to translate her strange resolve into action. At the instance of the leader of the Centre, whose practical mind was apt to repose upon a purely material basis, breakfast was in process of being prepared for four persons.

The two statesmen were insistent that she should share their modest meal. It was their intention, as soon as nature had been fortified, to repair to London. At the earliest moment they proposed to carry in person to the King the tidings of the all-important decision.

There could be little doubt that the public safety was assured. The knot had been cut by Rockingham's withdrawal. The ablest man in the country was now free to govern it. The moderate men of all faiths, the real backbone of the nation, had rallied to his standard. In spite of all the massed and subtle forces of reaction, a solution along the line of true development was now possible.

Having regard to the exigencies of the situation, the meal was surprisingly cheerful. Suspense it is that kills. The long night of doubt, of conflict, of divided counsel was at an end. Rightly or wrongly, for better, for worse, the course of the ship of state was now clear.

"Duchess," said Mr. Grundy as he handed her a boiled egg — the precarious nature of the inn cookery forbade anything more elaborate — "I think you deserve well of your country."

"Yes, I think she does," said Lady Aline, who was seated opposite to her.

The face of Evelyn Rockingham was suddenly flecked with colour. In the simple speech of the woman who had misunderstood her motives was the vindication of much that she had done.

"Thank you, my dear Aline," she said. "You cannot think what it means to me that *you* should say that."

"May I thank you also," said Mr. Draper.

"For what have either of you to thank me?" said Lady Aline.

"We thank you for your magnanimity," said Evelyn Rockingham.

"In misjudging one so much better than myself?"

"No, not for that," said Evelyn. "I say to you quite frankly that I cannot presume to claim the least superiority. Since last night you are so much more than you were."

"I pray, my dear Evelyn, that that may be said of us all," said Mr. Draper in his sombre voice. "It is hardly likely that any one of us can pass through such an ordeal without adding a cubit to our stature."

"I quite agree," said Mr. Grundy, helping himself to a second egg.

"One wonders if the same can be said of poor dear Robert," said Evelyn Rockingham in a voice that fell. "One wonders if he has added his cubit also."

"I am perfectly convinced of it, my dear Duchess," said Mr. Grundy. "Of course we none of us know our Rockingham, as I believe you are ever the first to allow, but there is just one thing I would like to say to you here and now. As one who has seen something of the duke during these negotiations, I would like to place on record that I believe him to be a very valuable asset to his country. He has the mind of a statesman, and the heart of a patriot, and that is much to say of any man."

Mr. Grundy's words were charged with a depth of feeling that surprised his hearers. Such a personality as that of Rockingham must have been antipathetic to him in almost every fibre. But throughout that long night of conflict these two alien natures had stood staunchly together in a last desperate attempt to stave off irreparable disaster. The goal had been won at the price of bitter sacrifice to one of them, and the leader of the Centre now paid homage to him whom a few hours ago he might have been tempted to judge very differently.

The silence which followed Mr. Grundy's words was broken at last by the deep voice of the Prime Minister.

"He is a man I cannot even begin to understand," he said with perfect simplicity. "But at least we will hope he has added his cubit also."

Evelyn Rockingham rose suddenly from the table.

"It is time I went to him," she said, "to find out for myself. Poor Robert! Perhaps he may have need of me." A feminine pang passed through her as she spoke.

She took an affectionate leave of the two statesmen. They were about to motor to London, to convey the decision to the King. Upon descending the stairs she found a car waiting for them at the inn door.

It was her intention to walk back to the house. It was less than half a mile distant, and she was shod and clad well enough to cope with a typical February morning.

As had been the case throughout the night, it was still raining steadily, but in no great volume. The air of the morning seemed delicious after the rather fetid atmosphere of the little inn sitting-room.

She had not left the neighbourhood of the inn door

before a second motor-car drove up quickly. A man alighted from it almost without waiting for it to stop. He was clearly taken aback by finding himself confronted by Evelyn Rockingham

"Halloa!" he said.

The man was Lord Loring.

"Is anything the matter, Loring?" she asked.

There was something in his swift descent from the car, in the way in which he spoke, in the look on his rather bucolic face, that somehow suggested that there was.

"Oh, no," he said curtly, and with an obvious effort to find words. "Tell me — have they started yet?"

"No; you will find them upstairs finishing breakfast."

"Thank goodness!" Loring's relief was evident. "I was afraid they might have gone already. I have something of importance to tell them."

"Is it anything that I can hear too?"

The face of Loring seemed to grow more perturbed.

"I would rather speak to them in private," he said curtly.

"Very well, I will go back to the house. I want to see poor Robert. I hope nothing has occurred to alter the situation."

She turned her head as she spoke and beheld Loring in the act of disappearing hastily through the door of the inn.

XXII

FOR a moment she stood on the inn threshold
in a state of acute indecision. She would
dearly have liked to turn and follow Loring. But a
very little reflection prevented her from doing this.
Instead, she set out on her walk to the house.

Her thoughts jostled one another in her head in a
strange medley. Even without the dramatic appearance of Loring at the inn door her overwrought brain
held matters sufficiently complex. But his arrival,
in a state of such obvious discomposure, served
somehow to bring a new uneasiness. What could
it mean? Had some new turn been given to a situation that still remained tense?

It was idle to speculate on such a slender premise.·
Accordingly, with that masculine resolution that
never deserted her, she dismissed Loring from her
thoughts for the time being, and allowed her mind
to envisage the situation as a whole. She was sufficiently in touch with it to know that the supreme
phase of the crisis was past. The leaders of
the three parties in common with the world at
large had been forced to recognize the genius

of the man who from the beginning she had blindly sustained.

As she walked up the avenue to the house her mind reverted to the irony of her own position. The triumph of her hero, in whose success she had borne so large a part, meant total eclipse for the man whose wife she was, whom she was now on the way to console.

In what manner would he receive her? They were still friends, as friends they had always been. She enjoyed the advantages of his name and status, for which as a young woman she had been unwise enough to marry him. Perhaps in those far-off days she had been dazzled by the glamour of the personality they embellished. Rockingham had always known how to wield a power over women. He was so much the *preux chevalier*. The *bel air* was so much in evidence. Few could resist a nobility of bearing that was the joy and the despair of the contemporary painter.

But when they came to know their Rockingham! was her comment on this glowing mirage of the fancy, which even after all these years of estrangement remained so luminously in her mind. But when they came to know their Rockingham, what was it that they found? They found an enigma, in one aspect unbelievably shallow, in another curiously subtle and deep.

Still the paramount question for her was, did anybody know their Rockingham? In spite of her opportunities she would be the last to claim so much. No, the man was an enigma to his wife, to his friends, to his country, perhaps most of all to himself.

On entering the house she had to pass through the spacious hall, round about whose large open fire-place all the men of the house-party with one exception, perhaps a dozen in all, were assembled. The exception was Rockingham.

As she came toward them she could hear the deep confused hum of their voices. They were pitched so low that she could not catch a word of what was said. And the moment they saw her they all ceased talking with an abruptness that was rather dramatic.

Evelyn looked from one to the other, but among them there was not the man she sought.

"Can you tell me where Robert is?" she asked.

At first no one answered her. But Mr. Maul-everer, who was seated in a chair some little distance apart from the others, rose and said in a peculiarly slow and impressive tone: "I believe Robert is in his room."

XXIII

"I WILL go to him," said Evelyn.

An odd silence followed her words. There was a lapse of a moment, and then Mr. Mauleverer spoke again — and again with his slow impressiveness.

"I don't exactly think I would do that," he said.

There was nothing in the tone to stimulate curiosity, yet the words themselves and the strange hush amid which they were spoken lent them an importance for which it was hard to account.

"Why not?" she said.

Mr. Mauleverer repeated her question in a musing tone, almost as if he would parry it.

"Yes, Evan, why not?"

Before the answer could be given, in whatever it might consist, there came an interruption. The sound arose of a door opening at the far end of the hall. The master of the house was heard and seen coming toward the group about the fireplace. He was followed by two others. A glance told Evelyn that one of them was Mr. Grundy and that the other was he who had been chosen Prime Minister.

It was a moment of high infinite tension, and somehow the faces of all declared it to be so. Loring came first. With a woman's quick, comprehending eye Evelyn saw that the bucolic Briton had been merged in the anxious mediocrity who is oppressively conscious of the fact that he is completely out of his depth.

He came right into the midst of his guests without saying a word. At a respectful distance, and strangely silent also, the two statesmen followed

All who were seated rose at once. But not one among them all could find a word to say. It was a moment of poignant intensity in which all stood awkwardly still. No one spoke or moved. And then, at last, almost it seemed in desperation, the spell was broken by the member for South East Leeds.

As became a man unfettered by subtleties of emotional experience, Mr. Ansell stepped forth suddenly from the midst of his colleagues with hand outstretched.

"Draper," he said in his hearty voice, "I welcome you. I am proud to be associated with you. I am sure you are the right man in the right place."

Such a speech in such circumstances was only possible to one wholly unfettered by delicacy. But such men often serve their turn. Where a fastidious feeling for the *nuances* kept others tongue-tied, this crude fellow was able to dispel an overpowering embarrassment by drawing a surprised attention upon himself.

James Draper was quick to respond. He took a step forward to meet the maladroit man of commerce who had saved the situation and promptly accepted the hand that was offered.

"Thank you very much, my dear Ansell," he said with a simplicity so unstudied that it could hardly have failed to disarm the most critical. "I am indeed proud to have you for a colleague. Gentlemen, I am proud and grateful to be associated with you all in the great task that lies before us."

There was something magnetic in the simple speech. A second individual detached himself from the group around the fireplace and took his hand.

And then followed a third, and then a fourth. Thus it went on, each in turn greeting the new leader, until only one was left. And he was the man who by attainment and authority should have been the first to step forward to bridge the gulf.

In the excitement of the moment it was hardly noticed that Evan Mauleverer had withdrawn from the others. Perhaps only Evelyn Rockingham was a sufficiently detached observer of the scene to perceive that the leader of the Right had seated himself and had taken up a newspaper.

Doubtless it was well that she only appeared to

notice it. A thrill ran across her nerves. Could it be that all was not yet won? Such an action at such a moment was almost intolerably significant.

A little sickly she turned away from the scene. Somehow it was more than she could endure. The frank acceptance of the new Prime Minister by the lesser lights still went on, but when all was said Evan Mauleverer was the man who counted. He must be gained, otherwise it might prove little better than a Pyrrhic victory.

The spectacle of the leader of the Right's aloofness started a new pain in her mind. Where was that other leader? Where was Rockingham? If the whole position had been yielded, ought not he to be there? Was it after all to be a capitulation merely in name?

She must go and see Rockingham. A small study in a distant part of the house had been placed at the disposal of the great man. It was in this rather remote place, not altogether easy of access from the main portion of the house, that he was said to have spent the night.

She made her way at once along the inner portions of the historic dwelling with which she had been familiar from her childhood, until at last the closed door of Rockingham's room confronted her. Upon trying to open it she found it was locked. She tapped smartly upon it several times, but no sound came from within.   She called the name of her husband, but again there was no response.

While she stood twisting the handle of the door, mentally debating what she should do next, there rose a sound of slow steps approaching along the corridor.   The tall, dignified form of Evan Mauleverer came into view.

"Robert is not here," she said.   "The door is locked and there appears to be no one in the room."

"Yes, he is there, Evelyn."

Suddenly she saw that the eyes of the leader of the Right were wet.

XXIV

MR. MAULEVERER placed his hand on her shoulder, as if he would soften the blow he was about to deliver.

"Robert has died by his own hand."

She accepted the stroke without a tremor.

Of the two she was by far the more composed. The shock was inevitably awful, inevitably tragic. But great strength of will was hers, and it never failed her in a crisis.

Moreover, she had never loved Rockingham; and the man who had worked and fought with him side by side in a common cause had loved him very deeply.

There was a silence while they stood close together, with something of the helplessness of a pair of children.

It was she who found the first words to speak.

"No, we none of us knew our Rockingham," she said at last.

"He has given his life for his country," said his friend, with the tears running down his face.

"Was there — was there no other way out?"

"There was no other way out for a gentleman."

"And yet ——? No, I suppose there was not.

And yet a woman can't be expected to understand these things."

"No, she cannot."

Again there was silence. Each was suffering acutely. Again it was the woman who spoke.

"Shall we go in?"

"Do you really wish to go in?"

"Yes."

He seemed to realize her great strength of will. Forlornly he turned on his heel.

"I will fetch the key," he said.

She watched the gaunt, haggard figure recede along the dimly lighted corridor.

She felt numb. There was a curious chill in her veins. But the strength of soul which carried her through everything was still at her command.

It seemed an age before Evan Mauleverer returned.

He swayed to and fro as he came toward her, like a man shattered in all his being.

Without an instant's delay he unlocked the door, and opened it for her to pass in.

"Don't look," he said.

But she had seen already.

He was lying across the hearthrug at the far end of the room, with the pistol still in his hand.

Again there was silence while she peered with calm eyes at the haggard face of the man of wisdom and mastery who had loved Rockingham.

"Will history speak of him?" she said.

Mr. Mauleverer shook his head mournfully.

"I fear not. The world knows nothing of its greatest."

"You think he is numbered among them?"

"Yes, in his death."

"He died to save England?"

"Yes."

The leader of the Right was weeping like a child.

Suddenly she placed a hand on his sleeve.

"Evan," she said softly, " we must see to it that he has not died in vain."

"I don't understand you, Evelyn."

In that presence, with the awful shock still upon them, it was not the moment for thought to leap to thought. But now that she had realized the nature of the sacrifice, she could not endure that its fruits should be lost.

Almost as if at the beck of the train of thought that was stirring in her mind her eyes strayed to the writing-table with its litter of papers and books. And there in a conspicuous place was a letter addressed in Rockingham's charcteristic hand to the chief among his friends.

She took it from the table and gave it to him.

He fingered it irresolutely.

"Read," she said.

A prophetic sense seemed to enthrall her.

He broke the seal, read the letter, and then handed it to her.

She read the following:

MONDAY MORNING, EIGHT O'CLOCK.

MY DEAR EVAN: You and I know that this thing has been played up far too high. We have fought a losing battle with our backs to the wall, and in death I say to you our weapons have not been clean. Do not think I have remorse. We have fought for a great stake against great odds, and we were not in a position to be delicate.

The decision you have reached is the only one possible in the circumstances. There is no disloyalty; I recognize that any other decision would have been disloyal to the Throne. Trust Draper. He is an honest man, and if you *all* stand by him he will save the country.

Good-bye, my dear Evan.   Yours in eternity,
ROCKINGHAM.

She handed back the letter. He stood dumb and tense, his eyes half closed. Not a word was spoken. The presence of the dead held them in thrall.

Yet again it was she who broke the silence.

"*Now* do you not see my meaning?"

He did not answer her.

"Will you remain in this room for a few moments?"

He inclined his head slightly but did not speak. She went out of the room, charged with sudden resolve.

XXV

IN a very little while she had returned to the room.

She was accompanied by him who three hours ago had been chosen Prime Minister. It was plain to tell by his face that he was fully cognizant of what had occurred. He entered the room with his usual straightforward air, but in every line was the instinctive good breeding that springs from the heart.

With Rockingham's letter still in his hand, Mr. Mauleverer received Mr. Draper with his stateliest bow. The bow was returned with equal ceremony.

"Mr. Draper," said the leader of the Right, "the duke has expressed a desire that I should enter your Cabinet."

The Prime Minister bowed again.

"I am prepared to respect his wishes," said Mr. Mauleverer.

"I can only say, sir," said Mr. Draper, "that by respecting the duke's wishes you will lay the country under a signal obligation."

"Upon that I am not altogether clear," said the leader of the Right. "But I feel that the country owes him so much, that as far as I am concerned personally I regard the least of his wishes in the light of a command."

"I rejoice, sir, that such is the case," said the Prime Minister. "Your decision will enormously strengthen his Majesty's Government. I at least am deeply grateful, and I am sure my colleagues will be no less so."

"Thank you, Mr. Draper," said the leader of the Right. Even he, apparently, was touched by the warmth and sincerity that breathed through the words.

"And perhaps, sir," said the Prime Minister, "it would not be improper at such a moment, and in the presence of him who is noble in his death, to record my own feeling about him. He was the bitterest of my adversaries, but I would say to you, sir, the first among his friends, that no man can realize more fully than I do that he is glorious in his death. He died to save England, and no nobler requiem can be claimed by any of her sons.

THE END

THE COUNTRY LIFE PRESS, GARDEN CITY, N. Y.

www.ingramcontent.com/pod-product-compliance
Lightning Source LLC
Chambersburg PA
CBHW032226010726
47494CB00002B/373